P9-DNG-391

THE LAWMAN: MASSACRE TRAIL

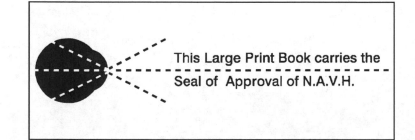

This Large Print Book carries the
Seal of Approval of N.A.V.H.

Mar 31, 2010

NEW PORT
RICHEY PUBLIC
LIBRARY

**LARGE
WESTERN
B8212law
BRANDT**

32288001338279

THE LAWMAN: MASSACRE TRAIL

LYLE BRANDT

THORNDIKE PRESS
A part of Gale, Cengage Learning

GALE
CENGAGE Learning™

Detroit • New York • San Francisco • New Haven, Conn • Waterville, Maine • London

Copyright © 2009 by Michael Newton.
Thorndike Press, a part of Gale, Cengage Learning.

ALL RIGHTS RESERVED
This is a work of fiction. Names, characters, places, and incidents are either the product of the author's imagination or are used fictitiously, and any resemblance to actual persons, living or dead, business establishments, events, or locales is entirely coincidental. The publisher does not have any control over and does not assume any responsibility for author or third-party Web sites or their content.
Thorndike Press® Large Print Western.
The text of this Large Print edition is unabridged.
Other aspects of the book may vary from the original edition.
Set in 16 pt. Plantin.
Printed on permanent paper.

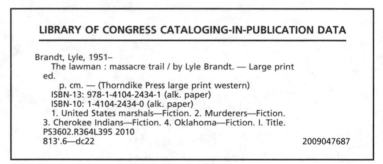

LIBRARY OF CONGRESS CATALOGING-IN-PUBLICATION DATA

Brandt, Lyle, 1951–
   The lawman : massacre trail / by Lyle Brandt. — Large print ed.
      p. cm. — (Thorndike Press large print western)
     ISBN-13: 978-1-4104-2434-1 (alk. paper)
     ISBN-10: 1-4104-2434-0 (alk. paper)
     1. United States marshals—Fiction. 2. Murderers—Fiction.
3. Cherokee Indians—Fiction. 4. Oklahoma—Fiction. I. Title.
PS3602.R364L395 2010
813'.6—dc22   2009047687

Published in 2010 by arrangement with The Berkley Publishing Group, a member of Penguin Group (USA) Inc.

Printed in the United States of America
1 2 3 4 5 6 7 14 13 12 11 10

For Sam Peckinpah

PROLOGUE

"It's *not* the wind," Joe Deacon told his wife, as he was pulling on his boots. "I know what wind sounds like. It doesn't spook the animals that way."

"But, Joe, it's *dark* out there," his wife replied.

"Of course it's dark out, Caroline," he answered, smiling with his back turned toward her so she couldn't see it and get angry. Then he couldn't help himself and added, "What do you expect at nighttime?"

"I expect you to stay safe in bed with me."

"I need to check the animals, that's all. It won't take long."

"Why can't it wait for morning, Joe?"

"Because whatever's bothering the stock could eat them up by then." He turned to face her in the soft, unsteady light of a short candle that he'd lit beside their bed after the whinnying of horses woke him. "Caroline, you *know* that. What's got into you?"

7

"I'm frightened," she replied. Almost a whisper.

"All the more reason for me to have a look around outside and see what's going on."

"He's right," a voice said from behind him, in the shadows. Joe was startled but he covered it, turning the little jerk into a pivot as he turned to face his mother-in-law.

"Will you sit with her, Ruth?" he asked. "I won't be long."

"Of course." Ruth Walker moved to take his place as Deacon stood up from the bed.

It was a milder version of his worst nightmare, having Ruth come between himself and Caroline in bed. She hadn't seemed to favor Joe when he was courting Caroline, and when her husband died — when Caroline had begged him, literally on her knees — to let Ruth come and live with them, he had anticipated trouble. Even now, after they'd been together under one roof for the best part of four years, it still made Joe uneasy, reaching out for Caroline at night. Wondering whether Ruth could hear them from her own small room.

That hadn't stopped him, though. Not even close.

And two-year-old Zerelda was the living proof.

Another reason why he had to have that

look around, outside. Zerelda and her older brother, Jacob, were more precious to him than the livestock. Anything or anyone who threatened them was automatically Joe Deacon's mortal enemy.

Now, on the other hand, if wolves should come along and snatch Ruth from the yard one of these days . . .

"What is it, Joe?" asked Caroline.

" 'Scuse me?"

"All of a sudden, you were smiling there."

Joe wondered whether she could see him blush by candlelight.

The lie came easily, from practice covering his thoughts about her mother. "I was just thinking," he replied, "it's probably a snake, maybe a fox. All this excitement over nothing."

"Then, for heaven's sake, come back to bed!"

"A snake or fox still has to go," he said. "I'd hate to lose the chickens or have any of the horses snakebit."

"You'll be careful, won't you?" Caroline demanded.

"Absolutely," Joe replied, taking his Henry rifle off the wooden pegs that kept it mounted on the wall.

Another squeal of protest echoed from the barn. Joe Deacon frowned and pumped the

Henry's lever action, making sure he had a cartridge in the firing chamber.

He had almost reached the door when Caroline hissed after him, "You'll need a light!"

He turned, one final time, and found both women watching him. "I've got the moon," he said. "It's one night shy of full. Now hush, before you wake the children."

It was something of a miracle that Jake, at least, hadn't already come to join them, full of questions. If he was forced to shoot a fox or snake, it *would* wake up the young ones, but by that time he'd be finished with the dirty work.

What if it's not a snake or fox? Joe asked himself and felt a little chill slide down his spine.

Most of the wolves and cougars had been killed or driven out by now. Coyotes were a possibility, and there were still supposed to be a few old bears around, though Deacon hadn't seen one for himself. Coyotes were the largest predators he should expect, Joe finally decided.

Well, at least the largest on four legs.

That brought him to the other problem: human beings.

Living off alone, the way his family did, Joe Deacon had to keep an eye peeled day

10

and night for strangers passing through. The Indians were more or less confined to reservations now, and any who resented it had managed to restrain themselves from going on the warpath during recent years.

White men were something else. All right in town, where everyone was civilized or made a practiced show of it, but out here in the country it was different. His nearest neighbor lived eight miles away, due west. Joe Deacon never trusted strangers on his property.

It won't be people, he decided. *But I'm ready for them if it is.*

Was he?

"Bar the door behind me," Deacon told his women, narrowing his eyes to slits against the candle's light before he stepped outside. He pulled the door shut with his left hand, steadying the Henry in his right, and waited until Caroline or Ruth had set the sturdy wooden plank in place, securing it.

Moonlight flooded the yard and showed him nothing.

Cautiously, holding the rifle cocked, he started for the barn.

The prowlers do not speak. They have rehearsed their gestures and the wordless hissing, clicking signals that direct each other to go here or there, do this or that.

Kill him or her.

The isolated ranch is new to them, but they do not feel lost or out of place. They make themselves at home wherever fate or fortune sends them, living off the land — or, preferably, off their fellow men.

Tonight they have the scent of easy pickings in their nostrils and they are immune to fear.

It was not always so, of course. They have been hunted in their time, with grim determination, by professionals and amateurs alike. They all have scars to show for it, upon their bodies and their souls.

But they survive.

The men who've hunted them are all dead now, unless some wearied of the task and went back home, defeated, to their wives and families. It makes no difference to the prowlers, just as long as they are left alone.

And they are hunters in their own right, culling weak and stupid members of their own herd as they move across the landscape, leaving only death behind.

Like now.

They're hungry, and the farm can feed them. There may well be money in the house; if not, there will be other items they can use or sell for cash, when it is safe. They hear and smell the horses that will help to speed them on their way.

In search of other prey.

They watch the farmer coming toward the barn. It's not the first time they have seen him, although he has never been this close before. They've seen his women and the youngsters, too, while counting the farmhouse occupants and calculating who is likely to fight hardest when it's time for them to die.

Not all at once, though. That would be a waste.

The farmer first, because he's armed and dangerous, within his limits. It's unlikely that he's ever killed a man before, dead certain that he's never faced an enemy like those who've found him now.

If so, he wouldn't be alive.

Halfway across the yard, the farmer stops, clutching the rifle to his chest and listening, turning his head from side to side the way a lizard will, tracking a fly. He hasn't seen them — there'd be no mistaking it, if that had been the case — but he's heard something, maybe smelled it on the night breeze washing over him.

Another hiss and click, followed by stirring in the barn. The nervous horses whicker, shifting in their stalls, stamping their feet. The farmer scowls by moonlight, moving closer. One step at a time.

He's cautious, but it isn't good enough. The farmer is a man whose world exists primarily in daylight. After nightfall, he is prone to jump at shadows, worry over sounds that do not threaten him, while missing silences that do.

It comes from being civilized — a handicap the prowlers do not share.

How best to kill him is the question now. A minimum of fuss and noise is preferable at the start of any siege. Take out the leader if you can, and leave the followers to crumble under pressure. It's a simple plan and has not failed the prowlers yet.

Of course, each situation varies, offers unique challenges. Cracking a house with occupants on full alert is not the same as falling on an open camp where everyone's asleep. There may be guns inside the prowlers haven't seen, and someone capable of using them.

In which case, there is always fire.

A waste of easy pickings, maybe, but it does the job as well as blades or bullets.

Still, screaming aside, a torch job spoils the game.

The farmer's reached his barn now, finally,

considering the best means of approach. He's wasting time, since there is only one way in or out, through double doors made by his own two hands.

One of those hands will have to leave the rifle while he's opening the doors. There is an opportunity to take him then, but maybe not the best. An unexpected visitor is waiting for him in the barn, prepared to strike at the first opportunity.

One of the doors creaks open and the farmer hesitates, then steps from moonlight into the dark cavern of the barn. Behind him, shadows gather and advance to cut off his retreat.

"What's taking him so long? He should be back by now!"

Ruth Walker put an arm around her daughter's shoulders, drew her closer on the sagging bed, and said, "It hasn't been ten minutes, Caroline. He had to check the horses, have a look around. Give him some time."

"I'm scared, Mama."

"Of what, child? Ghosts?" Ruth forced a smile but it felt brittle on her face. "I swear, you're like a little girl sometimes. It's hard to credit you've got children of your own."

"Not ghosts," said Caroline. "Wild ani-

15

mals . . . or worse."

"You're fretting over nothing. Wind and passing noises in the night."

"If it was *nothing,* Joe would be here with us. We hear *noises* all the time, without him taking down the Henry."

"He's a good man," Ruth replied. And she believed that now, although she'd definitely had her doubts at first. "A man sees to his family and property. You wouldn't want a coward lying next to you and shaking, with the covers pulled over his head."

"So, you *do* think something's out there!"

"Just what Joe already said, a fox or snake spooking the animals. He'll chase it off or kill it, and we'll all get back to sleep."

"The rifle's all we have, you know," said Caroline.

"It's all we need."

"But it's *out there.*"

"And safely in your husband's hands. You need to trust him, Caroline."

"I do! But . . ."

"What?"

"I don't know, damn it!"

"Caroline! Control yourself!"

Ruth saw the first tears leave bright tracks across her daughter's cheeks. "I'm sorry, Mama."

"Never mind. We need to listen close and

let the children sleep."

"All right."

But listening was nerve-wracking, as Ruth quickly discovered. Sitting still and tracking sounds at night could make you jump out of your skin.

No sounds of stirring from the loft yet, where the children slept, and Ruth considered that a blessing. They'd have been jabbering no end of questions, maybe even crying, if they'd seen their mother in her present state, and Ruth wanted no racket of that sort while she was straining to catch any sound of movement from outside.

Her first thought had been Indians, although she'd kept it to herself. There was no point in agitating Caroline beyond her present state, and Ruth knew that a raid by hostiles was unlikely. She'd seen Indians exactly twice since coming out to live with Caroline and Joe, both times in town while they were shopping for supplies. There'd been no trouble on the nearby reservation or around it, to her knowledge, for at least five years before she made the journey west.

One of the things she'd learned before making that trip was that a man didn't require red skin to be wicked. In St. Louis, where she'd lived until the move to Oklahoma Territory, there'd been thugs on every corner, wandering the streets in gangs, committing every crime a normal mind could think of and a few that strained imagination to the breaking point. The gangs fought over gambling dens, saloons, and brothels — or because one side was Irish Catholic, the other Protestant and "true American." A day seldom went by without reports of yet another victim shot or stabbed, left in the gutter where he fell.

Compared to that, the wild frontier seemed clean and peaceable. There was a church in town, no more than seven miles away, and while they had to start out early for the morning service, it ensured that Joe would get a day of rest from labor on the farm, as the good Lord intended.

But the Lord wouldn't protect them from intruders in the night. Joe had to do that on his own.

And if he failed . . .

"You stay right here," she said to Caroline. "I'll be back in a second."

"Where are —"

"Shhh!"

Ruth rose and stepped into the nearby kitchen. Nothing in the little house was very far away. She found what she was looking for and turned back toward the master bedroom. Felt her daughter watching her as she retraced her steps.

"Take this," Ruth said and handed Caroline the foot-long carving knife.

She kept the heavy cleaver for herself.

"Mama . . ."

"Hush, now. We won't be needing these, I'm sure."

"But why, then?"

"Just in case, child. Just in case."

The farmer stops when he is just inside the barn, with moonlight spilling in behind him, casting him in silhouette. The prowler who is already inside can't make out any features of his face, but from a kind of snuffling sound the farmer makes, it seems that he is sniffing at the air.

The hidden prowler doesn't realize that his musky aroma is distinct from that of horses and their dung, or any of the other smells the farmer may be used to in his barn. The prowler bathes whenever those who love him gather and demand it; otherwise, hygiene is not a subject that occurs to him.

He listens to the farmer sniffing, watches as the doomed man moves a little closer to his fate. The rifle is a threat, but it can only send a bullet where the farmer points it. If they play their cards right, he won't have a chance to fire at all — or else his one shot will be wasted on the walls, maybe the ceiling, when they take him down. There won't be time for him to cock the gun and fire a second time.

Unless they fail, in which case one or more of them may die.

Failure is always possible. The prowlers never know when one of their intended victims may resist with extraordinary strength or cunning. The fact that they have not failed *yet* improves the odds of trouble in their future, but the prowler hiding in the barn lives mostly in the here and now. His notion of great strategy is planning where to sleep tonight.

Already settled, once they force their way inside the house.

The prowler grins fiercely as shadows flit into the barn behind the farmer, breaking off to either side and finding deeper shadows to conceal them. Focused as he is on that new smell, the farmer doesn't notice their disruption of the moonlight in the doorway. If he had, he might have saved himself.

But it is too late now.

He's trapped; he just doesn't know it yet.

The prowler lobs a pebble overhand, striking the far wall of the barn. It spooks a horse, which neighs and scuffles in its stall.

As planned, the farmer turns in that direction, leveling his rifle as he edges toward the source of unexpected sound.

Perfect.

The hidden prowler draws his knife, a bowie, sharpened to a razor edge. Its wooden grip is satin smooth from frequent handling. The touch of an old friend who shares his taste.

The farmer, although cautious, seems more curious than worried. He is likely thinking *mouse* or *weasel,* unaware that he's about to die. His half-turned back invites the prowler to emerge from hiding, leap upon him, ride him down, and slash his throat.

But that is not the plan.

They have a certain way of doing things, sharing the wet work, that has proved effective over time. In fact, they are alive today because their discipline is still intact, despite adversity.

The prowler waits and watches, eyes tracking the farmer to the stall where he speaks softly to the horse, soothing its jangled nerves. The animal responds to him as to a lifelong friend.

Shadows move closer, inch by inch, to the distracted farmer. They are silent, skilled and studied in the art of taking

21

adversaries by surprise. Nothing is sure in life, except that most men struggle at the moment of their death, finding new strength in fear.

The answer to resistance, in the prowlers' personal experience, is overwhelming force and brutal violence.

The farmer senses something at the final instant, far too late. He turns to meet the hatchet blow that splits his skull with a ripe-melon sound, while other hands reach out and twist the rifle from his dying hands. Before his legs can buckle, knives rip into him, releasing crimson tributaries.

The hidden prowler joins them, stooping to perform his own appointed task. The bowie glides through flesh and muscle, skitters on a vertebra, then finds the slot he's looking for and cuts the spinal column, passing on through fat and cartilage to finish. Fresh blood warms his fingers as he holds the severed head aloft.

"Good work," another tells him.

"Come on, then," a third commands. "We're wasting time."

"He's coming back. I hear him, Mama."

"Hush a minute."

Ruth heard something, too, but if she'd had to guess, she would've said more than one person was advancing toward the house. That spun her mind off to a dark place where she didn't want to go, clutching the cleaver tight enough to make her knuckles blanch, and Ruth hoped that her ears were simply playing tricks on her.

One thing she *didn't* hear was Joe calling for Caroline or Ruth to let him in. Knowing the door was barred from the inside, he *had* to ask.

Instead, he knocked.

"Joseph?"

Caroline rose, but Ruth restrained her with a firm grip on her arm.

"Be still," Ruth cautioned.

"But —"

"Shut up!"

Looking as if she'd just been slapped, Caroline closed her mouth.

Just as a raspy voice beyond the door said, "Sweetheart, let me in."

"Oh, God!" Barely a whisper now, from Caroline. "Who *is* that?"

"No one that I plan to let inside," Ruth said.

The rapping was repeated, this time with a kind of growling sound that wrung a gasp from Caroline. Upstairs, five-year-old Jacob called down, "Daddy? Mama? Who's outside?"

Ruth moved to stand where Jacob and his sister, staring down at her with wide and frightened eyes, could see her in the candle's light. She raised her empty hand and pressed the index finger to her lips, demanding silence.

Like the good boy that he was, Jacob obeyed — and clapped a hand over Zerelda's mouth when she began to cry. Ruth pointed toward the nearest bed and they retreated, out of sight.

Ruth turned to face the door and found Caroline beside her with the carving knife gripped in both hands, held out in front of her, tip pointed toward the door and trembling.

Someone struck the door a mighty blow that made it jump a little in its frame. It held, but Ruth and Caroline backed up another step, as an unearthly snarling, howling sound erupted from the porch. It sounded like a wolf battling a cougar — or perhaps one of the great apes Ruth had heard about, from Africa across the sea.

It's just a man, she told herself, to stop the trembling in her hands. *I heard him speak.*

And confirming it, the harsh voice bellowed, "Open!" just before somebody struck the door another heavy blow.

"I have a gun in here," Ruth lied.

"Use it," the stranger answered, mocking her.

"Don't think I won't."

Disdainful laughter echoed through the night, before an ax or hatchet struck the door dead center, opening a crack through which its bright edge showed, before it was withdrawn to strike again.

Caroline tried to turn and run, but Ruth caught her and dragged her back to face the door. "Where are you going, Daughter?" she demanded. "Have you got somewhere to hide? Would you run off and leave your children helpless?"

"No!"

"Then come with me," Ruth whispered, moving closer to the door.

"What are you *doing?*"

"Keep your voice down, Caroline! Even if they chop through the door, they'll have to reach inside to raise the bar." She tapped her cleaver's blade against the bright steel of the carving knife. "It may not be so easy for them, without hands and arms."

Caroline's fleeting smile was bright with panic, but she followed Ruth and took a place to the right of the door, while Ruth stood to the left. No matter how the stranger tried to reach inside and raise the beam that blocked his entry, he would be exposed.

Take off the hand, he'll likely bleed to death,
Ruth thought. *Failing that, an artery runs up
the inside of his arm.*

God-fearing woman that she was, Ruth
Walker had no qualms about killing to save
her daughter, her grandchildren, or herself.
The Good Book said it plain enough, in
Genesis 9:6.

"Whoso sheddeth man's blood," she muttered, "by man shall his blood be shed."

Across the threshold from her, Caroline
whimpered, "Amen!"

The sixth or seventh hatchet blow snapped
off a foot-long piece of one board Joe had
used to make the door. Ruth guessed she
could have pressed her eye to it and seen
the man who threatened them, but what
would be the point? She meant to kill him if
she could, no matter what he looked like.

And the others?

Ruth decided she would deal with them
as necessary, hopefully one at a time. If they
were stupid, they'd keep trying to get
through the doorway, even after their front
man was bleeding out his life from bone-
deep wounds.

If they were smart . . . then, what?

She thought of fire and cringed inside.
Ruth half imagined she could hear young
Jacob and Zerelda screaming in the midst

of flames. It was a dreadful way to die —
but was it any worse than what awaited
them among the human beasts who'd killed
their father?

Joe was dead, of course. She had no doubt
of that. If he'd been living, no power on
Earth could have prevented him from standing up and fighting for his family.

I'm sorry that I ever doubted you, Ruth
thought, hoping that he could hear her
somehow, somewhere. *Please forgive me.*

Ruth stepped closer as a hairy crab-like
thing that must have been a hand thrust
through the jagged opening. She raised the
cleaver for a sweeping blow but wasn't fast
enough. The hand withdrew, and suddenly
a shot rang out.

Ruth staggered, felt her legs buckle as she
collapsed. After a flash of pain, her chest
felt numb, as if she had been punched hard
in the chest. The ceiling overhead spun
lazily, making her dizzy.

"Mama? Oh, God! Mama!"

Caroline, kneeling beside her, clutched at
Ruth. A sudden stab of anger cut the numb-
ness that was spreading from Ruth's chest,
throughout her body.

"Caroline! The door!"

Too late.

She heard the heavy bar drop, followed by

the clomping sound of footsteps on the wooden floor. Ruth saw the figures looming over her but couldn't focus on their faces. She regretted dying without wounding one of them, at least.

But she was lucky, in the end.

Sometimes dying is quick.

Sometimes it takes all night.

1

The Willock brothers didn't like their shackles. They'd been griping from the moment Jack Slade got the drop on them in Maple City, Kansas, where they had assumed that they were safe.

That hadn't been their first mistake.

Slade didn't know exactly where the brothers had gone wrong, originally, and he didn't care. One of the newfangled "alienists" he'd read about back East might blame their parents for abusing or ignoring them, and maybe that was true.

So what?

Slade's own parents had been distant, at best, though never overtly cruel. And aside from his gambling, a penchant for backing long odds, he had turned out all right, hadn't he?

At least, he'd never cut a sixty-seven-year-old woman's throat and stolen every penny she had saved throughout her life.

That's what the Willock brothers had been up to in Wakita, Oklahoma, three short weeks ago. Slade understood it wasn't their first crime, but when they stood before Judge Isaac Dennison in Enid, it was bound to be their last.

Tad Willock was older than his brother, Michael, by two years, and had served time in Yuma prison for a bungled highway robbery. The younger Willock either started thieving while his brother was locked up or else got caught for the first time, burglarizing a Wichita bank after hours. He'd forgotten about the night watchman and so was arrested before he stole anything, cutting his charge back to breaking and entering.

The Willocks reunited when they both got out of prison, roaming far and wide across a range that had included Kansas and Missouri, Arkansas and Oklahoma Territory. There were suspects in a Kansas City holdup and a rape in Little Rock, but with the Oklahoma murder charge against them, they could pretty well forget about those cases and whatever unknown crimes they'd pulled during the past two years.

Judge Dennison believed in swift and certain punishment, which cinched his reputation as a hanging judge. He needed evidence, of course, and there was plenty. Half a dozen witnesses had seen the brothers going home with Martha Satterfield the day before her corpse was found, ostensibly to do some work around her house.

And Michael Willock had been kind enough to drop an envelope that bore his name, while he was hiding Mrs. Satterfield's remains inside her privy.

Stupid.

Now they were bound to hang, unless they could persuade the president of the United States to intercede on their behalf. Slade didn't like their chances on that front, since President McKinley was distracted by his war to pacify the Philippines.

Slade viewed the Philippine campaign as a fool's errand, even though he understood the U.S. Navy needed fueling ports around the world. It seemed to him that Filipinos would resist the military occupation with a will that rivaled that of Texans at the Alamo — and they were not a handful of defenders trapped inside a crumbling mission.

Slade was glad he didn't have to fight that war.

His life was violent enough, already.

Tad and Michael Willock could've made it worse, forced him to kill them both, but they were cowards when it counted. They had been drinking when he found them and identified himself, showed them his U.S. marshal's badge, and gave them both a choice.

They could come quietly or try to use the pistols they were carrying. Even at two to one they hadn't liked the odds. Maybe because he wasn't sixty-seven, or a woman with her back turned when they made their move.

It was a three-day ride from Maple City back to Enid, making decent time without undue strain on the horses. When they camped at night, Slade chained the brothers to the largest tree available and let them eat in turns. Based on their comments and their odor, they were getting tired of beans.

Too bad.

They would be eating more of them in Judge Dennison's lockup and farting their way to the gallows, a joke that old Cromwell the hangman was known to repeat for the price of a beer.

Their last night on the road, stretched out beneath the stars, Slade closed his ears to the habitual complaints of damp and rocky ground, turning his thoughts toward Faith. It still came as a sweet surprise to him, how much he missed her when his work took him away from Enid, and it made him wonder why he hadn't popped the question yet.

Of course, he knew that answer going in.

Faith Connover had been engaged to wed Slade's brother, Jim, merging their ranches into one big happy ending, when a gang of rustlers killed Jim Slade. Jim's murder, even after years apart and barely speaking, had brought Jack to settle up the score.

He hadn't counted on Judge Dennison persuading him to don a badge before he started cleaning house, much less on taking to the job like he was born to it. And sure as Hell, he hadn't been expecting Faith.

Jim's ghost still passed between them at odd moments, and on rare occasions Slade still wondered whether Faith was drawn to him because he was Jim's identical twin. The real snag to proposing, though, revolved around Slade's job.

He'd been a gambler more or less since leaving home, favoring poker when he had a choice, and Slade was good enough with cards to make a living at it. That meant a life without deep roots, of course, because a dealer who keeps winning isn't loved by anyone for very long.

Now, while he still played poker when he could, Slade had become a lawman, ranging far and wide in search of fugitives. He had a home now, could send roots as deep as he desired in theory, but he and Faith both recognized the grave risks involved in his work. Each call out to arrest another thief, rapist, or killer placed him squarely in harm's way.

And what was more, Slade didn't mind. He'd come to like it, in a way, and feel that he was giving something back to civilized society, instead of taking all the time.

But what kind of life was that for a woman?

For a wife?

Slade reckoned he could think about it in the morning. They should reach Enid by noon, with any luck, and he'd have time to speak with Faith before another job sent him away. Meanwhile . . .

"Marshal!" Tad Willock called to him. "This ground's too hard for me to sleep."

"Enjoy it while you can," Slade said. "You're going to be planted in it soon enough."

Isaac Llewellyn Dennison had never planned to be a hanging judge. He hadn't started out to be a judge at all, in fact, but he had fallen into it somehow — an opportunity, someone had told him at the time — and everything had followed from that first decision to forsake a private legal practice and pursue what some called "public service."

Dennison supposed the men he was about to hang would disagree with any definition of that phrase he proposed. Their victims, could they speak, would certainly agree that hanging them was both a service to the living public and a form of closure for the dead, but Dennison was not required to take a poll before he passed sentence.

Responsibility was his alone.

Three men were up today, scheduled to pay for cruel transgressions with their lives. All three were murderers, and one had also raped the girl he'd killed right there in Enid, one week earlier. Some judges might've said that since she sold herself in a saloon she'd had no right to turn the man away — no right to live, in fact — but Dennison believed in absolute equality of victims.

And of punishment.

Some people, mostly in the East, protested against hanging. They claimed that it was no deterrent to potential criminals, and while the judge had few statistics to support his contrary belief, he knew that death deterred the living hell out of repeat offenses by the criminals who took the drop.

He'd never hanged a horse or cattle thief,

since federal law did not permit it, but he *had* hanged lynchers who presumed to place themselves above that law. The first time two of them had swung at Dennison's command, reports of vigilante action in his part of Oklahoma Territory had declined 60 percent.

Dennison thought it was a fair trade-off.

That didn't mean he'd won the war, by any means. Far from it. Dennison knew he would never live to see the territory — or the state, God willing — purged of violent crime. As long as there were human beings anywhere within its borders, Oklahoma would have scores to settle with its predators.

Dennison moved to stand before his office window. It faced down into a literal courtyard, surrounded on three sides by Dennison's courthouse, his jail, and the building where deputy marshals spent most of their time when they weren't on the trail, hunting men. The fourth side was open, providing a view from the street.

Dennison knew without looking that the passageway was clogged with spectators by now. He had two part-time bailiffs stationed there, to keep the gawping crowd from surging any closer to the gallows standing in the middle of the yard. His full-time bailiffs, armed, would walk the three condemned men to the platform when their time came, in . . . exactly three minutes and nineteen seconds.

They would not be late.

Some jurisdictions had so little call for hanging that they put up special gallows on the rare occasions when they were required, then quickly tore them down again, as if ashamed of what they'd done. In Enid, where the executions averaged one per week, the gallows were built sturdily enough to stand for years, exposed to sun, wind, rain, and snow. They were repaired as needed and kept in perfect working order at all times.

Two minutes.

Isaac Dennison had never been a great believer in the organized religions. He had seen too many self-styled Christians stand before his bench to trust that any book could truly save a man. Some of the worst ones took a shot at praying when the noose was snug around their necks, but Dennison wasn't convinced that it had done them any good.

And in the end, it made no difference.

Whatever waited on the other side of death — a fiery pit, a choir of angels, or a pitch-black void — the law required all men to answer for their deeds on Earth. When those deeds led to spilling blood, Judge Dennison or someone like him was required to set things straight.

Or, maybe, someone like Jack Slade.

There was a new job waiting for him, something Dennison had saved for Slade, holding it back until Slade brought the Willock brothers in. Dennison could've sent another marshal to investigate, and he might well have placed more lives at risk through his delay, but he believed Slade was the man to do this job.

Assuming *anyone* could do it.

If he failed . . .

No matter. They were bound to try — and try again, if they did not succeed at first. That could mean sending someone else, since Slade might not be coming back, but he was paid to take that risk.

It was time.

A door opened across the yard, and a bailiff armed with a shotgun emerged. He stood aside and waited for the prisoners, who shuffled out behind him in their manacles and shackles, each man rattling like Marley's ghost. Another bailiff came along behind them, with another shotgun, just in case the prisoners decided they would rather fight than hang.

In either case, they were about to die.

A minister, the Reverend Soames from Enid Southern Baptist, came along behind the others, reading something from his open Bible in a tone that didn't carry to Dennison's open window. No one seemed to pay the reverend any mind as they proceeded to the gallows, bailiffs standing off to flank the wooden stairs and cover their three charges without wounding one another in a cross fire if it all went wrong.

The hangman, Cromwell, waited for them on the platform. He'd already tested each rope, using sandbags, to ensure — at least, in theory — that they didn't snap off any heads or leave the convicts dangling, slowly strangling, for the crowd's amusement. Broken necks were the ideal, with greased ropes, knots secure behind left ears, and a measured drop to do the job. Each subject had been weighed and measured earlier, the measurement a double service for the hangman and the undertaker, who was finishing three coffins even now.

Dennison stood and watched the three men mount the steps to Cromwell's platform, followed by the bailiffs and the Reverend Soames. The bailiffs covered them and Soames kept praying, while Cromwell prepared each inmate for the drop. Leaving their manacles and shackles on, he bound their arms and legs with sturdy leather straps to minimize convulsions, then draped each neck with a noose and snugged them tight.

The hoods came last, after the Reverend Soames asked each man whether he had any final words. Two of them muttered short apologies, while number three — the rapist-slayer — spat toward the preacher's feet.

It was enough.

Cromwell moved back along the line, hooding each man in turn, then moved to stand beside the four-foot lever that would spring the traps. As always, he glanced up at Dennison and got the nod. A heartbeat later, three men fell through space, stopped short by ropes pulled taut and trembling.

Dennison could hear their necks snap from his second-story window.

It was one more job well done.

The head jailer in Enid was a wiry man named Warren Pike. He'd been a marshal for Judge Dennison until a shotgun ambush left him with a limp that slowed him down too much for man hunting. It hadn't slowed his hands or wits, though, and the prisoners who challenged him soon learned the error of their ways.

"These two cause any trouble?" Pike asked, as he took the Willock brothers into hand.

"I wouldn't turn my back on either one of them," Slade said. "But face-to-face, they're nothing."

"Killed that woman, didn't they?"

"The very same."

Pike gave the brothers an emasculating smile and said, "Come on, then, and I'll introduce your playmates."

Slade was retreating toward his roan when Pike called after him, "Oh, Jack! Judge wants to see you, soon as possible."

"What's up?" Slade asked.

Pike's smile was gone. "I'd better let him fill you in. Be careful, though. It's ugly."

Judge Dennison was fifty-something, Slade supposed, although he had the vigor of a many ten years younger. Since he'd taken on the marshal's job, Slade had collected bits and pieces of the judge's story, learning that he came from somewhere in Connecticut, born of a well-connected family, and that he'd held his first job as a magistrate in Mississippi, in the bloody days of Reconstruction following the Civil War. From there, the powers that be had moved him on to Arkansas, and finally to Oklahoma Territory, where he stood for law and order

41

in harsh land, barely civilized.

The judge answered Slade's knock with a commanding "Enter!"

Slade obeyed, opened the door, stepped across the threshold, and closed the door securely at his back. "You sent for me, Judge?" he inquired.

Dennison lingered near his window, peering down into the courtyard. "So I did. How are the Willock brothers? Give you any trouble?"

"Wore my ears out with complaining," Slade replied, "but nothing else."

"Good, good. That's good." Dennison drifted toward his desk and chair, telling Slade, "Please, sit down."

Slade sat, catching a puff of trail dust from his clothes. Trail dust and sweat.

"We have a problem, Jack."

Slade frowned at that, trying to guess which prisoner or free-world citizen had cooked up a complaint against him. Several candidates came instantly to mind, but Slade wasn't the kind of fool who leaped into an open trap.

"Over the past eight days," said Dennison, "there have been two attacks. Well, *massacres,* I'd guess we have to call them. Families on isolated farms slaughtered — men, women and children."

"When you say slaughtered —"

"It's exactly what I mean," Dennison said. "They weren't just murdered — which, of course, is bad enough. These folks were butchered, Jack. Cut all to pieces, scattered here and there. On top of which, it seems the women — and their children, girls and boys alike — were . . . *interfered* with."

"Raped?" Slade asked him, bluntly.

"Among other things. It's all in the report," said Dennison, sliding a sheaf of papers far enough across his massive desk for Slade to reach it. "Have a look at that, then we'll continue."

Slade read through the document and felt himself go cold inside. It told the story of two families and how they'd died screaming. Clinical language didn't help.

The Thompson family had lived a few miles south of Elmwood, in the panhandle. Frank Thompson and his wife, June, were expecting their fourth child when they were slaughtered — Dennison was right, that was the only word for it — like pigs or cattle in an abattoir. Neighbors had found them several days after the raid, five victims mutilated almost beyond recognition, while the unborn baby . . .

Slade moved on.

The Browning family was — had been —

larger, with five children. They'd lived east of Turpin, which in turn was west of Elmwood, farther out into the panhandle. All seven had been hacked and slashed with knives, hatchets, a pitchfork, and a scythe from their own barn. A note from Turpin's constable called it the worst thing that he'd ever seen, finding their heads stacked up on the front porch.

"What about robbery?" Slade asked, when he had finished reading through the grim list of atrocities.

"The constable thinks *maybe* there were horses missing," Dennison replied, "but since he really didn't know the Brownings, he's not positive. The folks who found the Thompsons are convinced they lost a mare. No one can tell about the houses. Both were ransacked, vandalized, turned into slaughterhouses. Maybe there was money, jewelry. We don't know."

It wouldn't matter anyway, Slade thought. Judge Dennison would want the killers swinging from a rope, not riding off to serve a prison term for theft.

"Whoever did this," Slade observed, "they're moving west."

"I noticed that. From where they hit the Brownings, they could head off into Texas, Kansas, Colorado, or New Mexico."

44

"They can't run far enough," Slade said. "Of course, I'll have to find out who they are."

"Some people seem to think they've got it all worked out," said Dennison.

"Oh, yes?"

"They're blaming hostiles off the nearest reservation. Kiowa, Comanche, or Apache, take your pick."

Slade frowned. "In that case, it's an army matter."

"*If* that's the case, you're right," the judge replied. "We need to prove that first, before I abrogate my own responsibility and hand it to the boys in blue."

"It's late for me to start today," Slade said. "But first thing in the morning —"

"Fair enough," said Dennison. "Find out who's done this, Jack. Find out, and if the bastards fall under our jurisdiction, bring them here to me. By any legal means available."

Slade's next stop was a barber's shop that offered baths for fifty cents. He lay neck deep in steaming, soapy water, his Colt Peacemaker within arm's reach, and thought about the judge's parting words.

By any legal means available.

The "legal" stipulation emphasized Judge

Dennison's insistence that the rule of law must be preserved at any cost. The rest of it, including his tone and the rare resort to profanity, told Slade that the family murders were preying on Dennison's mind.

In fairness, Slade knew that Dennison felt for *all* victims of crime, especially women and children. He would hang the Willock brothers without thinking twice — once jurors had convicted them, of course — and never lose a heartbeat's sleep over their fate.

But something in the latest massacres had touched the judge more deeply, or perhaps more *personally,* than the other cases brought before him on a daily basis. Slade couldn't be sure if it was the ferocity of the attacks, the large number of victims, or some other factor still unknown to him.

It didn't matter, though.

He had a job to do, and he would give it everything he had. To head off further bloodshed — or, failing in that, to run the killers down and make them pay.

Bullet or rope. In Slade's mind, their days were already numbered.

From the bathhouse, Slade walked to Delmonico's and paid a dollar for the largest steak he'd ever seen, with side orders of beans, potatoes, and black coffee. He was at the point of groaning when he finished, but

Slade cleaned his plate and managed to walk out under his own power, without assistance from the staff.

The Willock brothers would be having beans again tonight, and every night until they were condemned. Slade briefly wondered what they'd order for their last meal, then decided that he didn't care.

He had a room at one of Enid's two hotels — the cheaper of the two, but clean and warm, with indoor toilets — booked at monthly rates that were deducted from his salary. It was as close to home as any other place he'd occupied since adolescence, and superior to most. The room stood waiting for him at the end of each excursion Slade completed for Judge Dennison, and while he left nothing of value there, it was a place of sorts to call his own.

Packing in preparation for the morning's ride, Slade thought of Faith. She'd be expecting his return, and Slade knew that he couldn't just ride off again without explaining that he still had work to do.

In truth, he craved the sight of her, and if he should be privileged enough to touch her in the midst of all his staring . . . why, so much the better.

Slade figured that he could play it either one of two ways: stop by Faith's place in the morning, maybe catch her for a quick chat over breakfast prior to heading west, or make the ride tonight, when he had time to spare.

Tonight it was.

Downstairs, lugging his bedroll, saddle-bags, and Winchester, Slade told the hotel's manager that he'd be gone another week, at least. They wouldn't double book his room as long as they were getting paid — and saving on their laundry bill at the same time — but Slade always felt better when he'd spoken personally to the man in charge.

"More miscreants at large?" the manager inquired, eyes twinkling.

"It looks that way," Slade said and made his day.

It was a fair walk to the livery, where Slade knew he would find his roan well watered, fed, and rested up sufficiently to reach Faith's ranch without complaint. In fact, the horse never appeared to mind their long days on the trail, though if the situations were reversed, Slade thought he would've found them tedious at best.

Good thing I'm not a horse, he thought while saddling the roan.

Faith's place was two miles outside Enid, off to the northwest, which got Slade pointed in the general direction of his latest task. He couldn't guess where he would find the man or men he sought, how many of them there would be, or any other fact about the case until he'd nosed around in it and got a feeling for the murderers.

It wasn't something Slade looked forward to.

Nor was it anything he could avoid.

He took his time, riding through velvet dusk, and still reached Faith's doorstep before full night. Someone had seen him coming, warned her, and she met him at the door.

"You're late," she said.

"I didn't know I was expected."

"You still have a lot to learn." That smile.

"Well, anyhow, I had to make myself presentable."

"All right, then," she replied. "Present yourself."

2

Slade woke sometime past midnight and at first could not remember where he was. A soft mattress beneath him meant he wasn't sleeping on the ground, which canceled his split-second rush of fear that he'd forgotten to chain up the Willock brothers.

Reaching for his rifle, saddle — *anything* familiar — Slade found firm, warm flesh instead. The body moved, and a familiar voice said, "What, again?"

"Sorry," he whispered in reply. "Go back to sleep."

Faith found him with her hand and said, "I'd rather not."

The best part of an hour later, she was snoring angel soft within the circle of his arms. Slade worried that he might lie there, awake, until daylight crept underneath the bedroom window's curtains, but the sweet exhaustion overtook him, pulled him down, and carried him away.

He woke to Faith's warm kiss and reached for her again — remarkable, the stamina, at his age — but she ducked away from him this time and said, "Your breakfast's getting cold."

Slade found her fully dressed and standing over him, amazed that he had somehow missed her climbing out of bed and getting ready for her day.

"I think you drugged me."

"Is that what you call it now?" she asked, smiling.

"No. More like sorcery."

"Well, put your magic wand away and meet me in the dining room. I'm starving!"

Breakfast was a feast: fried eggs with ham *and* bacon, buttermilk pancakes awash in maple syrup, some delicious fruit juice Slade could not identify, and coffee strong enough to wake the dead. Slade dug into it as if he'd been starved for days.

"I don't know where you put it all," Faith said.

He smiled at that and raised an eyebrow.

"*Food,* you devil!" she said, laughing as she lightly slapped his arm. "Each time I see you eat, I wonder why you aren't as fat as Falstaff."

"Shakespeare's Falstaff, or that Hereford bull of yours?"

51

"I named one for the other. Take your pick."

"I'm not fat, ma'am, because my masters keep me toiling night and day."

She blushed at that, then said, "Well, if it's too much for you —"

"Which part?" he interrupted, teasing her.

"The daytime part," Faith answered, turning solemn. "Haven't you already done enough?"

"It doesn't seem so, when I hear about —"

"These crimes. I know. But, Jack, why *you?*"

Before he could respond, she rushed ahead, saying, "I understood, with Jim. And helping me. I love you for it. But you've *done* all that. You're not responsible for every person in the territory."

"While I wear this badge, I am," Slade said.

"And will you ever take it off? Or were you planning to be buried with it?"

"Faith —"

"No, wait." Her face had lost its color. For a heartbeat, Slade was worried she might faint and topple from her chair. "I'm sorry, Jack! That isn't what I meant to say at all. But —"

"Faith, I know you worry, and I'm sorry for it."

"Jack, I *worry* about weather and the cattle, wildfires and coyotes, sometimes next month's bills. When you're out hunting killers, I'm *afraid.* It's not the same at all."

"It's what I do," he said, hearing the words ring hollow even as he spoke.

"It doesn't have to be," said Faith, gripping his hand.

"My whole life," Slade replied, "I've only held two full-time jobs. The first was playing poker, if that even qualifies. I mean, I did all right and earned a living at it — most times, anyway — so it's a job. But nothing that would let me put down roots. Now, with Judge Dennison . . . since Jim . . ."

"It's not all you can do. You don't have to live in a hotel room or spend three weeks out of every month looking for murderers."

"They're not all —"

"Jack! I don't *care* what they're charged with. Any one of them could kill you. Now, you're going off to find these . . . these . . . *creatures* that annihilate whole families."

"To find and stop them. Yes."

"The judge has other marshals. They were catching men and he was hanging them for years, before you came along."

Slade knew where she was going with it,

and the notion was attractive. Sometimes, anyway. He could relax and put his feet up, be a rancher and a man of substance, sticking close to Faith and scratching trail dust off his menu.

He could do that.

And in time, Faith's ranch might even start to feel like it was his.

They'd had this talk before, but Slade felt bound to tell her, "I'm not Jim."

"I *know* that, *Jack*. You think I want to change you? Into *him?*"

"Well . . ."

"God, you're dense sometimes!"

He saw tears in her eyes now, knew he'd wounded her, and would have given everything he had to take it back.

"I love *you,* Jack," she repeated, stressing it. "And every time you leave this house to hunt another raving lunatic, I'm scared to death it will be the last time I see you."

"Faith, I'm always careful."

"So? The cemetery's full of careful men. You're not immortal, Jack. You sure as hell aren't bulletproof."

"Faith, can we talk about this when I get back from . . . this job?"

"See, there? You don't know where you're going, much less who or what you'll find. Suppose these killings were committed by a gang, and you're outnumbered ten, fifteen to one? Suppose it's Indians. What then?"

"The army handles Indians. If I find out —"

"Stop! Jack, listen to me. I love you with all my heart, the way I thought I'd never love again."

She'd raised the ante, saying "love" three times within a single conversation, tossing in her heart, and Slade was painfully aware that he hadn't replied.

It wasn't for a lack of feeling, God knew. Slade thought more of Faith than any other woman he had ever known, but part of him still wondered whether what he felt was *love*, or if he'd ever understand exactly what love was.

Trying to understand a feeling that had passed him by in childhood, and while he was growing up, he said, "I swear we'll talk about this when I come home. I mean, when I —"

Faith clutched his hand again, saying, "Don't ruin it. Home's good. Keep that in mind, will you?"

Good-byes were hard. Slade had discovered that, just recently, after long years of having no one, no place he cared to bid farewell. Drifting and gambling went hand in hand, unless you had your own casino.

In which case you weren't a gambler, just another penny-pinching businessman.

Between the night he ran away from home and the bright afternoon when he stepped off the train in Enid, Oklahoma, Slade had never stayed in one place more than six or seven months. He'd traveled where the cards and money carried him. Sometimes his reputation had preceded him, which could be good *or* bad. Sometimes it ran along behind him, nipping at his heels.

Now he was dropping words like "home" into his conversations, feeling like it might mean something.

What the hell?

Faith walked him out to where Slade's roan stood waiting for him, waited while he checked the cinches, the flank billets, canteen, his saddlebags. Slade knew his Winchester and Colt were loaded. Otherwise, they'd be no more use to him than a stick or rock he picked up off the ground.

At last, when he could put it off no longer, he turned back to Faith and found her watching him. The tears were gone, replaced by her incomparable smile.

What am I doing here? Slade asked himself. *Why am I riding out, away from her and all of this?*

But then he thought of Dennison's reports, the wounds described in detail, other violations only hinted at. He pictured a third family under the knife and hatchet, then a fourth, a fifth . . .

"I'll see you soon," he said.

"I hope so, Jack."

He couldn't have described her parting kiss as distant, but she didn't put her soul into it, either.

Who could blame her?

From the saddle, he reminded her, "We'll talk. I swear."

"I'll be here."

When he'd covered fifty yards, Slade reined in, swiveled in his saddle, raised his arm to wave good-bye once more.

But there was no one on the porch.

He thought about that, riding past the gate that marked Faith's property and turning westward when he reached the main road that would carry him from Enid, on across the panhandle and all the way to the Pacific Ocean if he let it. Weeks from now, he could be standing on a beach, knowing he'd ridden as far west as he could go.

And then, what?

Would Faith haunt him? Would he think about the job he'd left unfinished and the people who had died in agony because he'd

57

had enough of bloody work and wanted out?

They always needed gamblers out in California — or in any of the states he'd pass through on his way to get there. Slade had money in his pocket, new cards in his saddlebags. He'd simply have to drop his badge along the trail somewhere, release himself from carrying its weight, and ride on toward that sunset everybody talked about.

Or he could lose the badge and stay right there in Enid. What would be the consequence? Judge Dennison couldn't arrest him for resigning, couldn't hang him because Slade decided he preferred Faith's morning scent over the smell of gunsmoke.

You can always stay, he told himself. *It's what she wants. It's what* you *want.*

And he rode on.

Tom Gandy smelled the smoke before he saw its smudge against the cloudless sky. At first he thought it might be Caroline and Ruth preparing supper — there was a distinctive meaty kind of odor, mixed in with the smell of burning wood — but then he calculated there was too much odor for a simple family cooking fire.

And when he saw the smoke some minutes later, Gandy knew that he'd been wrong.

58

He reined up on a low rise, still a mile out from the Deacon spread, and watched the smoke blow eastward, moving out to greet him like a swirl of mud in running water. He could either ride to meet it, or forget his errand and turn back.

Which would it be?

His sorrel voted for leaving, shifting restlessly beneath him, snorting its impatience to be gone. He guessed the mare had smelled it before he did, likely smelled it *better,* and could've described what they were dealing with despite the intervening distance.

Damn. If only she could talk.

Gandy procrastinated for another moment, thinking that the smart move was to head for town. Or maybe double back to his spread first, collect his family, and *then* strike off for town with every gun he had.

That would be two — a Sharps rifle at home, above the mantel, and the Colt Navy tucked through his belt.

He'd never taken guns inside the Deacon home, which would've been a gross insult, but Gandy understood the risks inherent in the eight-mile ride to reach his nearest neighbor's house. Snakes and coyotes were the least of it, with all the renegades and border trash that drifted through.

And rumors made things worse.

For going on a month now, he'd been listening to rumors that his wife brought back from town. Stories of violence that consumed whole families and left no survivors to explain the crimes or name the killers.

The first massacre was written off as murder-suicide, a case of prairie fever where some rancher lost his hope and lost his mind at the same time, taking his wife and children with him when he went. The second raid changed that, being too much of a coincidence, but rumor had it that the law was groping in the dark for clues and getting nowhere fast.

How many massacres so far? Tom Gandy wasn't sure, since stories grew like mushrooms in the telling. If he'd understood the gossip passed on by his wife last week, there had been three or four raids up in Kansas, moving down to Oklahoma.

Coming right at Gandy and his family.

He'd hesitated when his wife said he should check on Joe and Caroline, then gave in to her pleading. He was thankful there'd been decent weather for the ride but now dreaded what he would find when he completed it.

Easing the Colt under his belt, to let him

clear it faster if need be, Tom Gandy urged his mare on toward the Deacon place. Somewhere along the way, the smoke cloud reached him and began to glide along his back trail, creeping in the general direction of his home.

Again, he felt the urge to turn and ride hell-bent for leather, back the way he'd come. Whatever had befallen Joe and Caroline was done. There would be nothing he could do, no way for him to help.

Unless they're still alive. Maybe the kids.

He gave the sorrel a gentle kick, rewarded with a jolting trot. He wasn't dawdling now, but there would still be time to pick out strangers, if they'd lingered at the scene.

Because Joe Deacon hadn't done this. There was just no way in Hell.

When he had closed the gap to a half mile, Gant saw that only Deacon's barn had burned. The house was standing, but he saw no sign of anyone moving around the place.

Nor livestock, either.

Gandy thought Joe might've taken Caroline, her mother, and the children into town after the fire, if it was accidental-like, to get supplies if nothing else. But would he take the extra horses out of the corral?

No way.

So there was trouble, and Tom Gandy

would be riding smack into the middle of it.

As he neared the house and smoking ruin of the barn, the smell got worse. He wondered now if Deacon's livestock — some of it, at least — had gone up with the barn. The other possibility was one he didn't like to think about.

It tested Gandy's nerve to ride the final hundred yards. He'd drawn the Colt Navy by then and held it braced against his saddle horn, thumb on the hammer, index finger curled inside the trigger guard. At the first sign of danger, he could cock and fire the pistol in an instant.

Whether he could hit his target, though, the way his hands were shaking, was a different story altogether.

Gandy reined up in the farmyard proper, equidistant from the house and smoking ashes of the barn. He hesitated briefly, fearing to make any noise, then called their names in turn. A mandatory ritual, all wasted breath and energy.

"Nobody home," he told the sorrel, but he knew that wasn't true. The Deacons wouldn't ride off, leaving their front door ajar.

There must be someone in the house. Someone who either couldn't answer or was disinclined to do so. Either way, it raised the short hairs on Tom Gandy's nape.

"Guess I'll just have a look," he said, and then dismounted. It took all the courage he possessed to cross the final twenty feet or so of scuffed-up dirt and mount the low porch steps. Another hesitation at the door, before he pushed his way inside.

And rushed back out a second later, pistol dangling useless, as he spilled his lunch into the dust.

Slade didn't mind the camping. Sleeping rough was part of any transient gambler's life, unless he won consistently, and who could honestly claim that?

He'd often camped out as a youngster, on the run from home. Later, on the occasions when he'd lost and couldn't rent a room — or when he'd been compelled to leave a town in haste — the open sky had been his roof, the ground his bed. At first, he'd kept a small knife close at hand, for self-defense. Tonight, Slade had his guns, with extra ammunition in his saddlebags.

To keep him safe from . . . what?

Whatever or *who*ever came along.

The Oklahoma Territory wasn't settled yet, by any means, though towns were springing up across the landscape and a larger portion of its soil was being tilled each year. Large tracts still qualified as no-man's-land, and little had been done to make the reservations any more hospitable than when the different tribes had been uprooted from their homes and moved to what was formerly designated as Indian Territory.

As in every other would-be state, defeated tribes had been graced with the least desirable land, compensated for the move with solemn promises that they would never have to move again. And as in every other case, white men had come along behind them later, gobbling up the territory, staking claims, killing off the game, laying their railroad tracks, demanding new concessions, adding new restrictions to the old agreements.

What would Slade have done, if he had been a red man?

Likely gone down fighting in the early days, he thought. Or if he had been born too late, after his people were defeated and their spirit broken, maybe he'd have run away from home and family — again.

One thing was certain. Many doors that had been open for him as a white man would've slammed shut in his face, if he had been an Indian. He couldn't have played poker for a living, since he would've been excluded from saloons.

What else?

Slade added more fuel to his small camp-fire and let his train of thought go up in smoke. Imagining a fabricated past with different skin achieved precisely nothing.

Biscuits and a strip of jerky made his supper, washed down with water he got from a small stream to quench his thirst and refill his canteen. The fire was for warmth and for show, warning strangers and predators alike that they didn't have the prairie to themselves.

Of course, in this part of the world, strangers and predators were often the same thing.

He'd thought about a cold camp, then decided that he didn't feel like shivering at midnight in his bedroll. If his fire attracted visitors, and they turned out to be the nameless, faceless murderers he sought, so much the better. They could have it out by moonlight and let right — or might — decide the issue.

Slade knew it was doubtful he would meet them on the trail, though. Even less likely to find them this far east. The killers had a pattern of attacking isolated farms with multiple victims in residence, mixing their business and pleasure.

If it was possible to plot a course from

two events, the killers should be moving in the general direction of a town called Paradise, still some fifty miles due west of where he'd camped. Without pushing the roan too much, he'd be there on the day after tomorrow, sometime in late morning.

Paradise was roughly equidistant from the Saline Reservation — so called for the widespread salt deposits on the ground — and from Fort Supply, the panhandle's main army base. Cherokees from Georgia had been marched off to the salt flats thirty years before Slade was born. Time enough, in Slade's opinion, for them to get settled and give up their dreams of revenge.

But who could really say?

Judge Dennison seemed skeptical of Indian involvement in the homestead murders, though he had no evidence to solve the riddle either way. Slade planned to keep an open mind and see where the evidence led him.

If there was any to see.

Paradise had a mayor and a marshal who might have opinions worth hearing. Slade could also talk to someone from the fort and find out what — if anything — the army knew or thought about the killings.

And after that?

He could investigate the crime scenes, but

from the descriptions in Judge Dennison's report, there wouldn't be much left for him to see. Whatever tracks might've assisted him in following the killers would be trampled over, blown away by wind, or muddied up by rain.

No matter.

He'd find something, even if he had to sit around and wait for the next killing. And there *would* be more. Of that, Slade had no doubt.

He'd known enough hard men while he was gambling, tracked and caught enough since he'd put on a badge, to know one thing for certain.

When a certain kind of hunter tasted blood, he never lost the taste for it.

He always wanted more.

Tomorrow started out like yesterday, except that Slade woke up on grass and dirt, instead of a soft mattress. When he shifted underneath his blanket, there was no warm shape beside him, welcoming his touch.

And just as well, he thought, since waking with a bobcat or coyote in his bedroll would've made a rough start for the day.

He ate a biscuit breakfast, skipped the jerky, and allowed his horse to drink its fill before they got back on the trail. It didn't qualify as any kind of road, not even wagon ruts to follow yet, but Slade kept track of his position from the sun, his compass, and assorted landmarks.

Farther on, he knew there would be proper roads connecting Paradise to Fort Supply and other towns, likely a wagon track for access to the reservation. Any place that didn't have a road, he'd make one for himself.

Riding along, he let his mind review the sketchy facts available from the two massacres. No firearms had been found at either site, which told him that the farmers' guns were stolen by whoever killed them. No one in his right mind traveled through or settled in the Oklahoma panhandle without at least one shooting iron to help him out of dire emergencies.

It also seemed that livestock had been taken in each raid so far. That told him that the killers weren't just maniacs intoxicated by their own bloodlust. They also stole things they could use or sell. If he could somehow trace the missing animals, maybe find out who'd purchased them, Slade would be that much closer to the people he was hunting.

And he made it plural in his mind, because it didn't seem to Slade that one man could wreak that much havoc.

No, scratch that. One man *could* do it — Slade had known a couple in his time who had been big and mean enough — but what he'd read about the two crimes made them sound like group endeavors. For example, would the same man who assaulted girls and women go for little boys?

Perhaps. And yet . . .

Neither of the murder houses had been burned, only their barns or other outbuildings. Inside the homes, their mutilated former occupants had been displayed, as if to shock whoever found them and the lawmen who were called out to investigate.

The killers would have better luck hiding their tracks if they had burned the homes and bodies, thereby cleaning up the evidence of wounds and vandalism. Not that Slade had *seen* the victims' injuries, but he could draw certain conclusions from their nature, number, and the sheer ferocity with which they were inflicted.

And there might be something else. In his description of the Browning murder scene, the constable from Turpin had remarked in passing that he'd found no women's clothing in the house, excluding what was ripped from Mrs. Browning's body prior to death. That struck Slade as peculiar, and he wished someone had thought to check the Thompson house as well.

Even the poorest farmer's wife would have at least three dresses: two for daily wear, so that she wasn't naked when she did the wash, and one for Sunday-go-to-meeting-type occasions. Most women, in Slade's experience, would scrimp and save to buy material they liked, then sew up different frocks in their spare time.

And it wasn't only dresses that were missing. Slade took the report to mean the constable had found no female garb of any kind scattered around the murder scene. No underwear. No scarves or bonnets. No stockings or shoes.

What did it mean?

There wouldn't be much market for used clothing, he supposed. Certainly nothing to compare with guns, cattle, or horses. So it must be something personal.

Slade reckoned that at least one of the killers had a lady friend. Someone he wanted to impress with gifts from time to time. Someone who either knew the line of business he was in or wasn't much inclined toward asking questions.

Did the female angle mean the killers had a base of operations where they could hide out between attacks, sorting their loot and planning where to sell it, looking forward to the next raid? And if so, why hadn't there been any previous reports of crimes resembling the Thompson and Browning attacks?

Slade knew it was a grave mistake to theorize before he had collected any evidence. A notion that intrigued him now might lead him miles out of his way, pursuing ghosts, if he ignored contrary clues. And so far, all the clues he had were jotted down on paper, summarized from statements by the individuals who'd seen the aftermath of slaughter for themselves.

It simply wasn't good enough.

Near dusk, when he was looking for a place to spend the night, Slade was surprised to see the small light of a campfire half a mile ahead of him. He paused and studied it, considering the risks of riding up on someone else's camp, weighing that risk against the possibility of sharing conversation with another human in the midst of no-man's-land.

And travelers might even know something about the crimes Judge Dennison had sent him to investigate. Granted, it wasn't likely, but it couldn't hurt to ask.

Slade aimed his roan in the direction of the campfire, gave its ribs a nudge, and limbered up his voice — parched from disuse the past two days — to make it suitable when he announced himself.

And he released the hammer thong that held his Colt snug in its holster.

Just in case.

3

"I'm sick of beans and fatback," Junior said.

"So leave it," Kate replied, as she continued filling up the other tin plates.

"But I'm hungry!"

"Well, then, *eat* it."

She was long accustomed to her brother's endless whining, barely heard it anymore, unless she was herself in a combative mood. That didn't happen often, thankfully for all concerned, but sometimes — like tonight, when she was extra-weary from her labors and the trail — she daydreamed about slitting Junior's windpipe while he slept.

"We've had the same thing for the past three days."

"Your 'rithmetic's improving, Brother."

"Well, why don't you *fix* it, then?" he argued. "Give us something else."

Kate turned to face him slowly, swallowing an urge to fling the crackling grease and hot beans in his face.

"Need I remind you that we'd all be eating turkey now, if you weren't such a miserable shot? Four birds, or was it five? And cockeyed Junior couldn't bag *one* of them. You want something else to eat, learn how to shoot."

Junior began to rise, scowling, then saw her hand drift toward the scalding pot and reconsidered. Plumping down again, he dug into his supper while he muttered to himself, a string of insults that she couldn't hear and thus would not be called upon to answer.

Junior *was* cockeyed, in point of fact. His right eye focused normally, while the left peered off at an angle of forty degrees, give or take, as if with a will of its own. At Junior's birth, their parents had assumed he would be blind in that eye, but he wasn't. They'd consulted doctors, but the surgery required to fix the wayward orb was too expensive, so they all forgot about it over time.

Except for Kate, when she was digging for an insult that would sting.

Her parents concentrated on the food in front of them, making no bid to mediate the argument. They'd seen enough of sibling squabbles in their time to let the dustup run its course.

Family always came through in the end.

Kate served herself a small helping of beans — *Watching my figure,* she'd have said, if anybody asked about her appetite — and eyed her parents surreptitiously. She had been doing more and more of that, lately, and wasn't loving what she saw.

The two of them were getting old. Late sixties for her father, anyway, and with the rugged frontier life they'd led, Kate thought it was remarkable they'd lasted this long. Both could still work when they had to, though they rested more between jobs, leaving heavy work to Kate and Junior. That was only normal, and she didn't really mind.

Not much. Not yet.

But they'd be gone soon, and she had to look ahead. Consider what was best for her in the long run. When both of them were dead, should she keep Junior or discard him?

It was one thing, dealing with an idjit brother in the bosom of your family, and quite another thing to drag him after you when he was all the family remaining in the world. She understood the human trait of judging by appearances and didn't want to be associated with her stupid walleyed brother in the public mind.

How could a lady of a certain age advance

herself, if she was forced to haul around a big, dumb anchor all the time?

It would be strange without him, granted, in the same way that new lodgings felt peculiar for a day or two. But she'd get used to it. The trick would be devising some way to prevent him tagging after her, since Junior rarely had an independent thought and looked to others for direction in the simplest things.

Oh, well, she thought, *small loss.* And waited for a pang of guilt that never came.

"Somebody's coming," Junior said, rising with supper plate in hand and staring off to eastward.

It was dusk, but light enough for Kate to see a plume of dust, perhaps three-quarters of a mile away. Junior had seen it first and hadn't even seemed to be watching the prairie, nose down in his beans and fatback. Kate made a note to remember that, when it was time to unload him.

"How many?" asked Papa, not rising, but scooting on his butt a little closer to the old Sharps rifle propped against the nearest wagon wheel.

Kate's mother didn't budge.

"Just one," Junior replied, "unless they're riding double."

"He'll have seen the fire," said Papa.

76

"May not risk it, even so," Mama replied.

"I'll bet he does," said Junior.

"Might be an outlaw," Papa said.

"You think?" asked Junior.

"Way out here? Why not?"

"*We're* way out here," Kate said.

"That's true," Papa allowed. "Can't hurt to chew the fat a little with a fellow traveler."

"Fat's something we got plenty of," Junior observed.

Kate almost said, *Between your ears,* but she resisted the impulse. It wasn't time now, with an unexpected visitor approaching, to provoke another spat with Junior. There'd be time for all that later.

Once they got the stranger sorted out.

Slade saw the campers watching him when he had shaved the gap down to a hundred yards or so. He raised a hand in greeting, but got no response. At fifty yards, he called out through the dusk, "Hello in camp!"

No answer, but all four of them were on their feet. Two men, two women, tracking Slade's advance. He held the roan at a slow walking pace and watched their hands for weapons, but saw none.

At thirty yards, Slade saw a rifle leaning up against their wagon — could it be a Sharps? — but no one in any kind of rush

to grab it yet. The wagon was, itself, something to see: covered on top and open at the
back, with rolled-up canvas flaps on either
side, resembling a larger version of an old-
fashioned stagecoach. Four sturdy horses
grazed off to one side, hobbled to keep them
from straying too far.

Scanning their faces, Slade called out,
"Sorry to barge in on you. I can move on, if
you like, and no hard feelings."

Finally, the younger of the women cracked
a smile — the first he'd seen from any of
them — and replied, "No need for that,
stranger. Come on and sit a spell."

Slade dismounted at twenty yards, walking his roan in the rest of the way. He waited
for the moment when they saw his badge,
gauging reactions as he often did, but none
of them seemed either nervous or relieved.

"A lawman," said the younger woman.
"You're a long way out from anywhere."

"Just passing through," Slade said.

"Like us."

Up close, he guessed that she was somewhere in her early forties, pretty in an
understated way that might've blossomed
with some help from rouge and other female
war paint. As far as Slade could tell, beneath
the dress and any hidden rigging, she appeared to have the body of a healthy woman

half her age.

Quite healthy.

"Jack Slade," he declared, by way of introduction.

"I'm Kate Bowden, Marshal Slade," their spokesmistress replied. "These are my parents, John and Helen, and the handsome one's my brother, Junior."

"*John* Junior," the brother said, and he was anything but handsome. Slade supposed that Kate had thrown that in to needle him, some kind of running thing between them.

No one offered to shake hands, making Slade glad he hadn't offered his. Instead, he told them all, "I'm pleased to meet you, out here where I didn't think I'd find a soul."

"You missing one?" Kate's father asked.

"That's good," Slade said, smiling. "I'll have to make a note."

"Won't charge you for it."

"Would you like to have some supper with us, Marshal? Only beans and fatback, I'm afraid —"

"The same as everyday," Junior observed.

Kate drilled him with a steely look and finished, "But you're welcome to it."

Slade returned her beaming smile and wondered if she meant the food, or something else.

"I won't deny I'm tired of jerky, ma'am. It's very kind of you."

"You can't have any if you call me 'ma'am,' " she said. "It's Kate, or nothing."

"Then you'll need to call me Jack."

"You've got a deal."

"I'll just see to my horse," Slade said.

"No rush at all. It's ready when you are."

Slade was about to lead his roan off toward the hobbled dray horses when Kate called after him, "Wait up. I'll show you where we found the spring."

She joined him, brushing shoulders as she led him toward a pair of weathered boulders, twenty paces from the fire. A second glance showed Slade that it was really just one slab of stone, split down the middle by some ancient cataclysm, with the left-hand side thrust higher than the right. Clear water burbled from the cleft between those halves and ran over a graveled bed for two feet, give or take, before it vanished back into the ground.

"You have a good eye, spotting this," Slade told her, while his horse began to drink its fill.

"I normally find what I need," she said.

"There can't be much out here," he answered, scanning the horizon as it flushed crimson with sunset and the shades of night began their swift descent.

"Depends on what you're looking for," she said. "Most places are for passing through, but you can still get lucky."

"You spend much time traveling?" Slade asked.

"My whole life, more or less," Kate said. "Junior and I grew up in wagons pretty much like that one. Always going somewhere else."

"You don't look like a gypsy," Slade observed.

"Sometimes you have to look inside," she said. "It's in my blood, I guess."

Slade wondered why a woman with her looks and evident endowments hadn't found a husband, but he didn't plan to ask. It would be impolite, for one thing, and he didn't want to open any doors in that direction, given how Kate looked at him when they were making small talk.

"Where'd you come from, Jack?" she asked.

"Most recently from Enid, where Judge Dennison holds court."

"The hanging judge?"

"Word gets around, I guess."

"It does. So, that's what? Two days on the road to someplace?"

"Paradise," he told her.

"And you're not there yet." She wore a knowing smile.

"Midday tomorrow, if my luck holds."

"And the creek don't rise," she said.

He glanced down at the spring and said, "I don't think this will give me any trouble."

"Trouble's everywhere out here, Jack. But you know that, right?"

"I've seen my share."

"It's in your eyes." She shifted topics suddenly, saying, "You ought to stay the night with us."

"I don't like to impose," he said.

"Feel free." She smiled again. "You've already agreed to eat our food. We don't have any claim on dirt and grass."

He glanced back toward the fire and found the others watching them. "Your family may not appreciate me staying on," he said.

"I'll talk them into it," Kate said.

And so she did. There wasn't much persuasion to it, really. She announced that Slade was sleeping over with them, and her father nodded, any twitch of smile or frown concealed by his snow-white mustache and beard. Kate's mother studied Slade as if he was a clothier's dummy in a window, but said nothing.

Only Junior Bowden seemed put off by the idea of Slade remaining in their camp after he ate the beans and salt pork Kate had piled onto his tin plate, with a cup of coffee to help wash it down. The big man glowered with one eye, then turned his head a little so the other one could take its turn. Throughout the scrutiny, he chewed his lower lip with large gray-looking teeth.

Kate sat beside Slade, close enough that he had trouble eating without giving her an elbow to the ribs. She didn't seem to mind, though, and kept up a nonstop stream of questions while he ate.

"Is it a lonely life, being a marshal?"

"On the trail, it can be. Not when I'm in Enid."

"Who's Enid?" asked Junior, with a cock-eyed leer.

"Enid's a *town,* you idjit!" Kate snapped at him, fierce eyes daring him to answer back. Instead, he shrugged and grinned.

Kate held the glare a little longer, then turned back to Slade. "You chase all kinds of bad men, I suppose?"

Slade chewed, swallowed, and answered, "Anyone Judge Dennison has warrants for."

"Will you be serving warrants on this trip?" Kate asked, leaning a little closer without shifting from her place.

"Not this time," Slade replied.

"What brings you out so far from home, then, Jack?"

"It's an investigation. West of here, another couple days, there've been some crimes. Killings. The judge sent me to have a look around and see if I come up with anything."

"What kind of killin's?" asked Kate's father.

"Families. Attacked and murdered in their homes," Slade said. "The last report was twelve or thirteen dead, depending how you count it."

"What's that mean?" asked Kate.

"Well . . . um . . . one of the ladies killed was in the family way." Slade dipped his head toward Kate's mother and said, "Sorry if that's upsetting to you, ma'am."

"I lost two younguns of my own," she told him, with a scratchy, brittle-sounding voice. "You just move on."

"Sounds like a pack of Injuns," Junior offered. "Killin' decent folk that way."

"It's been suggested," Slade admitted. "And I wouldn't be surprised to find the army looking into it when I reach Paradise."

"But *you* don't think so?" Kate inquired.

Slade's fork was halfway to his mouth when she turned toward him, and his elbow brushed the firm swell of her breast. He felt the color rising in his cheeks but couldn't think of any good way to apologize. Kate's smile seemed to suggest she didn't mind.

"I couldn't say, without investigating," he replied. "Judge Dennison has doubts. About the Indians, I mean."

"How come?" asked Junior.

"Mainly, I'd say, because there's been no raiding in the territory for the past ten years or so."

"You still can't trust 'em," Junior said. "The only good Injun's a dead Injun. Abe Lincoln said that."

"No, he didn't," Kate informed her brother. "It was General Sheridan, right here in Oklahoma. Could you *be* any more ignorant?"

"Whoever said it, it's the truth," Junior replied.

Kate turned away from him, her scowl inverting to become a smile as she faced Slade.

"How would you solve a case like that?" she asked.

"I've never tried before," Slade said. "Question the witnesses who found the bodies. Look around the crime scenes, if it's not too late, for any kind of clues. Keep my eyes open as I go along."

"Did you want seconds?" Kate asked,

glancing at his nearly empty plate.

"No, thanks," Slade said. "I don't know where I'd put it."

"Really?" she inquired and rubbed against his arm again as she relieved him of the plate. "I'll just take care of this, then."

"I don't mind helping with the cleanup," Slade said.

"You're a guest," Kate told him. "Just relax, while Junior helps me."

When her brother didn't get the message, Kate returned and said, "Junior?" Her tone fell somewhere in between cold steel and a whiplash.

Slade watched as the big man glowered, then stood up and followed Kate back toward the spring. They didn't speak until they were beyond the reach of firelight and their words were lost.

Slade tethered his roan to a stake near the spring, with enough lead to let the horse graze or drink as it pleased. He spent some time grooming the animal, giving the Bowdens time to talk about him while his back was turned.

They were a grim family, aside from Kate, but that was nothing new or special on the prairie. Half the farmers Slade had ever met seemed like they'd never learned to smile

— or, as he thought more likely, had forgotten over years of trying to coerce a living from the soil. Spending your whole life on the move would be a different kind of hardship, but he guessed people got used to it.

A glance back toward the wagon showed him that the flaps had all been lowered, granting privacy to Kate and Helen while they changed into whatever they would wear for sleeping. Junior and his dad, meanwhile, had wandered off into the darkness on the far side of the wagon, likely to relieve themselves.

Slade stole a private moment for himself, behind the chest-high boulders, staring at the wagon all the while, in case the women should emerge. He'd finished and was walking back when Kate appeared out of the shadows to his left, surprising him.

"Sorry," he said. "I didn't see you there."

And wondered what *she* might have seen.

"I love to walk at night," she said. "Don't you?"

"Can't say I ever thought about it," he replied.

"Well, think about it now, and join me for a little stroll."

She wore a scarf over a long-sleeved linen nightgown, hemmed at ankle length, but with a neckline cut below what Slade deemed modest. When she moved, the linen clung to her and gave Slade the idea that she wore nothing else beneath it.

"You're barefoot," Slade observed.

"It's warm out, yet."

He nodded. "Warm enough for snakes."

"You'll just have to protect me, then," Kate said, smiling.

"I suspect that you can take care of yourself," Slade said.

"You're right," she told him. "It's a talent — or a gift. Who knows? Still, every woman needs a man's help, now and then."

She looped an arm through his, her right breast nuzzling his biceps. Slade would have been something more or less than human if he didn't notice and react involuntarily, but he knew trouble when he saw it. And he didn't plan to let himself be sidetracked from his job, or from the loyalty he felt toward Faith.

"It must be dangerous, your job," Kate said.

"It can be," Slade agreed with her.

"You've had to kill men, I suppose."

"A few," he said.

"And does it bother you? Do you lose sleep about it, afterward?"

Slade answered with a question of his own. "Is this your notion of small talk?"

"I've always thought *small talk* was wasted breath," Kate said. "Chatting about the weather or the price of beef in Wichita won't tell you anything about a person, will it?"

"I guess not."

"Well, then?"

"Well, what?" Slade asked.

"My question, Jack."

He'd hoped that she might let it go, but no such luck.

"I lost some sleep the first time, though it couldn't have been helped," Slade said. "Now, with my job, it comes down to arresting someone or allowing him to go on hurting others. Maybe killing them. I give each one a chance. The choice they make depends a lot on what's in store for them."

"That hanging judge of yours," Kate said.

"He's hard but fair," Slade said, in Dennison's defense.

"And what about you, Jack?" she asked him. "Are you hard?"

"We'd better head on back to camp," he said.

"You're in a hurry?"

"I've been riding all day long. I need a break."

Kate laughed at that but still clung to his arm. "You don't know what you're missing," she informed him.

"I've a fair idea."

"You've been with women, then?"

His turn to laugh. "A few."

"Just like the men you've killed?"

"Except the women made me lose more sleep," Slade said.

"You've got a long night to recuperate."

"It's afterward that wouldn't sit right," Slade replied.

"All right, then. Back to camp it is."

As they approached the fire, Kate made a point of stepping out in front, letting its glow through linen emphasize that she was naked underneath. Turning to face him, she contrived to drop her scarf and bent down for it, trusting in the low-cut neckline to confirm it. As she straightened, Slade fancied that he could see her nipples poking at the fabric.

"Could be cold tonight," she said. "You're sure there's nothing else you need?"

"I'll be all right," Slade said.

"Good night, then, Jack. Sweet dreams."

Slade spread his bedroll near the wagon's falling tongue and gave his roan a final look before he slipped under the blanket, his saddlebags laid out to make a pillow. Junior Bowden slept beside the fire, already snoring, while Kate joined her parents in the wagon.

Slade tried eavesdropping, but they defeated him by whispering. Their voices carried, but the words were lost, a muffled hissing sound that made him think of snakes. He soon gave up and let sleep claim him, lying on his back, with one hand on his pistol and the Winchester against his thigh.

Slade woke to pale dawn's chill and stirrings in the camp. He had imagined, for some reason, that the Bowdens would be tardy risers, but they proved him wrong. Junior collected firewood, while his father lit the blaze and Helen sorted out the cooking gear they'd washed and stowed last night.

Kate was the latest of the family to rise, but even then, the new sun barely counted as a pink smear in the east.

"All rested up?" she asked.

"Fit as a fiddle," Slade replied.

"You don't sleepwalk."

Slade responded with a shrug. "Where would I go?"

"Maybe to Paradise."

"It's my next stop," he said.

Kate's mother brought fresh eggs from somewhere, fried them up with bacon, and the five of them consumed breakfast in silence. Slade had cleaned his plate before

Kate said, "We may head into town ourselves."

Both of her parents looked up from their plates, as if surprised. John Bowden said, "Nothing in there we need, right now."

"Maybe just have a look around," Kate said.

"Too far out of our way. We'll stop in at the next one."

Slade was half expecting Kate to argue, but she let it go, not looking at him as she finished off her eggs.

"There isn't much to Paradise, from what I hear," Slade said to no one in particular.

"Not what the Good Book says," Junior responded, talking with his mouth full.

"Boy's a joker," said John Bowden. "Always has been."

"It's a talent," Slade replied, thinking the cockeyed hulk could use some practice. Maybe get himself a book of jokes to memorize.

"Where are you headed, then," Slade asked, before Kate started to collect the breakfast plates.

"Wherever we end up," the elder Bowden said. "No place in mind. Just goin'."

"Fancy-free," Slade said, shooting for admiration in his tone.

"It gets old, I promise you."

Her father didn't seem to hear. "We never had no luck in towns," he said. "Too crowded, everybody hurrying around. Give me the open spaces every time."

"You found them here, all right," Slade said. "No one to help you if you hit a rough patch, though."

"We take care of ourselves," said Junior. "Don't cotton to rules or people sayin' where we oughta go and all like that."

Slade met his flat gaze one eye at a time and said, "I know a lot of people who agree with you."

"You hear this talk about statehood?" the old man asked.

Slade nodded. "Hard to miss it, but I'm guessing it's a few years off, at least."

"Lately, I'm thinking we'd be better off in Arizona or New Mexico. More room to breathe out west, there. Fewer people tellin' others how they oughta live."

"They'll all be states one day," Slade said.

"I'll never see it," Bowden answered. "Time's runnin' short on me, I'd say."

Returning from the spring with clean plates dripping wet, Kate heard her father's comment and said, "Papa, don't start *that* nonsense again!"

"Ain't nonsense, girl," the old man said. "Nobody walks out of the game. We all get carried out."

"Well, why don't you just dig yourself a hole right here, and pull the sod in after you?" she challenged him. "You talk about it so much, anyone would think you're looking forward to it."

"Dug enough holes in my time," her father said. "I'll let somebody else sweat over mine."

Slade rose, knees cracking as he stood, suddenly anxious to be on the move. "Well, folks," he said, "I want to thank you kindly for your hospitality. You've been most generous, but now it's time I earned my salary."

"Killers to catch," said Kate.

"Or track, at least," Slade said. "I'll just get saddled up."

"I'll help you," Kate announced and followed Slade as he moved to collect his gear. She took his bedroll, while he hauled the rest back to his roan and started getting ready for the trail.

"Pay no mind to my father," she remarked, as Slade settled his saddle on the horse and started fastening the cinches underneath its belly. "He gets in these moods and thinks he's dying any minute. I've been hearing it forever."

"But he still won't settle down," Slade said.

"We tried it, but it didn't work out for us," Kate replied. "I think he's talked himself into believing that he'll live longer if he keeps moving."

Slade tied his gear in place with saddle strings and slid the Winchester into its scabbard on the right.

"Some reason why you have to travel with him?" he inquired.

"Is that an invitation, Marshal?"

"Just a question."

"The answer is — we're family. We stick together."

"Could be worse," Slade said, considering the years of separation from his own.

"I doubt we'll meet again," Kate said, surprising Slade when she rose on tiptoes to kiss his cheek. "Be careful with your hunting."

He replied, "I always am."

Slade mounted, steered the roan around Kate where she stood, and used his heels to get it started, westward bound. A final wave to the assembled Bowdens only saw Kate's hand raised in return. The others watched him go, their faces deadpan.

Next stop, Paradise, Slade thought.

And wondered how far off the mark that name would be.

4

The sun was almost overhead, signaling noon, when Slade saw Paradise in front of him, a smudge of buildings in the distance, still at least four miles ahead. Breakfast with the Bowdens had inevitably slowed him down, and he'd refused to put the roan at risk for nothing, galloping in heat that had him sweating through his clothes by eight o'clock.

Their short breaks had been water only, and some fresh grass for the horse, but Slade had eaten plenty before leaving camp. Now, finally, his goal was within sight, but he continued at the steady pace he'd kept all morning, knowing that he'd be in Paradise around the time its people finished up their lunch.

No problem, then.

The dead could wait, and rushing now would put him no closer to those who'd claimed at least a dozen lives already. Slade still had to meet the men in charge of Paradise, examine crime scenes — which could take another couple of days, right there — and then digest whatever clues he found, striving to make a theory out of them.

Unless, of course, the army had decided it was Indians. In which case, Slade had wasted two days of his life to get here, with another two days spent on riding back to Enid.

Back to Faith.

Slade filled the time in front of him by picking through his thoughts. And since he'd gained no further information on the killings yet, those thoughts turned back to his experience with Kate and her peculiar family.

Slade understood the siren song of drifting, always chasing what was over the next hill, around the next bend in the road. When he was gambling for a living, he had gone wherever there was cash and men ready to lose it, keeping track of gold or silver strikes, riding a circuit that included half a dozen states.

He'd played in Phoenix, Tucson, Albuquerque, Amarillo, Wichita, Cheyenne, Laramie, Denver, and Colorado Springs, then back again to start the whole route over. In between, there'd been a hundred smaller towns or mining camps where Slade had risked his money and his life bucking the odds.

He'd even made it to New Orleans once, but found the city on the Gulf too organized to suit him. Gambling there was regulated by established syndicates, Italians versus Anglos, and it seemed to tremble on the brink of civil war the whole time Slade was there. A few weeks later, someone gunned down the police chief, blamed Italians for it, and the Anglo crowd had slaughtered something like a dozen of the immigrants after a jury found them innocent.

So much for being *civilized*.

In Oklahoma, if you saw a lynch mob coming after you, its leaders wouldn't be police in uniform. And as you died, at least you'd have the satisfaction of imagining Judge Dennison sending your killers to the gallows. Which, Slade guessed, was what they meant by thanking Heaven for small favors.

Overall, while drifting had been good enough for Slade until his brother's death — and some might say he was a drifter still, pursuing fugitives all over hell and gone — he wondered why a man John Bowden's age would shun society and drag his grown-up family along with him to share the lonely, rootless life.

None of your business, a small voice in his head reminded Slade, but he was bound to think about it, now that it had come to mind. Bowden wasn't a mountain man or hermit, one of those who found a cave or built a tiny shack somewhere and stayed off to themselves until they died. He wasn't any kind of migrant worker Slade had ever seen, nor did he travel for a living, like a gambler or a snake-oil salesman. He was simply on the go, dragging his family along to who knew where and endless empty vistas beyond that.

Maybe his wife, Helen, had known that when she married Bowden. Maybe it had even pleased her, somehow, for some reason Slade couldn't decipher. Fine. They'd have conceived their children on the trail, and Helen would've borne them, either by herself or with the help of others in whatever town was nearest when the moment came.

And after that?

Had either of the Bowden children ever been to school? Junior seemed slow, with just enough wit to enrage a drunken stranger or a small-town sheriff if he gave them any sass. Size might protect him in a fair fight, but he wasn't bulletproof, so maybe John and Helen minimized his contact with people outside the family.

Kate was a different story altogether. She was obviously bright — and passionate, judging from how she'd thrown herself at Slade — but was she educated in the formal sense? There'd been no call for any reading or arithmetic while Slade was with the Bowdens, so he couldn't tell if any of the tribe were literate. If only one of them could read and write, he'd definitely bet on Kate.

She'd been aggressive in a way that Slade had rarely seen outside saloons, where women earned their keep by making strangers feel special, each dusty cowhand off a drive welcomed as if he was a long-lost lover fresh home from the war. Except Kate wasn't being paid to cuddle with him, and Slade knew — despite what Faith said in their tender moments — that he shouldn't plan on winning any prizes for his looks.

So, was she desperately lonely? Or had something else prompted her offer of a bareback ride? And if the latter, what had been that *something else?*

"Who cares?" Slade asked the roan, predictably receiving no reply.

The Bowdens were behind him now rolling along their trail to nowhere, and Slade had no reason to think he would see them again. The odds against a second chance encounter dwarfed the risk of drawing to an inside straight.

He could forget about them now and focus on the job at hand. Finding the monsters who, with any luck, were still somewhere within his reach from Paradise.

The sheriff's office sat between a dry-goods store and a surveyor's office with a CLOSED sign in its window, more or less dead center in the heart of town. The rest of Paradise was four blocks long, with all the normal shops, a livery, a small church, and a three-story hotel. Construction still in progress at the north end of the street suggested confidence in civic growth.

As Slade had seen on his approach to town, Main Street ran on an east-west axis, while the homes of those who lived in town spread out to north and south on side streets. It appeared to be a growing town, not one already stagnant, waiting to dry up and blow away, but Slade imagined that some kind of stimulus would help.

An ore strike, maybe, or discovery of oil. Maybe a railroad line connecting Paradise to other whistle-stops from coast to coast.

And how much would a string of bloody murders set it back?

Slade dismounted outside the sheriff's office and tied his roan to a post beside a water trough. He left it guzzling as he stepped up to the door and passed inside.

The law in Paradise consisted of a small man, ginger-haired and freckled, whose mustache threatened to overwhelm his narrow face. He rose as Slade entered, blinked at Slade's federal badge, then sat back down again.

"Help you?" he asked.

"Jack Slade. I'm with the U.S. Marshals Service, out of Enid."

"Ardis Eastman. *Sheriff* Eastman."

"You're familiar with Judge Isaac Dennison?"

"Heard of him, sure."

"He sent me out to see about these homestead murders, so I'm checking in with you, first thing."

"From Enid, you've been riding — what? Three days?"

"Today makes three."

"You won't have heard the news, then."

"News?"

"About the latest killings."

For a second, Slade had hoped the sheriff was about to tell him that the slayers had been caught or killed. He didn't flinch at Eastman's news, but it was close.

"How many this time?" Slade inquired.

"Joe Deacon and his wife. Two kids. Mother-in-law."

Five more made seventeen — or eighteen, with June Thompson's unborn child.

"When did it happen?"

"Neighbor found 'em yesterday, but they'd been dead at least two days. Sumbitches left the front door standing open when they left. We had some trouble telling what was done by men and what by the coyotes."

"Have you buried them?"

"The funeral's at five o'clock," said Eastman. "You can see them at the undertaker's, if you need to. I don't recommend it."

"Any signs of theft?" Slade asked.

"As near as we can figure, Joe had six or seven horses. None left when I got there."

"Were they branded?"

"Neighbor didn't think so. I'd be going round to see if anybody's tried to sell 'em, but the council, in its wisdom, won't pay any deputies. So, here I sit."

"Somebody's checked the reservation, I suppose?" Slade said.

"First thing that Colonel Northcliff thought of, but he came up empty. Should you want to see him, by the way, he's over at the mayor's house. Save you riding out to Fort Supply, at least."

It was a good idea. Slade said, "I'll do that. Can you point me in the right direction?"

"Better yet, I'll walk you over. Make the introductions."

Sheriff Eastman rose, hitched up his loose gunbelt, and held the door for Slade.

"Down to your left, first side street," Eastman said. "Your mare's safe where she is."

"No thieves in town?" Slade asked him, making light of it.

"I wouldn't go that far," said Eastman, "but nobody's likely to try anything today. They're getting ready for the funeral, and the truth is that they're just shit scared."

"In town? The raids have all hit isolated ranches."

"So far," Eastman said. "O' course, that's only half of it."

"So, what's the other half?" asked Slade.

"The killers could be anybody, right? I mean, if they ain't redskins. Hell, they could be living right next door."

The mayor of Paradise lived in a white two-story house, painted sometime within the past six months or so, with flowers standing tall in window boxes. It was guarded by a token picket fence that only stretched along

104

the street, without extending to enclose the property on either side. They could have ducked around it, but the sheriff played it straight and entered through the waist-high gate.

Stones had been laid to form a path between the gate and the front porch. Slade followed Eastman up three wooden steps and waited while the local lawman knocked. A minute passed before a dark-haired woman answered, smiling when she recognized the sheriff.

"Ardis, they're nearly done," she said, flicking a hasty glance at Slade. "Rance didn't tell me you were coming over."

"Wasn't planning to, Miz Mathers. But I got a U.S. marshal here about our problem, and I reckoned he should meet the colonel. And the mayor, o' course."

"Well, then, why don't you both come in?"

Their hostess didn't ask Slade's name, just led them to a parlor where two men sat talking over coffee. One wore a colonel's eagle on the collar of his army uniform. The other was in shirtsleeves, with a vest strained by his paunch, hair thinning in an odd-shaped pattern on his scalp. He'd compensated with a set of bushy muttonchop sideburns.

Both men rose as the mayor's wife entered, breaking off their conversation in mid-sentence. It was plain from their expressions that they weren't expecting Sheriff Eastman, much less his companion. Something in the mayor's eyes told Slade that he feared more grisly news.

"Ardis, who's your friend?" he asked.

"I got a U.S. marshal here, sent out from Enid by Judge Dennison," Eastman replied. "Name's Slade," he added, glancing back for confirmation with an eyebrow raised.

"Jack Slade."

"Well, Marshal Slade, this is our mayor, Rance Mathers. And his company I mentioned, Colonel Northcliff, in from Fort Supply."

They shook hands all around. The mayor's grip had a little tremor to it, while the colonel's was a knuckle grinder. No one offered Slade a seat, which forced the others to remain standing.

"More coffee, anyone?"

The mayor had seemingly forgotten that his wife was in the room. He frowned and shook his head in answer to her question. "No, thank you, Colleen."

"I'll leave you to it, then."

When she was gone, the mayor said, "I suppose Ardis has told you that there's been another . . . incident?"

"He also mentioned that the victims'

106

missing horses didn't turn up on the reservation."

"Haven't turned up *yet*," the captain said, as if correcting Slade.

"You think your soldiers missed them?"

"We searched the main village and spoke to Chief Red Eagle," Northcliff answered, stiffly. "I don't have the manpower required to scour every corner of the reservation for stray horses."

It was Slade's turn to correct the soldier. "*Stolen* horses. And, apparently, the only evidence that might identify the killers in the latest *incident*."

"For all I know, the nags have already been butchered and consumed," Northcliff replied.

"Times must be hard out on the rez, if Cherokee are stealing horses for their meat," Slade said.

"It wouldn't be the strangest thing they've done, Marshal. But without evidence —"

"You can't hang any Indians," Slade finished for him. "And the job comes back to me."

The mayor's small eyes pinned Slade. "Marshal, do you have any reason to believe it *wasn't* Indians?"

"I've only been in town for half an hour," Slade replied. "The way it works, I normally investigate *before* I start accusing anyone."

"You think *white* men could do something like this? The butchery and . . . and . . ."

"I've seen enough to know that *men* are capable of anything, regardless of their color. Colonel, you admit you've got no proof these murders were committed by an Indian?"

"No proof *so far.*"

"Well, if you find some, let me know. Meanwhile, according to the law and my instructions from Judge Dennison, I'll be examining the evidence myself."

"Such as it is," said Sheriff Eastman.

"I'll take what I can get," Slade said.

"Ardis will get you started, then, I'm sure," the mayor announced. "Whatever Marshal Slade requires, yes, Sheriff?"

"Be a pleasure," Eastman said, without enthusiasm.

"Now," said Mathers, "if we're finished, Marshal, I just have a few more incidental matters to discuss with Colonel Northcliff. Various security precautions for the town, and so forth."

Recognizing a dismissal when he heard it, Slade trailed Eastman from the parlor, out the door, and through the whitewashed picket gate.

"You really don't think Injuns did it?"

asked the sheriff, as they walked back toward his office.

"Sheriff, you're the one who said the killers could be living right next door."

"I didn't really *mean* it, though. Jesus! It's what some folks say, 'cause they're scared."

"That's good," Slade said. "A little fear may help them stay alive."

Angus McCallister struck a match and held its flame an inch below the blunt tip of his huge cigar. When he was puffing like a locomotive, satisfied, he deigned to give the officer in blue his full attention.

"I'm not following you, Colonel," he remarked. "How does this lawman passing through affect us, one way or the other?"

"First, sir," Hollis Northcliff answered, "he's a U.S. marshal, sent from Enid by Judge Dennison."

"I heard that part."

"And he has doubts that redskins are behind these killings."

"He has doubts? So what?" McCallister frowned through a cloud of acrid smoke. "Are you in charge, or not?"

"I am in charge of Fort Supply, and I can search the reservation for incriminating evidence — which, you'll recall, we so far haven't found. Beyond that, as you know —

or should know — this man's federal badge trumps my authority."

"Don't tell me what I *should* know, Colonel. What I *do* know is that I've invested in you and your future as a prosperous civilian. I intend to get my money's worth, unless you're telling me I've backed a loser."

"No, sir! I'm not saying that, at all."

McCallister could see Northcliff's regret at stopping by the ranch to brief him on the day's events, but what choice did the soldier have? He had accepted money from the single largest landowner within a hundred miles, and in return had promised certain things. McCallister couldn't care less if it was difficult to keep those promises — as long as they *were* kept.

"What *are* you saying, then?" McCallister demanded. "Are you telling me *you* doubt these murders were committed by redskins?"

"It doesn't matter what I think, Mr. McCallister. I have to *prove* they were involved, before I can suggest specific remedies to my superiors in Washington."

" 'Suggest,' my ass," the rancher sneered. "Where would we be today, if our forefathers had *suggested* that the Injuns get the hell out of their way? I'll tell you where: we'd have seventy-six million white people

110

squatting in slums along the East Coast, with ninety percent of America going to waste."

"I don't make rules," Northcliff replied.

"And I don't want to hear about them," said McCallister. "Whatever happened to the army's fighting spirit, Colonel? Do you think that Chivington concerned himself with rules at Sand Creek? What about Custer, at Washita?"

"Colonel Chivington was court-martialed and left the service in disgrace," said Northcliff. "And you may recall Custer's come-uppance at the Little Big Horn."

"Jesus Christ!" McCallister rose from his place behind the ornate desk and stalked around its bulk to face Northcliff. "Are you afraid of getting slaughtered by the goddamn reservation Cherokee?"

An angry rush of color stained the colonel's cheeks. "No, sir," he said, between clenched teeth. "However, I don't aim to see our private dealings aired in front of Congress or a military court — which I can guarantee *will* happen if I try to stage another Sand Creek massacre."

McCallister pinned Northcliff with his cold gray eyes.

"I want the redskins off that land, Colonel. I *need* them off that land. These killings are our best hope to achieve that, as you formerly agreed while standing in this very room."

He didn't add, *With my cash in your pocket.* Northcliff wasn't likely to forget the bribes he had accepted, even if he now wished that he *could* forget them.

"I'm in full accord with your intent, Mr. McCallister," the colonel said. "But every move my soldiers make is in the public eye. We can't just move the Cherokee because we feel like it. They must at least *appear* guilty, and so far, I have nothing in the way of evidence."

"Then, I'd suggest you find some, Colonel. Sooner, rather than later."

"I can't find what doesn't exist," Northcliff said.

"Don't be so sure."

"What's that supposed to mean?"

McCallister responded with a question of his own. "What kind of proof would close the deal?"

The colonel frowned, clearly uneasy with the new direction of their conversation. "Obviously, something that connects the murders to the reservation," he replied.

"Well, *obviously,*" said the rancher, with another sneer. "Give me specifics, Colonel, if it's not too much to ask."

"We haven't got specifics," Northcliff said. "As far as personal effects, we can't tell whether anything was stolen from the scenes — or if so, what they might have been. We *think* livestock was taken in each case, but the reports from different neighbors are confused."

"So much the better," said McCallister.

"How so?"

The rancher shrugged. "If you have different descriptions of a missing horse, for instance, who's to say the one you find out on the rez isn't the very horse you're looking for?"

"Which brings us back to what I told you in the first place," Colonel Northcliff said. "We found no unexplained horses or cattle on the reservation."

"No," McCallister agreed, then smiled around the girth of his cigar as he added, "not yet."

The undertaker's name was Hezekiah Grimm. Slade wondered if he'd made it up to fit his chosen trade, but thought it would be impolite to ask.

On second thought, he noted that the name matched Grimm himself, as well as his profession. He was tall and gaunt, with sunken cheeks accentuated by a set of poorly made false teeth. Slade guessed that when he dressed up in his mourning suit and top hat, Grimm would give a fair impersonation of an animated skeleton.

But his latest customers were far from animated.

Truth be told, some of them weren't entirely *there.*

The Deacons had been slaughtered, one and all. Viewing the injuries they'd suffered, Slade wished that he could've skipped it, but he had to learn something about the crimes that wasn't spelled out in Judge Dennison's reports.

What kind of mind — or *minds* — would wreak this kind of bloody havoc on another human being?

Slade had seen his share of gruesome crimes. He'd read about the raw brutality of war and how some soldiers ran amok in combat. From the War Between the States, Fort Pillow and the raid on Lawrence, Kansas, came to mind. He'd also heard the tales of Indian atrocities and knew that some of their more barbarous behavior — scalping, for example — had been learned from white men.

Was there anything about the corpses of the Deacon family to tell Slade whether knives, axes, and other weapons had been clutched in red hands or white ones?

If so, he didn't see it.

Slade knew that no arrows had been recovered from the latest murder scene, or any of the others. Likewise, there had been no moccasins or feathers, buckskin clothes with classic beadwork — nothing, in short, that screamed "Indian!"

And what of it?

Was he dealing with red killers who were smart enough to cover their tracks? White slayers too stupid to off-load the blame on convenient scapegoats?

Or were the men he hunted from a different breed entirely? Something more — or less — than human?

Slade didn't believe in monsters of the supernatural kind, werewolves and such, but he had seen enough human depravity and viciousness to wonder if some people didn't qualify as throwbacks on the Darwin evolutionary scale.

From the undertaker's parlor, Slade went to the livery and got his roan settled in for the night. The hostler had plenty of room and let Slade reserve a stall indefinitely for his open-ended stay in Paradise.

And he'd been right about the name, it seemed.

So many frontier towns began with high

hopes, drawing names from scripture or adopting one that seemed appropriate to their intended future. In his drifting days, he passed through towns with names like Glory, Eden, Hallelujah, Lucky Strike, and Rainbow (in the middle of the Arizona desert). Most of them had likely blown away by now, or withered into whistle-stops no one remembered as their train sped past.

Slade didn't deal in prophecy. He couldn't say if Paradise would prosper or evaporate, but one thing was certain: its people were learning to live with fear.

From the livery, Slade walked back to the Excelsior Hotel and booked a room on the second floor, overlooking the street. The town's one saloon was a full block away, and Slade reckoned that was far enough to let him sleep through any racket it produced.

Next stop, the restaurant, which happened to have a Mexican chef. Slade took a chance on the carne asada and found the steak perfectly grilled, with enchiladas and beans on the side. The waitress tossed in a smile for dessert, and Slade left the place with his hunger sated.

He thought about whiskey, then decided to pass. The honk-a-tonk piano music didn't suit his mood, and Slade was in no mood to socialize, much less to answer strangers' questions about when or how he planned to make their nightmare go away.

So he walked back to his hotel and went upstairs, availed himself of the indoor facilities, then settled down to make an early night of it. More riding faced him in the morning, and there would be risks involved.

He meant to have a look around the reservation for himself.

Slade hadn't shared his plan with Colonel Northcliff, for the reason that he didn't want an army escort to the rez. Bluecoats would likely either frighten or enrage the Cherokee, and either way it wouldn't put them in a mood to tell Slade what — if anything — they knew about the killings.

Slade had no good reason to suspect them, at the moment, but he could be wrong. In which case, he might run into a pack of renegades intent on killing him. Still, he could not claim to investigate the crimes without at least considering the reservation's occupants.

After a troubled half an hour, Slade drifted off to sleep, hoping he wouldn't dream of tomahawks or scalping knives.

5

Breakfast was eggs and sausage, fried potatoes, thick-cut bread with strawberry jam,
and coffee. Slade was among the restaurant's first diners, and he paid little attention to the others. They seemed happy to
ignore him in return, except for Hezekiah
Grimm, who smiled and nodded at him
from across the room.

Hoping for another customer, Slade thought
and wondered if the undertaker was about
to get his wish.

Riding out to the Saline Reservation on
his own might not turn out to be the smartest move he'd ever made, but Slade was past
changing his mind. After he'd cleaned his
plate, he walked down to the livery and
claimed his horse, checking both the cinches
and the stirrup leather before he mounted
and rode out of town.

Slade had a map but didn't think he'd
need it. He already knew the reservation's

border lay eight miles northwest of town, linked by a wagon road to Paradise. He was a bit surprised the townspeople had put down roots that close to people whom they obviously feared, but Slade wasted no time trying to work it out.

The Saline's population easily outnumbered residents of Paradise today, but that would change with time, if the town kept growing. Slade had only visited a reservation once before, but he knew something of the life its captive inmates led.

Confined to land they'd never love, where game was often sparse and rations from the government verged on inedible, the reservation was no place where anyone would thrive. Children were born there, certainly, but some of them died young, while others grew up frail, with broken spirits. Liquor, although banned by law from reservation land, still found its way to people thirsty for oblivion, who turned their rage on one another while the rightful targets lay beyond their reach.

Slade knew the recent homestead murders *could* have been committed by a band of renegades, but even if that turned out to be true, it didn't mean they'd come out of the Saline Reservation. Aside from Cherokee, Oklahoma's various reservations contained

Apache, Arapaho, Caddo, Cheyenne, Chickasaw, Choctaw, Comanche, Creek, Delaware, Fox, Ioni Kichal, Iowa, Kansa, Kaskaskia, Kickapoo, Kiowa, Lipan, Miami, Modoc, Great and Little Osage, Oto, Ottawa, Pawnee, Peoria, Piankashaw, Ponca, Potawatomi, Quapaw, Sauk, Seminole, Seneca, Shawnee, Tonkawa, Towakoni, Wea, Wasco, Wichita, and Wyandot.

All uprooted from their villages, with friends and loved ones slaughtered in the process, marched under the gun to new "homes" where the Great White Father did his utmost to forget that they existed.

Slade imagined there was ample hate to go around — and nothing to prevent an outside band of renegades from some adjoining territory from deciding Oklahoma made a happy hunting ground.

Slade hoped it wasn't Indians.

He didn't want the army making matters worse.

And, truth be told, he hoped to deal with the sadistic murderers himself.

The trick would be not killing them, but presenting them alive before Judge Dennison and giving him the chance to hang them high.

The judge's words came back to Slade. *By any legal means available.*

Which meant, *Don't gun them down unless you have no choice. But if they force it on you . . . well, too bad.*

Not quite a hunting license, but the next best thing.

The road from Paradise out to the Saline Reservation basically consisted of a rutted track carved out by wagon wheels. No one had cleared or leveled it, which Slade supposed was symptomatic of white attitudes toward reservations everywhere across the country.

People knew the Indians were there, but didn't want to think about it. Didn't want to know if they were happy or well fed, if they were suffering from some disease that didn't bother white folks any longer, or if they were wobbling on the razor's edge between explosive rage and suicide. That willful blindness stretched from local burgs like Paradise, to the state capitals and legislatures, on to Washington, Congress, the president.

Stealing America from its original inhabitants had been a long and bloody job, but it was done now. And the victors sought to wash their hands of all responsibility. What better way than to put the survivors out of sight and mind on barren land, while waiting hopefully for them to die?

121

Slade, with his federal badge, would be a symbol of the government that had defeated and abused the Cherokee, which had deposited them here, so far from home. He wouldn't blame the Indians for holding it against him, but he hoped it wouldn't come to killing, when he only meant to help.

"Guess they've heard *that* before," he told the roan and thought its little whicker might've been a laugh at his expense.

Slade couldn't change the world, beyond his own small part of it, and even there his powers were limited. His badge wasn't a magic talisman. He couldn't brandish it aloft and stop the evildoers in their tracks. It couldn't even save him from a bloody death.

Slade had to do all that himself.

Beginning now.

"You know my goal," Angus McCallister declared.

"Yes, sir, I do," Cletus Paxton agreed.

As if his foreman hadn't said a word, McCallister pressed on. "I want the redskins shifted off the Saline Reservation, set up somewhere else. Give them New Mexico, for all I care."

"Yes, sir."

"Now, I've spoken to our friend, the

122

colonel. He's in full agreement with our aim, but feels his hands are tied without sufficient evidence to make a case in court — or, at least, to defend an inquiry.

"What kind of fishin' evidence?" the foreman asked.

McCallister sat dead still for a moment, frozen in the act of striking a match. It took him five heartbeats to work out what Paxton was asking him.

"I said *sufficient* evidence. It means enough to get the job done. Look it up, why don't you?"

"Where'm I supposed to find it, sir?"

"Oh, for Christ's sake, just forget it! Where was I?"

"The colonel."

"Right. He won't move without *evidence,* so I've been thinking we should help him find some."

"Sure thing, Boss. You want some of the boys to have a look around the rez?"

McCallister sat staring at his foreman, seated on the far side of his desk, and wondered why in Hell he'd ever chosen Cletus Paxton for the job. It clicked a heartbeat later, memories of certain dirty jobs Paxton had done for him without complaint, eliminating obstacles that stood between McCallister and what he'd craved from childhood.

Money. Power. Absolute control of everything within his grasp.

The rancher calmed himself, drew deeply on his fine cigar, and made a point of spelling out his answer.

"No, Clete," he replied. "I don't believe a look around the rez will do it. Say the redskins hid the evidence too well for us to find it, or you got caught trespassing on reservation land. Bad business, either way."

"Or if they didn't even kill them folks," Paxton suggested, with a crooked smile.

McCallister leaned forward in his high-backed chair. "Are people saying that?"

"*I* said it, Boss."

Jesus!

"I *know* you said it, Clete. Are people saying it *in town?*"

"I mighta heard a couple of 'em talkin' in the Long Branch," Paxton said, referring to the one saloon in Paradise.

"*Might have,* or *did* hear them?" McCallister demanded.

"Did, Boss. Yes, sir, it's as plain as day now, in my mind."

"And what was said, exactly?"

"Well . . . I don't know whuther I can give the words exact."

"Then do your best."

Paxton put on a frown, as if the task of resurrecting memories was painful. For a moment there, he actually closed his eyes, as if the answer might be printed on the inside of his eyelids.

"One old boy," he said at last, "was talkin' about how he don't know who to trust these days, with all the killin's goin' on. Guy sittin' with him says it could be anybody doin' it and layin' it on Injuns."

"That was all?"

"The kernel of it. They went round and round a couple times, then got off into cattle."

"So, you see my problem, then."

"Uh . . . sure, Boss."

"What I'm getting at," McCallister explained, despite Paxton's reply, "is that folks need to be convinced the redskins are responsible for these atrocious crimes. A few may always question it, but at the very least, we need the colonel and his various superiors to be convinced."

"That way, they'll take the Injuns somewhere else," said Paxton, with his trademark smile.

"Correct."

"But you don't want me and the boys to look around the rez for evidence, 'cuz it's too risky."

Calm, McCallister repeated to himself. *Stay calm.*

"What I was hoping, Clete, is that you might locate some evidence we could *deliver* to the reservation, where the boys in blue could *find* it."

Paxton seemed to get it, finally. His smile widened, and he was nodding while he made a little chuckling noise.

"You wanna frame 'em, then," he said.

"I think of it as helping justice find its way," McCallister replied. "Can do?"

"It needs to be somethin' the redskins woulda taken when they hit those homesteads," Paxton offered. He was getting smarter by the second, now that there was active crime involved.

"Something that *could* be from the homesteads," said McCallister. "From what I understand, the only items stolen were some women's clothing and livestock."

"Shouldn't be hard to get some dresses," Paxton said, grinning. "Maybe some bloomers, while I'm at it."

"But they'd have to match clothes that the victims owned," McCallister explained. "Something a neighbor might've seen, for instance."

"Oh."

"The livestock, now, that might be easier."

"You think so, Boss?"

"This last deal, at the Deacon place. I understand from Sheriff Eastman that the raiders got away with six or seven horses. Seems the owner never got around to branding them."

"What kinda horses were they?" Paxton asked.

"Their neighbor, same one found them dead, says that the animals were mostly brown."

"Brown horses," Paxton snickered. "Who'd a thought it?"

"So, we understand each other, then?"

"Let's see. I needta find some nags that ain't branded, then sneak 'em on the rez and tell the army where to find 'em. Right, Boss?"

"Let me take that last part, Clete. The colonel may need some persuasion, and I know you get frustrated with his kind of people."

"That's a fact."

"As for the rest, I'd say we're set to go, as soon as you can manage it."

As Paxton rose to leave, he said, "Maybe there'll be more killin's. Speed the whole thing up that way."

McCallister was stern as he replied, "Don't let another soul hear you say anything like that, for God's sake. Do you want to be the guest of honor at a necktie party?"

"I just meant —"

"Forget it. Loose talk's bad for business, Clete. Remember that. And it's a hazard to your health."

Slade didn't have to guess when he had reached the outskirts of the reservation. Someone had been kind enough to post a sign beside the wagon track, approximately three feet square, reading:

SALINE INDIAN RESERVATION
ENTRY PERMITTED ONLY ON
OFFICIAL BUSINESS
BY ORDER OF THE U.S. GOVERNMENT

Slade hadn't asked permission, but his business was official and his badge came from the same federal government that had paid for the sign, so he nudged the roan onward.

It must have been his apprehension or imagination, Slade supposed, that made the atmosphere seem different on the reservation. Obviously, the same sun was beaming down on him, making him sweat, and he still breathed the same warm air. The ground beneath his horse's hooves was still rutted by wagon wheels, with grass and weeds sprouting between the furrows.

All the same.

Except that when he looked off at a distance, to the front and either side, Slade now saw white patches of crusty soil amidst the grass and scattered wildflowers. The farther he proceeded, the more prominent those patches grew.

He'd found some of the salt that gave the Saline Reservation its distinctive name.

There would be more, and plenty of it, on the land allotted to the Cherokee by Washington. Slade wondered how much salt they used on any given day, and whether there was any process for collecting it to sell the excess. Were the reservation's penned inhabitants even entitled to earn money from the soil where they'd been dropped and told to call it home?

Slade didn't know the first thing about salt, except that he enjoyed it on his food. He'd read somewhere that it was mined, but now he guessed that it could also be scraped up from open ground. As for the cost of transportation and processing, he was clueless, but he guessed that whites would find a way to cut the Cherokee out of the profit-making end, if organized collection started on the Saline Reservation.

Not my problem, Slade recalled.

He was a U.S. marshal, not an agent for the Bureau of Indian Affairs. Judge Dennison had sent him to find killers, not ensure fair treatment for the Cherokee.

If he could prove they weren't to blame for any of the homestead murders, maybe that would help somehow.

And if they were responsible . . .

Again, it wouldn't be Slade's problem. He could pass his information to the army and let Colonel Northcliff deal with it.

An hour past the army's warning sign, Slade got the feeling he was being watched. He scanned the rolling hills around him, saw no obvious lookouts, then focused on a stand of trees a quarter mile in front of him and offset to his left. It made a decent hiding place from which to watch the wagon trail, without being observed, and Slade's eyes couldn't penetrate the shadows pooled among the trees.

So be it.

He was bound to meet the Cherokee sometime. It's why he'd come out to the reservation, after all — to find them and discover, if he could, whether rogue members of the tribe had carried out the recent deadly raids. Slade had assumed some of the tribesmen must speak English. Whether they would speak to *him* was still a question waiting to be answered.

When he'd closed the gap between himself and the free-standing clump of forest to a hundred yards, four riders broke from cover and fanned out across his path. All four were obviously Indians. One held a Springfield Trapdoor rifle, while the other three were armed with bows.

Slade kept his roan from shying, held it to a steady pace as he approached the waiting Cherokee. He saw them spot his badge and wondered what, if anything, it meant to them, when they were used to dealing with the cavalry.

At last he reached them, reined up, and eyed each somber face in turn as he informed them, "I'm a U.S. marshal, here to see your chief."

"Why should he speak to you?" the rider with the Springfield asked.

"This badge gives me authority to see him," Slade replied. "I have some questions about crimes committed off the reservation. If the answers satisfy me, maybe I can find a way to keep the army off your backs, at least for now."

The leader thought about it for a moment, then said, "Follow me."

■ ■ ■ ■

Rance Mathers paced the sheriff's office, roaming back and forth in front of Ardis Eastman's desk. "What do you think about the new man, Ardis?" he inquired.

"Nothing *to* think, so far," Eastman replied, giving his loose gunbelt a tug. "Sent out to have a look around, just like he said."

"Was he?" The mayor shot him a sidelong glance and kept pacing, watching foot traffic on the street outside.

"You don't think he was sent about the killings?" Eastman didn't have to feign confusion.

"Oh, the murders brought him here, all right. But, still . . ."

"Still, *what?*"

"There might be something else."

"Mayor, with respect, you ain't making a bit of sense."

Mathers stopped dead and spun to face him, hands thrust deep into his pockets. With the bright windows behind him, casting him in silhouette, those muttonchops made Mathers look as if his head was swollen, getting ready to explode. And from the way he had been acting, Sheriff Eastman wondered if it might be true.

"Just think about it," Mathers said. "Why would he show up here, just now?"

"Because Judge Dennison got word about the second batch of killings, I suppose."

"And now, there's been a third!" Mathers replied, as if that proved some point the sheriff couldn't understand.

"You reckon *he* took out the Deacons?"

"Oh, for God's sake, Ardis! Use your head! Listen to what I'm *saying!*"

"I've *been* listening for twenty minutes now," Eastman retorted, waspish in his sudden irritation. "And you haven't given me one reason you're suspicious of the marshal."

"Don't you see? They wouldn't send him out if it was Indians behind these murders. It's the army's job to handle renegades."

"So? I already told you what Slade said. Judge Dennison ain't sure the redskins are behind it. If they're *not,* it won't be army business."

"Thanks for that." Mathers resumed his agitated pacing. "I know damn well what it means. And if the killers *aren't* redskins, what happens to our town? What's to become of Paradise?"

"You lost me now," Eastman admitted.

"I mean, what happens if the murderers are *white?*"

"We hang 'em."

"No, no, no. They'll hang in Enid, if he catches them alive. Hell, if he catches them *at all.*"

"Dead's dead," Eastman replied.

"And dead is what this town could be, if it turns out we've had these monsters living in our midst the whole time, smiling at us on the street and trading in our shops like . . . like they were *human.*

"I don't see you in church, Ardis," said Mathers, shifting topics suddenly.

"I'm not a praying man," the sheriff said.

"You've read your Bible, though?"

"A bit."

"For then shall be great tribulation, such as was not since the beginning of the world to this time, no, nor ever shall be."

"If you say so."

"That's from Matthew, Ardis. Chapter twenty-four, verse twenty-one."

"I'll take your word on that."

"It's possible we're living in that final day of tribulation, here and now."

Eastman began to wonder, for the first time, if the mayor of Paradise had lost his mind.

"You figure someone from the *Bible* did these killings?"

"No, goddamn it! What I'm saying is, we

may be living in those final days. If not for all mankind, at least for Paradise."

"Mayor, I believe you need to calm yourself. People get killed, okay? If this was happening in Arkansas or Texas, hell, you wouldn't even *know* about it, much less have yourself worked up like this about some old-time prophecy."

"But I —"

"Besides," said Eastman, interrupting him, "we've had nobody killed at all, in town. I'd say that's *good* news. You would, too, if you were thinking straight."

"You likely think I'm crazy now," said Mathers, sounding winded.

"Well . . ."

"My faith supports me, Ardis."

Don't forget your salary, the sheriff thought but kept it to himself.

"There's nothing wrong with faith, Rance, in its place. But when you start in seeing demons where there's only wicked men, I'd say you need to take a step back from the pulpit."

Red-faced, Mathers opened the door, as if to leave, then hesitated on the threshold.

"There's more trouble coming, Ardis. Mark my words."

"They're marked. You bet."

Eastman watched Mathers close the door

135

behind him and hurry off along the sidewalk with his head down, muttering. The folks he passed were bound to wonder what was wrong with him.

Behavior of that kind could jeopardize a man's career, make people think they might be better off with a new mayor.

The sheriff leaned back in his chair and put his boots up on a corner of his desk, considering the possibilities.

Slade's escort with the Springfield Trapdoor led him for another two miles, over gently rolling ground patchy with salt deposits, to a village that surprised Slade. He'd expected tipis — and there were some, made of sewn-together hides — but a majority of the incarcerated Cherokee appeared to live in shacks or huts constructed out of wood and tar paper. There was no standard size or model, and the unpaved streets laid out between dwellings were haphazard at best.

A crowd of some three hundred Cherokee came out to see the new arrivals. One in every twenty-five or thirty of them had a carbine like the rider's, while the rest appeared to be unarmed except for knives worn on some of their belts.

It wouldn't matter, though, if they got riled and rushed him. Even if he fired off every bullet in his Colt and Winchester, Slade couldn't stop one-tenth of them from reaching him.

He made a point of riding half a neck behind his guide, not pushing it, and scanned the mob of faces without focusing on anybody in particular. Slade didn't know the rules, and didn't want to give offense before he'd had a chance to speak his piece.

The mounted scout led Slade past homes that wouldn't qualify as chicken coops in Oklahoma City, stopping when they reached a larger, better-built house situated roughly in the center of the village. There, his guide dismounted, gesturing for Slade to do likewise.

Young men pressed in around him as he stood beside his roan, not touching Slade, but clearly ready to spring forward if his hand moved toward his holstered gun. Some of them muttered back and forth in what he took to be their native language, unintelligible to his white man's ears.

Slade's escort was about to knock on the door when it opened, revealing an elderly man with long gray hair framing his deeply lined face. He wore a red shirt over faded denim pants and hand-tooled moccasins, with a colorful blanket draped over his shoulders. His dark eyes found the badge on Slade's vest, then moved up to scan his face.

"First soldiers, then a lawman," said a voice like creaking leather.

"I'm not with the soldiers," Slade replied and introduced himself without presuming to shake hands.

"I am Red Eagle, chief of the Echota Cherokee. You come to us because white blood is spilled."

Slade nodded. "I was sent out from the U.S. district court, to give the judge there my opinion of the murders."

"You think Cherokee did these things?" asked Red Eagle.

"I've seen nothing to suggest it, but I have to look at every angle."

"Come inside."

Slade did as he was told. His escort from the trail began to follow him, but Red Eagle held up a hand to stop him.

"Little Wolf has done enough, for now," the old man said. "Wait here."

That earned a scowl for Slade, but he ignored it, following Red Eagle to a small-ish kitchen where a table and two chairs stood near an old wood-burning stove. The day was warm enough outside that no fire had been lit.

"You sit."

Slade sat, Red Eagle facing him across the table.

"I tell you," the old man said, "my people have not done these things. Our war against the white man ended long ago."

"I hope you're right," Slade said. "But some of your young men may not agree. How can you be so sure?"

"I have decreed it. I am chief. My word is law."

"My people have their chiefs and laws, as well," Slade said. "It doesn't stop them from killing, when the mood comes over them."

"White men are damaged in their souls," Red Eagle said. It didn't seem to be intended as an insult, just a plain statement of fact.

"You reckon it's impossible for anyone to leave the reservation and commit these crimes without your knowledge?"

Red Eagle considered it for all of thirty seconds.

"I am old," he said. "I stay here, mostly, in this house. I don't see all the reservation, all my people, every day. You ask if it is *possible* some Cherokee could come and go, I say yes. But to kill so many whites, endanger all of us, and none of the Echota tribe tells me? That is *not* possible."

"A raiding party from some other reservation, then?" asked Slade. "Maybe not even Cherokee?"

Red Eagle shrugged. "I speak for the Echota people, not for Kiowa, Apache, or the rest. I know them if we meet, but they don't come here. Look for them among their own people, not mine."

Slade thought himself a fairly decent judge of men, and he believed Red Eagle was sincere. As to the old man's knowledge of what happened when he wasn't there to see it, well . . .

"Tell me," Red Eagle said. "Were these whites killed as if by red men?"

Frowning, Slade replied, "I'm not sure what you mean."

"Was their suffering extended? Were their scalps or fingers taken? Were their houses burned?"

Slade wondered how much he should share with Red Eagle. At last, he said, "The men were killed outright, women abused in private ways before they died. Some of the children, too. There was a lot of butchery, but none as you describe. None of their homes were burned."

"Not Indians," Red Eagle said, with quiet confidence. "You look for white men. Damaged souls."

With nothing left to ask, Slade said, "Well,

thank you for your time. I'll pass on what you've told me to the court."

Red Eagle walked Slade to the door and said something to Little Wolf that made the young man frown some more. After the chief had closed his door, Slade's escort said, "You wish to search our homes, now?"

"I'll be leaving, if it's all the same to you," Slade said and walked back to his roan.

No conversation passed between them, as the two men traveled back the way they'd come. Slade left his silent escort at the stand of trees where they'd originally met, continuing alone toward Paradise.

He was halfway there when he saw black smoke rising from the skyline, half a mile away.

6

Slade held his roan at a gallop the first quarter mile, then slowed on the approach to what had clearly been a homestead, until recently. The house was still standing, but fire had consumed the barn. Its ashes were still smoldering, and Slade's nostrils picked up a roast-meat smell that told him it had not been empty when it burned.

He circled wide around the place, outside of rifle range, taking his time as he examined every angle of the silent house. He had his Winchester across his saddle horn, finger outside the trigger guard, but ready at the first sight of a hostile figure on the property.

So far, the only creatures stirring were some chickens pecking in the yard. A small corral, close by the barn, stood empty with its gate ajar.

Slade spiraled closer to the house, watching its windows and the single open door. He'd never understood why many of the farmhouses he'd seen during his travels had only one exit. If the floor plan was supposed to help defend the home against outside attackers, it did not appear to work. And if some danger — fire, whatever — blocked the front door, how would occupants escape?

Not through the windows, which were firmly shuttered now. That meant Slade couldn't peer inside the house, but it was doubtful he'd have seen much anyway, standing in sunlight, looking at the dark interior.

Someone inside the house could still watch *him,* of course, through small slits in the shutters that allowed a barricaded farmer to observe his enemies, while they were laying siege and plotting ways to smoke him out. A gun barrel could fit through one of those slits, too, but Slade suspected that the occupants of this farmhouse were long past putting up a fight.

From fifty yards, he called out to the silent house, giving his name, explaining that he was a lawman, while the prairie breeze tattered his words.

No answer from the house.

At last, Slade rode up to the porch, conscious of muscles clenching in his back and shoulders, willing them to just relax. When no one challenged him, he climbed down from the saddle, tethered his roan to one of the porch roof's support beams, and stepped toward the threshold.

Slade smelled it, then.

The scent of death warmed over.

Bodies start to cool the moment hearts stop beating, blood stops circulating, and the brain shuts down. Muscles relax, then start to stiffen up again, beginning with the head and neck, proceeding downward toward the feet. Within six hours, rigor mortis makes the body timber-stiff, remaining that way for a day or so. Then it begins to loosen up again, starting as it had stiffened, from the head. Slade didn't understand the chemistry involved, but he knew doctors used a corpse's flexibility to help them guess the time a person died.

The smell of death warmed over was another thing, entirely. Stiff or slack, a corpse that had been lying in the sun — or in a warm, dark place, like an abandoned farmhouse in the early summer — commonly produced a ripe-yeast odor that foretold decomposition setting in. It didn't wait for lifeless muscles to relax and could advance quite swiftly in the right conditions, helped along by scavengers and insects.

Slade used one boot toe to push the door

open, holding his rifle tight against his hip and well back out of grabbing range. Despite the fact that there were dead folks stinking up the house, a possibility remained that someone else was waiting for him in there, too.

Maybe the killers, for this clearly *was* a murder scene, and very little from the other crimes had suggested that the murderers were sane. Why not remain inside a house of corpses to surprise another victim, if a whim dictated it?

The swinging door let sunlight penetrate the house and showed Slade two bare legs off to his right. Shifting positions on the porch, he craned his neck and saw a naked woman lying there — or, rather, what was left of her — spread-eagle on the bloody wooden floor.

Slade swallowed hard to keep his breakfast down and shouted once more into silence, answered only by the echo of his voice. He had a choice to make, then: either cross the threshold or climb back aboard his roan and ride straight back to Enid, hand his badge back to Judge Dennison, and let somebody with a stronger constitution take his job.

He stepped inside.

Flies rose and fell in humming waves around the bodies, like dust devils formed by whirlwinds in the desert. These small storms were living, though, driven by ancient urges — feed and breed — to seek out flesh abandoned by its own life force. The buzzing got inside Slade's head and set his teeth on edge.

The flies went first for open wounds — plenty of those, all shapes and sizes — and then for normal body openings where moisture lingered and the flesh was softer. They obscured Slade's view of what the woman and her family had suffered, kept the finer details from him, and he felt a sudden urge to thank them for it, worried that the urge itself was proof he'd lost his mind.

Three dead inside the house. There'd been two children, one still in its cradle, and the other dragged from underneath a bed if Slade's take on the scene was accurate. Granted, the rage of crazy vandalism made it difficult to say, with any certainty, but Slade guessed that the child — a boy of six or seven years — had tried to hide when the attackers started hammering the door.

Its metal bolt, store-bought, had failed to keep them out. A splintered door frame showed where application of brute force had torn screws out of timber, scattering them across the floor.

Slade left the house of death and walked

back to the ruin of the barn, seeking the woman's mate. The fourth and final corpse lay close to the corral, cut down en route from house to barn, likely to check on some disturbance that had roused him in the middle of the night.

A pattern, then?

Slade didn't know enough about the other murder scenes to say that much, with any certainty, but it made sense. None of the houses had been torched, and logic told him that the men were lured outside for slaughter, while their wives and children stayed behind.

How else had the intruders cracked four isolated houses in a row, without a shot triggered in self-defense?

Dumb luck or skill, it all played out the same.

He'd seen enough — or thought so, anyway, until he walked back toward his horse, ready to ride back and alert the law, such as it was, in Paradise. He'd been watching for traces the killers had left, and saw nothing that might help him single them out.

Slade almost missed the wagon tracks.

Four wheels with two-inch rims, nothing unusual about them. Slade supposed someone could figure out the wagon's weight and wheelbase from the tracks, but Slade's skill at arithmetic extended more toward calculating odds and counting cards. The wagon had been drawn by good-sized horses and had left the homestead traveling in a southwesterly direction.

Had it been driven by a killer? Or a neighbor stopping by to visit sometime prior to the attack?

Slade couldn't say.

Torn between following the wagon's tracks and turning back toward Paradise, he chose the latter course of action. It was more important, in his view, to warn the town and rally help for any search he planned, than to pursue a trail that would be waiting for him when he made his second visit to the farm.

As for the victims, time had lost all meaning.

None of them were going anywhere.

Lately, it seemed to Ardis Eastman that his job was getting harder by the day. Before the homestead murders started, he had jailed a rowdy drunk or two on weekends, let them sleep it off, and maybe read the riot act to some young sneak thief when the need arose.

There's never been a homicide in Paradise since Eastman was elected sheriff, running unopposed three years before. His term was up next summer, August thirty-first, and lately Eastman had been thinking that it might be time to try another line of work.

He'd done some farming in his time, but never really made a go of it. The good news was that when his farm went belly-up, his nagging, shrewish wife had fled back home to file for a divorce and start life over with some "real man" she had yet to meet.

Eastman wished the poor bastard luck.

He'd need it.

After hanging up his plow, Eastman had spent six months working as a railroad conductor on the Arkansas and Oklahoma Line. One scorching afternoon, sick of the toadying to thoughtless passengers, he'd disembarked in Paradise and then refused to get back on the train.

The rest, as someone said, was history.

So what if he'd embellished his accomplishments and reputation when he heard the town was looking for a lawman? They were past the point of checking references, and it was true that he could fight, despite his size. Bullies had come to grief by underestimating Eastman all his life.

Hoisting the gunbelt up around his narrow waist, Eastman was grateful that he'd never had to shoot a man. He didn't question his ability to pull the trigger, but still hoped it wouldn't come to that. And lately, he'd been thinking that the best way to make sure it didn't was to give up his position as the law in Paradise.

It wasn't that he feared the killers would start hunting folks in town. That clearly wasn't how they operated. But if Colonel Northcliff and the mayor were wrong about the crimes, if white men *were* responsible, it threw the whole mess back in Eastman's lap.

Granted, they had the federal man from Enid on the case now, sniffing here and there, but how much could he really do alone? If Marshal Slade discovered who the killers were, he'd naturally expect help from the man whom local voters had selected to protect them from that sort of danger.

That, in turn, meant going up against some kind of crazy man — or crazy *men,* more likely — and God only knew who'd still be standing when the smoke cleared.

Eastman had already given thought to clearing out before his term expired. He could pack up and leave that very night, while Paradise was sleeping, and who cared what anybody thought about him after he was gone? Start over fresh, in some town where he had no reputation to defend or to live down.

He'd sworn an oath, of course, but what was that, compared to getting killed? He never would've run for sheriff in the first place, if he'd known a gang of maniacs would turn up in the neighborhood and start to butcher homesteaders like they were livestock. No one could anticipate a thing like that, and damned few in his personal experience would relish such an event.

The three cells in his back room were deserted, no jailbirds requiring his attention if he left his tin star on the desk and simply rode away. He wouldn't even try collecting on his last month's pay, since that would mean explaining his decision, facing down Rance Mathers and whoever else might corner him before he had a chance to disappear.

The more he thought about it . . .

It was hot inside the office, even with the door open to catch a breeze. He stepped outside and slumped into a chair he kept beside the doorway during office hours, leaning back in it with shoulders pressed against the wall.

Eastman believed it made people feel more secure, seeing their sheriff on the job and watching over them. He'd never had occasion to come bolting from his chair and interrupt a robbery — or any other crime, for that matter — but he supposed it never hurt to show the badge and gun. Maybe a stranger passing through would see him and think twice before he started raising any hell in Paradise.

Or maybe one of the affable shopkeepers who saw him from their windows was a madman, looking forward to the next time he could ride out after nightfall, hunting humans.

Eastman hoped that next time, when the killers struck, they would come up against a family of sharpshooters and meet a bloody end. It would relieve him of a burden that was threatening to break his spirit.

What he never doubted was the *next time* part of it.

He knew the maniacs would strike again, if not outside of Paradise, then somewhere else.

People like that enjoyed the killing. And they never quit till they were caged or killed, themselves.

A rider was approaching from the northern end of town, reining his horse back from a gallop to a trot. Eastman pushed off the wall, put all four chair legs back onto the wooden sidewalk, and leaned forward, resting elbows on his knees.

He recognized the federal man and stayed where he was until Slade pulled up in the street and sat there, staring down at Eastman from his place astride the roan.

"How soon can you be saddled up?" Slade asked.

"Where am I going?" Eastman said.

"With me, back to a spread due north of town," Slade said. "There's been another raid."

For the second time in thirty-odd hours, Slade walked with Sheriff Eastman to the mayor's house. He understood the politics of Eastman speaking to the man in charge of Paradise as soon as possible, and didn't argue that it was a waste of time.

The latest victims in the string of homicides weren't going anywhere.

There was no telegraph in Paradise, and any letter Sladc sat down to write would have to wait for the arrival of the weekly mail coach, so he couldn't warn Judge Dennison about the third and fourth homestead attacks. As for the series of events that followed his report to Sheriff Eastman and the mayor, Slade knew they'd soon take on a strange life of their own.

Concern — or outright panic — would compel a certain course of action by the principals involved. Mayor Mathers would alert the troops at Fort Supply, where Colonel Northcliff would assume that Cherokee or some other "redskins" had carried out the latest raid.

Northcliff would lead or send another group of soldiers to the reservation, seeking evidence or vengeance. They'd be on the prod, frightened and angry, itching for a chance to settle scores. The younger troops among them might be looking for a chance to prove themselves in battle, hoping it would be the same one-sided kind that always seemed to happen when the cavalry attacked a village.

And from that point, once the deadly fuse was lit . . .

They'd reached the mayor's front porch while Slade was lost in thought. The mayor's wife, Colleen, answered the sheriff's knock as seemed to be her habit. Slade wondered how many times in any given day she had to smile at townsfolk and invite them to her parlor, where they'd wait to ask for favors or complain about some problem in their lives, expecting Rance Mathers to make it go away.

"Ardis — and Marshal Slade, was it?" she asked.

"That's right, ma'am," Slade replied.

"You must be here for Rance. Please, come inside and have a seat. He'll be right with you."

If she read the bad news on their faces, she was practiced at concealing it. Her smile remained in place, and if it seemed a shade brittle, or left her eyes untouched, Slade guessed that sociability had turned into a business for Colleen Mathers. Her smile and personality were now adjuncts to her husband's political career.

The lady of the house went off to fetch her husband, but did not return with him to offer drinks or snacks. The mayor himself looked like a man who'd passed a nearly sleepless night.

"Sheriff. Marshal," he said. "What brings you back so soon?"

"There's been more killing," Eastman blurted out, before Slade could respond. "Out north of town. Sounds like the Hascomb place."

"Dear God!" Mathers picked out a chair, dropped into it, and waved the lawmen toward their own seats in the parlor. "Tom and Betty Hascomb? Are you sure?"

Slade spoke up then, before Eastman could spin out any speculation. "I can't give you any names," he told the mayor, "but I can tell you where the homestead is, or show you."

"How far out?" asked Mathers.

"Three miles as the crow flies, give or take. The wagon road won't take you there, directly."

"That's Tom Hascomb's place, all right," said Mathers. "Jesus! And you say they're *all* dead?"

"All that I saw," Slade replied.

"Did they . . . I mean . . . were they . . . ?"

He faltered. Slade knew what he wanted and replied, "I didn't see the other murder scenes, but someone torched the barn and left the house. As for the wounds, they fit with what I saw at Grimm's and what I've read about the other raids. I'm guessing that it happened late last night, or early on this morning."

"So you think it was the same gang then?" asked Mathers.

"I can't speculate on who's responsible," Slade said. "But on the commonsense side, call it two men, minimum."

"Same hands in all four crimes?" the sheriff asked. "I mean, it *has* to be, wouldn't you say?"

"I'd hate to think it was a trend that's catching on," Slade said.

He'd heard of crazy people imitating

certain crimes for pleasure and of clever ones who masked their guilt by following a pattern someone else established. Slade knew that some novelist back East had called such imitators "copycats."

He seriously didn't want to think there was a copycat — much less a *gang* of them — in Paradise.

Was madness catching? Could it possess a man who witnessed or examined cruel behavior? And if so, why wasn't every lawman in the world insane?

Maybe we are, Slade thought. *Crazy to take and keep this job, at least.*

"Will you go out to see them, Mayor?" Slade asked.

"*See* them? Why . . . no. What purpose would that serve?"

"You could confirm identity, for one thing."

"That's the sheriff's job. I'm sure you understand, Marshal, that my authority does not extend beyond the boundaries of Paradise."

Slade nearly asked about his common decency, but let it slide.

"I *will* help, though," Mathers pressed on. "The first thing that I'll do is send a messenger to Fort Supply. Colonel Northcliff knows how to deal with things like this."

Like he'd "dealt with" the other killings, Slade thought. But he said, "There's still nothing suggesting this was done by Indians."

"Well, who else, Marshal? I mean, honestly!"

"That," Slade replied, "is what I'm hoping to find out."

Angus McCallister had started pacing furiously when the messenger departed, and he kept it up until the next knock sounded on his office door. That stopped him, freezing his thoughts in place. He took the time to light one of his big cigars before he said, "Come in!"

There was a smile on Cletus Paxton's face as he entered the room and closed the door behind him.

"Jared passed the word that you were lookin' for me, Boss," he said.

"That's right, Clete. Have a seat, will you?"

"Sure thing." Still smiling, as if neither of them had a single problem in the world.

McCallister remained standing while Paxton sat. It gave him an advantage, staring at his foreman down the short slope of his nose.

"Remember what we talked about, last time?" he asked, trying to keep it casual.

"Sure do, Boss," Paxton said.

"What kind of progress are you making?"

"Well, sir, I've been lookin' for some horses we could take out to the rez, but all the ones I've seen so far got brands on 'em, so that's no good."

"And have you thought of any way around that?"

"Um . . . you may not like it, Boss."

"We won't know till you spell it out," McCallister replied.

"Well, sir, we can't use any horses from the spread, here. Most of 'em are branded, and it might start someone talkin' if the others disappeared. So . . ."

"What, Clete? Spit it out."

"I'd need to get 'em . . . somewhere else. Not buyin' 'em, you see. We wouldn't want the seller comin' back on us and tellin' anyone about it, later."

"So you'd mean to *steal* them," said McCallister.

"Well, um . . . if you want to put it that way."

"How else would I put it?"

Paxton had begun to look nervous, eyes shifting here and there around the office.

"Boss, I thought . . . from what you said last time . . . I mean . . ."

"Clete, look at me."

159

The foreman did as he was told, licking his lips the way a lizard might, when it was too long in the sun.

"Have you done anything about this plan of yours?" McCallister inquired.

"Not yet, Boss. I was gonna —"

"Did you pay a visit to the Hascomb spread last night, by any chance? Or send someone out there on your behalf?"

"Hascomb? No, sir. He's got some horses, though, I think. If you —"

"He doesn't have them anymore, Clete."

"Huh?"

"In fact, he's dead. His missus, too. And kids, from what I hear."

The color drained from Paxton's face, then came back in the form of blotchy red spots on his pitted cheeks.

"You think *I* kilt 'em? Jumping Jesus, Mister —"

"It's coincidence, I guess," McCallister cut in. "The night after we had our little talk — which, it appears to me, you misinterpreted completely — this thing happens, almost in our own backyard."

The foreman saw where he was headed. "Hey, now, Boss . . . we both know what you told me yesterday."

"Do we? It sounds to me like you're suggesting I told you to go out and commit a crime."

"Well —"

"And you know damn well that if that got around, I'd be obliged not only to deny it, but proceed against whoever spread such stories in the first place."

Paxton shut his mouth, waiting.

"I'm not concerned about the sheriff, mind you," said McCallister. "That Ardis couldn't find his ass with both hands and a posse. Colonel Northcliff . . . well, you let me deal with him. The problem is this U.S. marshal."

"Slade, somebody said his name was."

"I don't give a hoot in Hell about his name," McCallister replied. "The point, from what I understand, is that he doesn't blame these massacres on redskins. He thinks *white* men may've done it, and for all we know, he may find some."

"Somebody'd do a thing like that," said Paxton, "must be crazy."

"There are crazy people in the world," McCallister observed. "Right now, I'm hoping that I don't have any on my payroll."

"Boss, I swear to God, I had nothin' to do with this."

The rancher searched his foreman's eyes,

trying to peer inside of him and find the truth.

"Clete, I'm prepared to take you at your word — for now. But understand one thing: I cannot — *will* not — be associated with a crazy man. If I find out you were responsible for any of these heinous crimes, I'll string you up myself."

"Don't worry, Boss. My hands are clean."

McCallister knew *that* was stretching it. Paxton had done things for him in the past that were unethical, some of them criminal, all going toward the greater good. Which, in this case, meant the enhancement of McCallister's prestige and fortune. It wouldn't do to have those stories surface, and he pondered whether it would be advisable for Clete to have an accident.

Not yet.

"All right," he said, relaxing as he walked back to the chair behind his desk. "Forget about that business with the horses, now. We need to think of something else."

"Like what, Boss?"

"If the soldiers can't find evidence lying around the reservation," said McCallister, "maybe they need to catch the redskins somewhere else."

"Like, off the rez, you mean?"

"That's what I mean."

"They don't go into town," said Paxton.

"No. But if they had good reason — say, if something riled them up so bad, they couldn't let it go or trust the army to take care of it — that just might change."

"Something to make 'em fighting mad," Paxton replied.

"That's it."

"Like what?"

"Let's think about that," said McCallister. "Shall we?"

Slade had to wait while Sheriff Eastman went around the shops in Paradise, up one side of Main Street and down the other, seeking men to join him on the ride out to the Hascomb spread. The bad news ran ahead of him, somehow, and by the time he finished on the street's west side, shopkeepers on the east were mostly standing in their doorways, anxious to delay him further with a swarm of questions Eastman couldn't answer.

Slade planned to wait outside the sheriff's office, but when people started drifting over, asking *him* questions, he went inside and shut the door. His job didn't involve public relations, and he didn't have to scrounge around for votes. More to the point, nothing he'd seen and nothing he could say would reassure the frightened folk of Paradise.

Eastman returned to find Slade sitting on

a corner of his desk. "I stopped at Grimm's," he said. "He's coming with us, for the bodies."

"Anytime today?" asked Slade.

"Mister, you may be used to things like this, but here in Paradise, we're not. This is the fourth raid in a month."

"Which means you *should* be getting used to it," Slade said. "Or, at the very least, have some kind of response prepared."

"I'm doing what I can," Eastman replied. "You want to rush ahead and ride out there alone, go on and be my guest."

"I've *been* there, Sheriff, just in case it slipped your mind. The killers didn't hang around."

"They might come back. I read somewhere that crazy people do that, sometimes."

"In which case, we should be there to meet them, don't you think?"

"I only have one deputy. He'll have to stay and watch the town till we get back."

"And if the killers come back, like you say, we'll have a barber with us, to take care of them? Somebody from the general store?"

"Good people from the town who give a damn about what happens here!" said Eastman. "Folks who won't be riding out tomorrow or the next day, and forgetting

165

they were ever here."

Beyond the open doorway where the sheriff stood, Slade saw townspeople gathering. The murmur of their voices quickly rose in volume. It reminded Slade of buzzing from a hornet's nest.

"Your public's waiting," he told Eastman.

With a parting glare at Slade, the sheriff stepped outside and raised his hands for quiet, waiting while the voices from the crowd before him slowly died away. Slade loitered in the doorway, watching as the small-town politician went to work.

"Now, folks, I know you're all upset about what's happened," he began. "We all are. But the best thing you can do for Paradise and for your families is to stay calm."

Good luck with that, Slade thought.

"I'm riding out with Marshal Slade, here, for a look around the Hascomb place. We need to find out anything we can about the men — the *animals* — who did this thing. Some of you men want to come with us, as a posse, you'll require a horse and gun."

"We'd be sworn in?" a fat man in the front row asked.

"You will," Eastman replied. "For this day only, and I can't afford to pay you."

Slade hoped that would weed out half the prospects, anyway, but no one left. Questions bombarded Eastman until he was forced to raise his hands again and call for silence.

"What I need to emphasize —"

"We only want four men," Slade interrupted him. "It's not a picnic or a hunting party. You *will not* be chasing anyone around the countryside or handling evidence at the crime scene. You will most *definitely* not be taking any souvenirs."

While Sheriff Eastman gaped at him, before the crowd mind could respond, Slade let them have the other barrel.

"Those of you who are concerned about your families and property, I understand," he said. "It's only natural, although the killers haven't come within two miles of town."

"So far!" the fat man down in front called out.

"That's right," Slade said. "So far. And if you think they're coming here, the smart thing for you all to do is stay near home. You can't protect your families by riding off into the hills and leaving them alone."

"Some of us got no families," a slender, balding fellow said. "We only want to help."

"I say again, we can take four men. That's the limit. Do you have a horse and gun?" he asked the man who'd spoken last.

"I do. And I can handle both."

"That's one. Who else? Let's narrow it to single men."

Four hands went up, including the fat man's. Slade picked the other three.

"Get armed and saddled up, then come back here, quick as you can," Slade told them. "We've already wasted time we can't afford. The rest of you, go on about your business."

Eastman reached out to grip Slade's arm, then seemed to reconsider it. Red-faced, he hissed, "Mister, this is *my* town. You can't start giving orders like —"

"In fact, I *can,*" Slade cut him off. "You're free to send Judge Dennison any complaints that come to mind, assuming that the mail coach ever gets here. In the meantime, there are killers on the loose who show no signs of getting tired or slowing down."

"And we'll be going after them with just four men?"

"*We* won't be going after them at all," said Slade. "I told you, they're long gone. If I thought there was any chance of them returning to the Hascomb ranch, I would've waited there."

"So, why — ?"

"Are you and I going to see the mess they made? Three reasons. First, I want to have another look around the place before night falls. Second, the bodies should be brought back here while something's left to bury. Third, you represent the law in Paradise. You *need* to see it."

"I've already seen what they can do," said Eastman, looking almost sickly now.

"You need to see *each one,* and keep in mind what happens if you can't hold up your end."

"You can't blame *me* for this!"

"The killings? No. But if you let things fall apart while you're in charge here, it comes back to you."

Behind them, Hezekiah Grimm arrived with his morgue wagon, dressed in black from head to toe. "Gentlemen," he greeted them. "Whenever you're prepared . . ."

"We're waiting for the sheriff's posse," Slade replied.

It took another twenty minutes for the four men Slade had chosen to arrive. Two were already mounted, while the others led their horses by the reins. Three carried rifles, and the fourth had found himself a double-barreled shotgun. All of them wore hats and grim, determined faces.

"Now, then," Eastman addressed them. "Who's been out to Hascomb's place before? Nobody? Well, just follow me and

169

Marshal Slade. Stay together, you should be all right."

"One other thing," Slade said. "If we meet anybody going out or coming back, nobody draws a gun without my order."

"His or mine," the sheriff added.

Slade let that one pass and mounted up, while Eastman spent another minute fiddling with his saddle, dragging now to show the locals he was still in charge.

The street was lined with somber people as their party headed out of town. Without discussing it, the posse fell into a loose formation. Slade and Eastman rode in front, with Grimm's wagon behind them, and the other horsemen flanking it, two on a side. Eastman had sworn them in as promised, standing at his desk, and each had spent a moment polishing the tin star he received.

Nobody spoke as they paraded down the length of Main Street, though a few townspeople waved and were acknowledged in return. Slade had a sense that they were riding off to war, like volunteers before Bull Run in 1861, instead of going to collect the bodies of a slaughtered family.

Slade had been truthful when he told Eastman that he desired another look around the crime scene, but he had no realistic hope of finding evidence he'd missed first time around. Rather, he felt as if another visit to the ranch might give him some insight into the killers' thought processes — though he wasn't sure a sane mind could approximate a madman's rage and violence.

Slade had about convinced himself that one man couldn't wreak such havoc on a family. If he was wrong on that point, then all bets were off.

And if the killers *weren't* insane? What, then? What could their motive be? Why slaughter fifteen people for a few head of livestock?

Too many questions.

No one in the mounted party spoke until they were well clear of Paradise, then Sheriff Eastman said, "The mayor's asking for soldiers to come out and meet us at the ranch. The fort is ten miles farther out, so it could take a while."

Slade calculated that the messenger would still be riding hard toward Fort Supply, even if he'd departed within minutes of their meeting with Mayor Mathers. Ten miles out from town, then add the time for organizing a patrol, and ten miles back. Call it five hours, give or take, and that would put it sometime after six o'clock before the bluecoats finally arrived.

So be it.

"I suppose they'll want to check the rez again," Slade said.

"Well, wouldn't you?"

"I was out there this morning," Slade informed him.

"You rode out to see those redskins by yourself?"

"Why not?"

The sheriff shook his head, but offered no reply.

"I've tried to think of some reason for Cherokee to start this killing, and I can't come up with one," Slade said.

"How 'bout the fact that they hate white men?" Eastman asked him. "Far as I recall, that's always been enough."

"Some might suggest they have good reason," Slade replied, ignoring Eastman's sour expression. "But considering their ancestors were packed off to the Saline Reservation more than sixty years ago, it seems a little late for them to start resisting, don't you think?"

"Never too late," Eastman replied. "They've got young bucks out there who'd slit your throat as soon as look at you."

"And when's the last time that happened? Since you've been sheriff? Since the town was built?"

"Well . . ."

"I did some looking into this, before I left Enid," Slade said. "The latest Indians arriving in the territory were the Kickapoo, from Mexico, in 1883. That's sixteen years ago, and their reservation sits a hundred miles from here, to the southeast."

"You still think it's white men doing this?"

"I think, if it *is* white men, blaming their kills on Indians would be a smart idea."

"Then, why not quit while they're ahead?" asked Eastman. "Why keep killing in the same place, time and time again, with risk of getting killed or caught."

"We don't know if they *are* ahead," Slade answered, "since we don't know who they are or what they want."

"It's rustling, right? I mean, they're taking livestock."

"So it seems."

The sheriff peered at Slade from underneath his hat brim. "Well, the stock *is* gone. Can we agree on that?"

"Gone *where* would be the question. If they're selling it, who's buying? And is that the only reason for the killings?"

"What else would it be?"

Slade shrugged, matching the rocking motion of his roan. "Who gains if homesteaders are killed or scared away from Paradise?

173

What happens to the land?"

"Goes up for auction, I suppose," Eastman replied. "Nobody's done a thing about it, yet."

"And who's most likely to step in? There can't be many in the neighborhood who could afford that kind of acreage, even at a bargain rate."

"Now, wait a second."

"What?"

"You can't start pointing fingers at a man because he's managed to make something of himself."

"You have a name in mind, then?"

"No, sir. None who'd even think of doing such a thing as this."

"Okay. I'll ask around when we get back to town."

"Damn it! Loose talk don't mean a thing."

"I always take it with a grain of salt," Slade said. "But I can't clear a man before I find out who he is."

"Just let me think about it for a minute, will you?"

"Take your time, Sheriff. We've got a long day still ahead of us."

The messenger from Paradise was in a lather, like his chestnut horse, when he reached Fort Supply. There was a holdup at the gate, while soldiers questioned him and listened to his nervous answers; then they pointed him toward the command post.

Colonel Hollis Northcliff was considering retirement, as he often did these days, when voices raised outside his office drew his mind away from counting dollars in his head. Someone was coming, and he turned from his window to face the door, hands clasped behind his back and booted feet slightly apart.

At ease, they called it, but that wasn't how he felt.

Northcliff's staff sergeant knocked, then opened the door without waiting for Northcliff to answer.

"Colonel, sir," he said, "we've got a rider in from Paradise to see you. Got important news, says he."

"By all means, show him in, Sergeant."

"Yes, sir."

The sergeant disappeared, replaced on the threshold a moment later by a slender man in his mid-twenties, whom Northcliff had never seen before. The stranger held a hat in front of him, around groin level, kneading it with anxious hands.

"Come in, please," Northcliff said. "You are . . . ?"

"Ken Darby, mister . . . sir. I just rode in

175

from Paradise, sent by the mayor."

So, not McCallister. The colonel wasn't sure if he should feel relieved or worried.

"For what purpose, may I ask?" He'd found that stiff formality was best for keeping yokels in their proper place.

"There's been another murder. Well, a massacre, I guess you'd say. Out to the Hascomb place."

Northcliff managed to keep his face deadpan, but he could not suppress the churning in his stomach. Soon, the acid would be in his throat and scalding him.

"I see," Northcliff replied. "Do you have any further details?"

"No, sir. Rance — I mean, the mayor — just sent me out to tell you. I expect they'll need some help."

Help for the dead?

" 'They' being . . . whom, again?"

"Well, Sheriff Eastman and the marshal out of Enid, I suppose. Whoever else went with 'em, out to look around the place."

"How long ago was this?" Northcliff inquired.

"I left before they did," the rider said, "but they was only ridin' two miles to my ten. They should've been there for a while, by now, guess. Takin' the bodies back to Grimm's, and all."

Northcliff had no idea what that meant, and he frankly didn't care. Bodies were no concern of his. He dealt in *policy,* which sometimes overlapped with judgment and revenge.

"I'll send some men out to the scene, of course. Or, better yet, I'll lead the troop myself."

"Okay."

"Where did you say this happened?"

"At the Hascomb place."

Northcliff regarded the young man as if he was an idiot — which, he supposed, was possible.

"You understand, I don't know where that is?" the colonel asked.

"Oh, well . . . a couple miles from Paradise, heading northwest a bit, you —"

"Never mind," the colonel cut him off. "I take it you can lead us there?"

"Oh, sure. I need to rest my horse some, though, after a ten-mile gallop."

"Go see to it, then," said Northcliff. "Oats and water, a good wipe down. You'll have time, while we get organized, and we'll be going slower on the way back."

"Yes, sir."

"Wait outside a moment, then. And tell the sergeant that I need to speak with him."

"Will do. Thank you."

The sergeant stood before him seconds later, not quite at attention. Soldiers his age, who had been promoted, busted down, then re-promoted countless times, took rigid discipline with several grains of salt.

"Yes, sir?"

"Our guest needs oats and water for his horse, Sergeant. After you've seen to that, select a dozen men to join me on an outing. To the Hascomb place, no less. Sounds charming," Northcliff told him. "Everybody's dead."

"I'll get right on it, sir."

"Ready to ride in half an hour, yes?"

"No sweat, sir. Good as done."

Alone once more, Northcliff could feel the lure of the whiskey bottle he kept in the bottom right-hand drawer of his old army desk. The sergeant likely knew about it, but he wouldn't dare to steal a taste. And if he talked about it to the other men, so what?

Another thirteen months, and Northcliff would be out of uniform for good. Retirement loomed before him like a wall, had worried him no end for half a dozen years, until Angus McCallister had shown him where the door was in that wall and how to open it.

A new world lay beyond the roadblock that had frightened Northcliff so. He simply

178

had to take advantage of a golden opportunity that Fate had handed to him, run with it, and then cash in his chips at the conclusion of the game.

The best part was that, if he did it properly, Northcliff would be a double winner. He'd not only have a bankroll and position with McCallister ready and waiting for him in civilian life, but he would also be a hero.

Never before, in his twenty-eight years and nine months of military service, had Hollis Northcliff been accused of heroism. He had been too young for service in the Civil War, and by the time the war with Spain had rolled around, last year, he'd been assigned to Fort Supply. There'd been a couple of skirmishes with the Apaches before that assignment — and Northcliff thought he'd actually shot an Indian on one occasion, storming through a Cheyenne village, though he couldn't prove it — but it would be nice to finish on a high note.

He could be the officer who solved the Oklahoma homestead murders and eliminated those responsible. Congress was bound to go along with forced removal of the Saline Reservation's Cherokee, if he could prove they were responsible for killing whites.

How many was it now? He hadn't thought

to ask, assuming that he'd find out soon enough.

The bad part was examining another murder scene, but if the messenger was right, the bodies would be packed off long before he and his men arrived. As for the rest, well, he could handle it.

He was an officer and gentleman.

Northcliff knew how to play the part.

The smell of death had ripened by the time they reached the Hascomb ranch. It didn't help, learning the names or hearing members of the sheriff's makeshift posse talk about how nice Tom Hascomb was, or how his wife took honors for her cobbler at the county fair.

Slade didn't need to mourn the victims or discuss how Paradise had lost a fine, upstanding family. In fact, he doubted whether Sheriff Eastman and the others riding with him ever thought about the Hascombs, unless they were seen in town, handing their money to some shopkeeper. They had been neighbors only in the sense of occupying an adjacent space. But for the most part, Slade imagined, they'd been out of sight and out of mind.

Now, death had made them memorable for a day or two. And when they were recalled, briefly, in future, it would always be for how they'd died, rather than how they'd lived.

That was a part of human nature, Slade supposed. His job was not to grieve or eulogize the dead. He was supposed to find their killers and prevent some other family from going the same way.

And so far, he had nothing that would help.

Except, perhaps, a set of wagon tracks.

"Hold up a minute," Slade commanded, when the party still had something like a hundred yards to go before they reached the charnel house. "I found a set of wagon tracks when I was here, before, but couldn't see a wagon anywhere around the place. I don't want anybody trampling over them right now."

"What good are wagon tracks?" one of the flanking riders asked.

The sheriff answered for him.

"If the Hascombs didn't have a wagon, Tim, the killers might've used one, haulin' off their goods. We'll have to ask their neighbors, see if anyone was over here to visit, in the day or so before they died."

"I never heard of Injuns using wagons," said the one called Tim.

"They've got 'em, but it *would* be odd,"

181

another said, "bringin' a wagon on a war party."

"You're catching on," Slade said and left them chewing over that as he rode slowly forward, toward the house.

There was no way to spare the wagon tracks entirely, while removing corpses from the ransacked home, but Slade directed Eastman and the rest not to disturb them outside the immediate farmyard. Judging from visible hoof marks and other signs, it seemed the wagon had approached from the south and left heading northward.

Sheriff Eastman spent a moment with Tom Hascomb's corpse, then went inside the house. Slade saw him start to take his hat off — force of habit, fingertips already on the brim — before the sheriff caught himself and left it on.

The lady of the house was in no shape to be concerned about such things. Manners were lost on her, now and forever.

Two riders from Paradise followed their sheriff through the open doorway, but they both came out a minute later, vomiting their lunch into the dusty yard. It was enough to set one of their friends off, without seeing anything except the body near the burned-out barn, but number four managed to keep his vittles down.

As for the undertaker, Hezekiah Grimm had seen it all. Nothing fazed him, though he made sympathetic clucking sounds over Tom Hascomb, then went on to view the carnage in the house. When he emerged into the fading daylight, Grimm stood with his eyes closed for a moment, as if sending up a prayer.

It couldn't hurt, Slade thought.

But then again, it wouldn't do much good, either.

"I'll need help putting the bodies," Grimm announced, "getting them in the wagon. Four hands each should do it fine."

When no one volunteered, Grimm pointed out the four civilian members of the posse, sending two of them to fetch Tom Hascomb's body, while the others joined him in the house. They slouched in, muttering, as Slade ignored a pleading look from Grimm.

You couldn't wait to see it, Slade thought. *Here's a chance to get your hands dirty.*

While Slade checked out the wagon tracks again, confirming first impressions of their general direction, Sheriff Eastman walked around the farmhouse, eyes lowered, as if expecting clues to spring from nowhere. Slade ignored him, left him to it, well aware that people dealt with violent death in different ways.

Hezekiah Grimm had all four bodies in his wagon, and his four reluctant aides were busy scrubbing bloodied hands under the farmyard's pump, when Slade observed a rider pounding toward them, from the west. Slade didn't take him for a threat, but slipped the hammer thong off of his Colt Peacemaker, just in case.

The horseman had a farmer's look about him, from his floppy hat and stubbled chin to scuffed, worn boots. He wore no pistol, but had a Henry rifle braced across his saddle horn. His wild-eyed look settled a bit, on seeing Slade's and Eastman's badges.

"Sheriff," he addressed Eastman, "what's happened here?"

Slade pegged his age somewhere in the mid-twenties. Vaulting from his saddle, he appeared unsteady on his feet and had to catch his horse's reins to keep from stumbling.

"It's bad news, Ferris," Eastman said.

"Tell me!"

"Someone hit the place last night, or early on this morning," Eastman said. "Same as the other homesteads, it appears."

"Oh, Jesus! Is that Mr. Grimm?"

"He's helping us with the removal, Ferris."

"Jesus, God!"

184

The new arrival bolted for Grimm's morgue wagon and climbed in through the open rear, before Eastman could stop him. In another heartbeat, he came tumbling out again, face blanched and looking stunned.

"Where is she?" he demanded.

"Where is *who,* boy?" Eastman asked him.

"Jenny! Is she in the house, or — ?"

"There's nobody left inside," the sheriff said.

"Well, where *is* she, goddamn it?"

Slow on the uptake, Slade asked, "Are you saying someone's missing?"

"Jenny Hascomb. She was . . . we were . . . Jesus, don't you all know *anything?*"

8

The new arrival's full name, Slade soon learned, was Ferris Chalmers. He lived with his parents and three younger siblings on a ranch located five miles west of what had been the Hascomb place.

"You think we ought to question him?" asked Sheriff Eastman.

Slade replied, "As soon as everybody else is gone."

"Gone, where?"

"Taking the bodies into town. We don't need escorts for the ride back, do we?"

Eastman took a moment to consider it, then shook his head reluctantly. "Guess not," he said.

The other posse members were divided when it came to leaving. Two protested, maybe half enjoying their proximity to someone else's death, while their companions hemmed and hawed about the undertaker needing some protection on the trail.

Eastman played off of that and finally convinced the holdouts to move on.

Slade wondered, briefly, why the sheriff didn't simply tell all four to go about their business, but he kept it to himself. Lawmen who had to beg for votes to keep their jobs apparently had problems when it came to exercising their authority.

When Grimm's wagon and its flankers were a hundred yards away and dwindling, Slade turned back to Ferris Chalmers. Eastman read his look and told the young man, "Ferris, we all need to have a talk."

"You need to be out finding Jenny," said the farmer's son.

"We'll get to that," Slade said, already more than halfway certain that they'd never find the missing girl alive.

"Then *get* to it!" Chalmers snapped back at him. "Why are you standing here? God only knows what they'll be doing to her."

"Who is 'they'?" Slade asked.

The young man blinked at him, then swept an arm to indicate the murder house and blackened ruin of the barn. "Who do you think? The ones who did all *this*, for Christ's sake!"

"Mind your manners, boy!" the sheriff growled. Apparently, he wasn't worried about this one's vote.

Chalmers muttered something underneath his breath.

"What's that?" Eastman demanded.

"I said, fine! Go on and ask your questions."

"First," Slade said, "I need to know what brought you here today."

"I came for Jenny," Chalmers said. "To call on her, I mean. We're not engaged or anything, but I was hopeful."

"And she felt the same?" asked Slade.

"She said so."

"You don't sound convinced," said Eastman.

"We both wanted to get married, Sheriff. You can take my word or not. I never thought to have her write it down."

"Ferris . . ."

Slade interrupted to inquire, "Were you expected then, today?"

"No, sir. I finished early on some chores at home and thought I'd take a chance."

"Packing a Henry rifle," Slade observed.

"I don't go anywhere without a weapon, since these killings started. There's a Winchester and scattergun at home, so I brung that."

"When was the last time you saw Jenny Hascomb and her family?" Slade asked.

Chalmers shifted his feet, toeing the dirt

with eyes downcast. He might've just been counting backward through the weekdays, but Slade didn't think so.

"Well?" he pressed.

"Last time I saw her," Chalmers said, "she wasn't *with* her family."

"Explain that," Eastman ordered.

"She snuck off awhile, all right?" The young man blushed, but forged ahead. "It was on Sunday afternoon, so that's five days ago? Yeah, five." A finger count confirmed it.

"So what happened?" Slade inquired.

"She went to pick some flowers for the supper table, like she'd always do on Sundays. Only this time, we had worked it out ahead of time to meet and . . . talk."

Slade bought it, all but the last word.

"So where'd you have this talk?" he asked.

"Not far from here. They got a little river over that way," Chalmers said, pointing northwestward. "Say a quarter mile or so. There's lots a flowers there, shade trees. Soft grass."

His eyes were glazing over, but Slade pulled him out of it. "After you finished *talking,* then what happened?"

"She was worried that we'd been too long and all, thinking her folks might be riled up, or even come out looking for her. Time just got away from us, you know?"

Slade knew, all right.

"So she walked home alone?" he asked.

"I couldn't very well go with her, could I?"

"And that's the last you saw of her, before today?" the sheriff asked.

"The last I saw of her *at all*," Chalmers corrected him. "She isn't *here* today."

Eastman pursued his point. "You had no way of knowin' whether she caught blazes from her daddy, over Sunday's little chivaree?"

"That's right," Chalmers replied.

"So you just rode out here today and — how'd you say it? Thought you'd take a chance?"

The young man nodded.

"With friend Henry, there."

"I told you —"

"Ferris," Slade cut in, "do you know anyone who'd want to harm the Hascomb family for any reason?"

"No, sir! They were fine, upstanding people, every one of them."

"And the first thing that you knew of any trouble was . . . ?"

"Seeing the barn down, and you people milling in the yard."

"That's all for now," Slade said. "Stay

close to home the next few days, in case we need to talk to you again."

"I will."

Eastman watched Chalmers ride away, saying to Slade, "He coulda done it. May not seem like much, but with his blood up —"

"What? Killed off the girl's whole family, carried her off somewhere, and then *came* back to have a chat with us over the ashes?"

"Well . . ."

"And what about the other killings? Did he do them all, or fake this job to blame it on some other lunatic?"

"You put it that way," Eastman said, "I guess it don't make sense."

"Not much."

"We headin' back now?" Eastman asked.

"Not yet."

"How come?"

Slade pointed to a smudge of dust on the horizon, growing larger by the minute.

"It appears," he said, "we've got more company arriving."

Colonel Northcliff led the file of cavalry himself, wearing a holstered pistol on his right hip and a saber on the left. A dozen soldiers trailed him, riding two abreast. Beside the colonel rode a young civilian whom the sheriff seemed to recognize.

"Ken Darby, out from Paradise," said Eastman, speaking from the corner of his mouth. "Mayor sent him to the fort for help."

"Just what we need," Slade said.

"You don't think so?"

"Depends on *how* he helps."

"Want to explain that?"

"Let's just wait and see," suggested Slade.

When he was twenty yards out from the house, Northcliff pulled up and raised a hand to stop his troopers in their tracks. Slade noted that the colonel wore a pair of leather gauntlets, as if worried that the reins might chafe his palms.

"Sheriff. Marshal," he said, peering at each of them in turn. "What have we here?"

"Same as before," Eastman replied. "Just change the names and numbers."

"*Not* the same," Slade contradicted Eastman. "There's a girl missing this time. Carried away somewhere."

"Bound to be dead by now," the sheriff said, frowning. "Tomorrow, we'll ride out and watch for buzzards circling."

"*Maybe* dead, not bound to be," said Slade. "They've never kidnapped anyone before, as far as we know, so we're starting off from scratch on this one."

"Well, it seems to be a good thing that I'm here," Northcliff remarked, "since civil law enforcement can't seem to agree on anything."

"We're in agreement she was taken," Slade replied. "It's kidnapping until we find her dead. My call."

Eastman shot Slade a sidelong glare, which Slade ignored.

Northcliff dismounted, passed his reins up to the nearest soldier, and approached the two of them on foot. Before addressing them, he had another thought and turned back toward his waiting guide.

"You may as well go back to town," he said. "We know the way from here."

Ken Darby bobbed his head, then turned and rode away toward Paradise.

"Now, gentlemen," said Northcliff, facing Slade and Eastman, "if you'd be good enough to share the details of this tragedy?"

Slade let the sheriff lay it out. Four dead. The missing girl. Livestock presumed stolen. Slade wished that he'd asked Ferris Chalmers about missing horses, but the point had slipped his mind when Eastman focused on the young man as a suspect.

"I believe it's clear what must be done," said Northcliff, when the sheriff's recitation ended.

"Chase the wagon tracks?" Slade asked.

"How's that?" The colonel looked confused. "What wagon tracks would those be?"

"Over there." Slade pointed. "Coming in from the northeast and going off to the southwest from here. The victims didn't own a wagon."

"So? A neighbor likely stopped to visit, who knows when? I seriously doubt that Cherokee would bring a wagon on the warpath, Marshal."

"You think Indians did this?" asked Slade.

"Of course. Don't you? I mean, isn't it obvious from all the . . . savagery?"

"The marshal thinks it's white man's work," said Sheriff Eastman.

"Does he, now?"

"Ask me, you want to know what's on my mind," said Slade.

A hint of angry color tinged the colonel's cheeks. "All right, I'm asking."

"I rode out to the reservation earlier today and talked to Red Eagle," Slade said. "I don't believe he knows who's doing all this killing."

"Ah. *You* don't *believe* he knows. And if he lied?"

"I'd like to have his poker face."

"Well, let's assume he told the truth for once," said Northcliff. "What does that prove? He's an old man who can barely feed himself. Should we assume that he knows *everything* that happens, on and off the reservation?"

"Where his people are concerned, I'd say it's pretty close," Slade answered.

"You have some sympathy in that direction, I suspect. Toward *his people.*"

"My sympathy lies with the victims," Slade replied. "That's why I want to find the killers, not just chase some Indians around the reservation for the hell of it."

"Now, look here —"

"Colonel," Slade cut through his protest, "if you have some kind of evidence against the Cherokee or any other tribe, the play's all yours. Until you have that evidence, the U.S. Marshals Service calls the shots."

"I'll find the evidence, *Marshal.* In fact, I'm on my way to do that very thing, right now."

"The rez, again," Slade said.

"Where else."

"You won't mind if I ride along, then."

"Would it matter?" Northcliff asked.

"Not one iota," Slade replied.

"And what about you, Sheriff?" asked the colonel. "Would you care to supervise, as well?"

Eastman considered it for all of half a

second, then said, "Nope. I've got my work cut out for me in Paradise." Turning in the direction of his horse, Eastman half smiled at Slade and said, "You're on your own."

Slade nodded, thinking to himself, *What else is new?*

Given Colonel Northcliff's attitude, Slade saw no point in making small talk on their ride out to the Saline Reservation. They were wasting time, in his opinion, when he could have chased the wagon tracks leaving the Hascomb spread, but Northcliff had him worried.

In his present state of mind, Slade wouldn't put it past the colonel to exaggerate — or even fabricate — some bit of "evidence" against Red Eagle and his Cherokee, in order to support a move against them. He wasted no time speculating over Northcliff's motives and did not delude himself into believing he could stand between the U.S. Army and the Cherokee for any length of time.

In this one case, however, Slade *could* stop Northcliff from muddying the waters and allowing the real killers to escape while framing Indians to close the case. If he accomplished nothing else, in fact, that would be something.

But it wouldn't be *enough.*

Slade didn't see himself as a detective — certainly, he didn't have the mental powers of the fictional crime fighters created by Poe or the Englishman Doyle — but certain facts seemed obvious.

Red Eagle had not ordered any of the homestead raids, nor — in Slade's personal opinion — could he name the individuals responsible. If they'd been Cherokee, he thought the chief would either give them up or find some way to punish them himself.

And if the murderers were white, Colonel Northcliff would never find them. *Couldn't* find them, much less prosecute them, even if he wanted to, since his authority was limited to Fort Supply and the surrounding reservations.

Slade reckoned that one key to running down the killers would be finding out who bought the livestock they had stolen on their raids. They would be damned conspicuous dragging a remuda of horses around the Oklahoma badlands, and Slade seriously doubted that they were devouring all the rustled cattle.

He had tried to make that point to Sheriff Eastman, more than once, but Eastman didn't seem to hear him. Or it could be that he didn't *want* to hear it.

197

Slade had an impression of the sheriff as a man who ran a tidy town and dealt with lawbreakers according to the standard small-town formula. He would walk softly with the locals who controlled his fate around election time — particularly those with the authority to gut his budget — but he would pull out the stops if strangers overstepped themselves in Paradise.

He seemed to be a cookie-cutter lawman, one who wouldn't buck the odds or the majority opinion if he wasn't guaranteed a profitable win. Of course, Slade couldn't swear to that, but first impressions in a case like this were generally all he got.

And though he'd never served a day in uniform, he also knew a bit about the colonel's type. He'd met some army officers at poker tables, riding trains and stage-coaches, and even chasing Indians across the vast Southwest. Slade knew that some exalted duty over anything — or any*one,* including their own wives and families — while others looked beyond their discharge papers, sketching an imaginary life of ease and plenty.

Slade pegged Northcliff as one of the latter, though he couldn't see the colonel's angle yet. Northcliff did not seem like a man whose prejudice against red skin would make him close his eyes to mass murder committed by whites, but that prejudice *could* tip the scales of his judgment on any close call.

What did the colonel stand to gain by rousting Red Eagle's Cherokee off the Saline Reservation? Was he acting on behalf of someone else, or did the plan — whatever that might be — originate with him? Slade couldn't find an answer looking inward, so he tried to put it out of mind.

They'd reached the reservation, anyway. He recognized some of the landmarks, even with the first vague gloom of dusk descending, and Slade knew he wouldn't get to chase the troubling wagon tracks that day. He didn't want to lose the trail, for one thing; nor was he encouraged by the thought of meeting his intended quarry in the dark.

What difference did it make, in any case?

A fully loaded Conestoga wagon, moving at a normal pace, covered some fifteen miles per day. A smaller vehicle, less burdened, could improve on that — but by how much?

Before he started in the morning, Slade would be a day or more behind his targets, but that didn't make them safe. They didn't know it yet, but he was coming for them. And he wouldn't stop.

Not if he had to follow them to Hell.

■ ■ ■ ■

"What brings you out this way, Sheriff?" Angus McCallister inquired.

Eastman was tempted to reply, *My horse,* but knew instinctively that being flippant wouldn't help him here. Not that he *needed* help, just passing on the latest news, but standing in the rich landowner's presence, overlooked by trophy heads on all four walls surrounding him, made Eastman feel as if he did.

"Just wanted to make sure you'd heard the news," he said, "and that you're battened down for any trouble."

"Oh, I'm always set for trouble," said McCallister. "By news, you mean this business at the Hascomb place?"

"That's it," Eastman agreed. "I don't suppose the scum who did it will try anything with you and all your men around the spread."

"I almost wish they would, Sheriff."

"Might solve my problem, anyway," said Eastman, "if your riders took 'em out."

"I guess it would. Cigar?"

"No, thank you, sir."

McCallister lit his and spent the best part of a minute puffing on it, fogging up the

200

room around him. When he spoke at last, the rancher's voice had taken on a thoughtful quality.

"What *is* your problem, Sheriff? I mean, besides the obvious."

Something told Eastman it was unwise to share his darker thoughts with someone whom he didn't really know, but he'd gone too long now without a sympathetic ear.

What could it hurt?

"One problem," Eastman said, "is Marshal Slade, from Enid. He thinks white men did these killings, and I have to wonder if he might be right?"

Frowning, McCallister asked, "Why is that?"

"There's nothing I can put my finger on, right now. More like, it's things that *should* be there, but aren't. Know what I mean?"

"I'll need a few more clues, Sheriff."

"Well, sir, what's missing is a sign of anything that redskins might've left behind while they were killin' white folks in the middle of the night. So far, there hasn't been an arrow or a feather, not a footprint from a moccasin. No gunshot wounds to match the few old Springfields they're allowed to keep out on the rez, for hunting. No one scalped, even when they were cut to hell and gone."

"But surely," said McCallister, "they must be smart enough to cover up their tracks."

"That's how I felt, at first," Eastman replied. "But *smart* ain't killin' families this way, within a few miles of the rez. Who else would they suppose I'm gonna look at, first? And what's the army gonna do, except ride out and give 'em hell?"

"Sheriff —"

"And what about the livestock?" Eastman interrupted. He was on a roll now, even though it felt peculiar, hearing Slade's words coming out of his own mouth. "When you think about it, where do they keep hiding all those animals?"

"How many are you missing?" asked Mc-Callister.

"We still aren't sure. It must be pushing twenty head, before last night, horses and cattle all together."

"Twenty head's not much," McCallister observed.

"It would be, on the rez. They'd stand right out."

"Unless they're stashed somewhere."

"Such as?"

The rancher shrugged and blew a plume of smoke. "I wouldn't know. They've likely got a few box canyons on the reservation. Wooded patches, here and there. I mean, it's not *all* salt, is it?"

"More likely, they've been sold," Eastman replied.

"Who'd buy them from a redskin, when all this is going on?"

"Exactly," Eastman said.

McCallister scowled at the trap he'd baited for himself. "Well, Sheriff, it appears you need the buyer, then. Find him — or *them* — and you'll be one step from the killers."

One hell of a long *step,* Eastman thought, but he was nodding, just the same.

"Of course," McCallister added, "you'd actually have to *find* the buyer, in the first place. Any thoughts on how you'd pull that off?"

Eastman supposed the rancher meant to rile him, maybe make him feel all foolish and embarrassed, but it didn't work. Because the sheriff *did* have an idea. In fact, now that he wasn't focused on Red Eagle's Cherokee to the exclusion of all else, he had a suspect's name in mind.

"You're smiling, Sheriff. Did I make a joke?"

"No, sir," Eastman replied. "I'd say the joke's been on me, all along."

No scouts came out to meet the cavalry

patrol. Slade didn't need a guide to find the village, though, and neither did the soldiers trailing Colonel Northcliff. Fifteen minutes brought them to the clutch of dwellings, whose inhabitants stood waiting to receive them.

Slade scanned hostile faces, noting that the men — including Little Wolf, who'd met him on the reservation earlier that day — displayed no weapons in the presence of the bluecoats. Seeing that, Slade understood that someone must have seen the cavalry approaching and raced on ahead to warn the Cherokee.

Red Eagle stood outside his home with two more tribal elders, as the troops approached. Their faces had a kind of timeless quality, but Slade guessed that both flankers must be older than the chief himself.

Had they been on the Trail of Tears as children, when their people were uprooted from ancestral lands in Georgia and compelled to march five hundred miles through Dixie, to a place where they would never truly be at home?

Slade let the question slide and focused his attention on Northcliff, as he began to speak.

"Red Eagle, it appears you were expecting us," the colonel said.

The chief said nothing, which appeared to irritate Northcliff. Of course, the colonel hadn't asked a question. Why should anyone respond?

Trying another tack, Northcliff inquired, "Are you aware that there has been another massacre of homesteaders, within a short distance of where we stand?"

"I know nothing of any white man's crimes," Red Eagle said. "My people know nothing."

"Indeed?" The colonel shifted in his saddle, leather creaking underneath him. "Are your warriors all accounted for?"

"There are no warriors here, but yours," Red Eagle answered. "We wish nothing but to live in peace."

"I see. Does it *disturb* you that these murders have occurred? Are you not fearful for the safety of your people?"

"White men kill each other every day," said Little Wolf, speaking out of turn.

Slade felt a shifting in the mounted ranks, but Red Eagle ignored the soldiers, pinning Little Wolf with a stare that made him flinch and look away.

Northcliff leaned slightly forward, hands braced on his saddle horn. "I'm waiting for an answer, *Chief.*"

Red Eagle took the thinly veiled insult,

ignored it, and replied, "We have done nothing wrong. We have nothing to fear."

Slade reckoned it took nerve to say that, in the face of uniforms and rifles, looking back on history. In any clash between white men and red, even when they were in the right, the Indians had suffered catastrophic losses.

"I have only your word for that," said Northcliff, "and it isn't good enough. In light of the most recent crime, we are required to search for evidence that may identify the man or men responsible. You understand, I'm sure."

No answer from the chief.

He understands, all right, thought Slade. *He sees that Northcliff's looking for a reason — any reason — to unleash his men and punish someone for the massacres.*

From where Slade sat, it didn't seem that Northcliff cared much about punishing the guilty, only making sure that those who felt the weight of so-called justice had red skin.

When Red Eagle kept silent, Northcliff said, "All right, then. Since we're in agreement, let the search begin. Sergeant! Take half the men, fan out, and check the houses. We need —"

"No."

The single word from Slade brought

Northcliff's head whipping around to face him.

"What was that, Marshal?"

"You're after cows and horses, Colonel. If you see a house that's big enough to hide some, I'll go in and search it for you. Otherwise, your men look only where they might find livestock."

Crimson blotches stained the colonel's cheeks.

"You dare to countermand my orders, sir?"

"When they're in violation of the law, I do."

"The law? *What* law?"

Slade said, "You may have heard about the Constitution at West Point. If not, I'll fill you in. The Fourth Amendment bans unreasonable searches, and pretending you expect to find livestock in one of these houses is what I call unreasonable, Colonel."

"Marshal, I propose to carry out my duty."

"Then remember what it is," said Slade. "You're stationed here to keep the peace, not to provoke a war with no excuse. Judge Dennison won't sanction bullying —"

"Judge Dennison is not in charge of —"

"— and I'm betting that the newspapers will hang you out to dry, before it's over."

"Newspapers?" Above his crimson cheeks,

the colonel's eyes had narrowed down to slits.

"Imagine what they'll write," Slade said, "if you touch off a massacre tonight *and* let the homestead killers get away, besides. Won't be the smartest move you ever made."

Northcliff considered it, his soldiers flicking glances from their boss to Slade and back again, waiting.

"Sergeant!" he said at last, gruff-voiced.

"Yes, sir?" the answer came back from a grizzled trooper with three yellow hash marks on his sleeve.

"Proceed to search for any place where livestock might be kept. Avoid the homes . . . for now."

Slade let himself relax a bit, but only just. He'd made an enemy of Northcliff, and most probably of every man at Fort Supply. As for the Cherokee, he found the elders and Little Wolf eyeballing him with blank expressions, totally inscrutable.

It was a victory of sorts, but Slade did not feel like a winner.

Truth be told, he felt as if he had a bull's-eye target painted on his back.

9

Jenny Hascomb woke believing she was blind and paralyzed. She had been struck a vicious blow across the head that rendered her unconscious, that much she remembered, and such things could steal a person's eyesight, even rob her of ability to move her limbs.

But, no.

When Jenny *tried* to move, she felt muscles responding in her shoulders, back, and arms, her thighs and calves. Her fingers wiggled and her toes flexed. Finally, she recognized the bite of rope wound tightly around wrists and ankles, knotted so that she couldn't untie them.

Even if she could have *seen* the knots.

Nor was she blind, as Jenny realized a moment later. Rather, she was blind*folded,* with some kind of rough cloth wound about her head and tied in back. She felt that knot, as well, when she attempted to turn over and relieve some of the achy feeling in her arms.

And she was gagged, as well. Another piece of cloth was wadded in her mouth, held there with yet another strip around her face, tied off behind her neck. It wasn't choking her — not *yet,* at least — but Jenny knew she must be careful not to swallow.

A flood of memories washed over her. She saw her parents in the farmhouse, huddled close and whispering by candlelight. She heard her father's warning to remain inside, stay quiet, and bar the door, before he took his gun and slipped out into darkness.

In her mind, she heard the shot a moment later, waited trembling at her mother's side until a scratching sounded at the door and someone — was it some*thing* — started whimper-whining in the night.

She felt her mother's arms around her, heard her little sister crying, while their brother — quite the little man at ten years old — cursed at the prowlers, telling them to go away and leave his family alone.

She made a muffled sobbing sound, and someone close at hand replied, "Hush up!"

It was a gruff male voice, one of the men who'd burst into the house, grinning and making noises like wild animals. Despite her terror, Jenny tried to speak. Instead of words, it came out sounding like the rooting noises of a hungry piglet.

"I said hush!" the man repeated, and a pair of calloused fingers pinched her nostrils shut.

At first, she thought he simply meant to twist her nose, to hurt her, but the grip remained in place and Jenny realized she couldn't breathe. She couldn't smell the musty odor of the rocking wagon any longer, couldn't purge the stale air from her lungs, or draw fresh to replace it.

Jenny bucked and wriggled, thrashed her head from side to side, but couldn't shake the fingers clamped over her nose. The gag stopped her from breathing through her mouth, and within seconds she was starved for oxygen. Bright specks of light swam in the dark behind her covered eyes.

Jenny was on the verge of passing out when he released her, let her draw a grateful breath. He pinched her breast as a cruel afterthought, then seemed to reconsider it and stroked her. Jenny made a moaning sound as he began to lift her nightgown's hem, but then the wagon stopped.

His hand withdrew.

"We got some business needs attending to," the man half whispered, leaning close enough for her to feel his hot breath on her ear. "You make another sound, I'll gut you like a fish. Just think of all the fun you'd miss."

He left her then, the wagon creaking with his weight as he moved down its length, then vaulted to the ground. Jenny was trying to decide a course of action, when she heard another shifting sound and felt someone beside her.

Felt the unseen watcher staring down at her.

The slap across her face surprised her totally. It bounced her head against the rough bed of the wagon, nothing but a thin blanket between herself and rigid boards. A second, harder slap silenced her muffled protest.

"That's for tempting him," a woman's voice informed her. "You'll get worse than that, if you don't stop it!"

Then the woman left, as well, and Jenny heard voices outside the wagon, strained her ears to listen. Hampered by a ringing in her ears, both from the slaps and momentary oxygen starvation, she could only pick out bits and pieces of the conversation.

". . . less than last time," said a man's voice that she didn't recognize.

"How much?" asked the woman who had slapped her. Jenny knew *that* voice, right enough.

". . . dollars a head," the stranger answered.

". . . need more," said the man who'd pinched her nostrils.

". . . somewhere else." The stranger standing firm.

They must have struck a bargain, since the conversation ended. Then, a moment later, Jenny heard the wagon's canvas flaps shifting and heard the stranger ask, "What else you got back here?"

"Nothing for you," the woman who had slapped her answered, in a voice as cold as polished steel.

"Awright, don't get your knickers in a twist," the man said, chuckling at his own joke. "I'm just lookin' for a deal, the same as always."

"We've already made our deal. Pay up," the woman said.

"I'll get your money," said the man. "You all go on and put my horses in the barn."

Jack Slade rode back to Paradise alone. Northcliff's patrol was heading back to Fort Supply without a shred of evidence linking the Cherokee to any of the homestead massacres, and Slade had read the fuming anger on the colonel's face when they were finished scouring the village.

It was clear to Slade that Northcliff had desired a confrontation with Red Eagle and his tribe, something to justify retaliation and allow him to report that he done something in the wake of so much carnage.

But was that the full extent of Northcliff's motive?

Slade was no mind reader, but he had to wonder if the colonel had some hidden program of his own in mind that would involve the reservation. Lacking any clue what that might be, however, Slade dismissed it from his mind.

Night overtook him on the prairie, north of town, but Slade wasn't concerned about riding alone through darkness. The killers, whoever they were and wherever they'd gone, didn't prey on lone riders as far as Slade knew.

Too bad, he thought, frowning.

At least, if they had ambushed him, he'd have a chance to end it — or, at least, to see their faces. One glimpse over gunsights would be satisfactory, just long enough for Slade to aim and pull the trigger.

It would disappoint Judge Dennison, if none of those responsible wound up before his bench for sentencing, but more than anything, the judge wanted them stopped.

By any legal means available.

With that in mind, Slade couldn't creep up on their camp — assuming he'd known where it was — and shoot them in their bedrolls while they slept. He couldn't hand them over to the citizens of Paradise for lynching, either.

If it came to that, and Slade was able to arrest the killers without shooting them, he'd have to think about skirting the town on his return to Enid. It was one thing, keeping prisoners alive in custody, but if he locked them up in Sheriff Eastman's jail, however briefly, and a mob formed . . .

Could Slade bring himself to fire on them, in the defense of men who'd slaughtered more than twenty people that he knew of? Who had snatched a girl out of her home and might be doing God knows what to her right now?

Slade wasn't sure that he could pull the trigger in a case like that, when all his sympathy was with the mob. Of course, he knew Judge Dennison's opinion on the matter, without asking for it. Dennison would hang lynchers — or, at the very least, send them to spend their lives in prison — without thinking twice about the motive for their crime.

That was part of being *civilized*. A man could kill in self-defense, or to protect his family and property, but punishment — the bit that trailed after a crime and tried to put things right again — remained the sole preserve of government.

The state could kill for any number of accepted reasons, using soldiers, lawmen, and the courts to get it done. All duly authorized, investigated, filed in triplicate for future reference.

If Slade killed someone in performance of his duty, he explained it to Judge Dennison, and Dennison decided whether it was justified or not. If not, the judge could fire Slade, or suspend him without pay, even file charges that could land Slade in a prison cell or on the gallows.

So far, the judge had rubber-stamped the split-second decisions Slade had made in life-or-death encounters on the job.

So far.

Civilians in the badlands, on the other hand, were constantly at risk from every quarter. If attacked, they could fight back, of course. But if they sought revenge beyond the letter of the law, then *they* became the criminals, subject to punishment.

Slade pushed the foibles of the legal system from his mind and concentrated on his quarry as the lights of Paradise came into view. Tomorrow morning, he would ride back to the Hascomb farm — for the last time, he hoped — and trace the wagon tracks as far as possible.

And if he lost them, he would try to think of some other approach. Something besides waiting around for yet another family to be butchered, and another after that.

Slade couldn't guard all of the districts farms and rural homes. He couldn't wait and watch at each of them in turn, for madmen to come calling in the middle of the night. How many homesteads were there in the country around Paradise? A hundred? More?

And if he knew the number, what good would it do?

Slade's stomach growled, reminding him that he was hungry. He would make his first stop at the restaurant, then back to his hotel room for a night of fitful sleep. He could be on the road at dawn, with any luck.

Good luck for me, this time, I hope, Slade thought.

Bad luck for them.

"Thank you for stopping by, Colonel."

Angus McCallister poured two glasses of whiskey, handing one of them to Hollis Northcliff.

"We were passing by," the colonel said,

"returning to the fort. I thought you'd like to hear the latest news."

"Which is?"

"More farmers dead," Northcliff replied, after a sip of liquor, "and I've still got nothing that will make Red Eagle's Cherokee look responsible."

"You've been out to the rez again, I take it?" asked McCallister.

"We were."

"And searched it all again?"

"As much as possible."

The rancher frowned. "What's that supposed to mean?"

"A federal marshal was already at the murder scene when we arrived," said Northcliff.

"Slade." McCallister pronounced the name as if it was a curse.

"The very same. He seems to think —"

"That the redskins are innocent. I've heard it," said McCallister.

"Then you won't be surprised to hear he rode along with us to see Red Eagle."

"So?"

The colonel shrugged. "Before my men could search the hovels where these savages reside, your Marshal Slade insisted that we only look for stolen livestock in conventional locations."

"Can he do that?"

"Can, and did," Northcliff replied. "You should have seen him on his high horse — literally, that is — spouting off about the Constitution. God, you'd think the Cherokee were *citizens,* the way he carried on."

"And you just took it?"

Northcliff stiffened.

"I'm obliged to follow certain rules and regulations, even in my dealings with the Indians. No one listens to their complaints, alone, but if a U.S. marshal testified to violations of the law . . . well, let's just say that neither one of us needs *that.*"

"No, no, you're right," McCallister agreed. Thinking, *We don't need Slade, in fact.*

"So what's the next step, Colonel?"

Northcliff drained his glass, then said, "I've done all that I can do, for the moment. If we'd found some kind of evidence the Cherokee were raiding homesteads, I could punish them. We'd have a good case for evacuation of the Saline Reservation. Failing that . . ."

The colonel spread his hands, a helpless gesture.

"Failing that," McCallister echoed. His thin lips formed a scowl. "I have to tell you, Hollis, *failing's* not a word I like to hear. At least, not where my plans and money are concerned."

"I understand, but —"

"I'm not sure you do," the rancher interrupted him. "We have a deal. Or, should I say, we *had* one? Are you backing out on me? Are you a *quitter,* Hollis?"

Northcliff had to notice that McCallister had stopped using his military rank, but he raised no complaint. His right hand trembled slightly, as he clutched his whiskey glass — whether from rage or fear, McCallister could not have said.

But either one would do.

"Angus, you know me and you know my record. I'm not backing out of *anything.* I'm simply telling you that I don't have authority to raid the reservation without cause. If I did that, three things would happen. Can you guess what those might be?"

"Tell me," McCallister replied.

"First, I would be relieved of duty pending an investigation by the general staff — and probably by Congress. When I can't show cause for any moves against the Cherokee, I'll be court-martialed."

"And the job I promised would be waiting for you."

"I'm not finished! Second, if the military or congressional investigations turned up any link between us indicating a conspiracy, then they'd be coming after you, as well."

"What evidence, there's no —"

"And third, you've still got Marshal Slade, snooping around for old Judge Dennison. They want to hang whoever is responsible for all these murders, and they're bound to find someone. Suppose they focus in on you?"

McCallister gaped back at him, cigar and drink forgotten. "What the hell . . . ? On *me*?"

"On *us*, then," the colonel amended. "Why not? We've been using the murders as leverage against Red Eagle's Cherokee — or trying to, at least. They might go one step further and conclude we *planned* the crimes."

"Conclude, my ass! We didn't *do* it. There's no evidence to back it up."

"Juries are fickle things," said Northcliff. "Once twelve farmers hear some of the things we *have* done, they could hang us for the hell of it."

McCallister's voice had a stony edge as he inquired, "Who would they hear that from, Hollis?"

"I won't hang over this, Angus. Not for retirement pay. Not so that you can make another million dollars bagging salt."

"Hanging isn't the only way to die," Mc-

Callister reminded him.

Northcliff set down his empty glass and stepped in closer to his host. The colonel's hands weren't trembling now.

Between clenched teeth, he said, "And threatening my life won't get you anything but trouble, Angus. Do you *really* think that you can win a fight against the U.S. Army? Have you lost your goddamned mind?"

McCallister knew when he'd gone too far. Backpedaling, he told Northcliff, "I'm not proposing any kind of war, Colonel. My business *is* business. But when I pay a man to do a job, I want it done — or else, I want the money back. In full. With interest on the loan."

"I'll say again, we have a deal. But I can't make a move with U.S. marshals breathing down my neck."

"One marshal," said McCallister.

"He's plenty," Northcliff said. "You ought to meet him. Educate yourself."

McCallister inhaled cigar smoke and replied, "I just might do that very thing."

"So, now you're telling me you think it *isn't* Indians?"

Mayor Mathers looked confused, and Ardis Eastman couldn't rightly blame him.

"I'm not sayin' that, exactly," he replied.

"But thinkin' on the livestock that's been stolen, knowin' that the colonel's soldiers couldn't find them on the rez, I started wondering."

Eastman had stopped off at the mayor's house on his way home from his visit to the Hascomb spread. The smell of death and ashes clung to him, making Rance Mathers flinch away when they were shaking hands, but Eastman didn't care.

So far, the mayor's involvement in the homestead murders had been that of a concerned bystander. Nothing had occurred within his jurisdiction, and he hadn't lost a single voter to the rash of crimes occurring outside Paradise. Mathers would love to see the killings stop, of course, like anybody else. But when push came to shove, his job was the first thing he thought about.

Sometimes, Eastman suspected that it was the *only* thing.

"And your idea is . . . what, again?" asked Mathers.

"To go out and find whoever bought the animals," Eastman replied.

"You plan to ride all over hell and back, looking for cows and horses?"

"If I have to. But the fact is, I've already got a name in mind."

Mathers blinked at him, leaning forward

on his sofa cushion. "What? You *do?* Who *is* it, Ardis?"

Eastman shook his head. "I can't say, yet, in case I'm wrong. I won't make anybody live under that kind of cloud, if I can't charge 'em with the crime."

"So it's someone I *know.*"

"I'll say no more about it, Mayor. It still might be the Cherokee — or, hell, some other buncha redskins off another reservation. I just need to check this out, to satisfy myself."

"And if it doesn't fly? What, then?"

"I'll keep on looking for the buyer," Eastman said. "These animals are goin' *somewhere,* right? There never was a gang that rode around collectin' stock without reason."

Mayor Mathers frowned. "Something you ought to think about," he said. "I mean, assuming that you're right and these horrendous crimes were perpetrated by white men. Maybe the stock *was* taken for a reason. Not to sell, but to build up the killer's spread."

Eastman considered it, then said, "Too risky. Keepin' evidence of murder at your house is askin' for a noose. Oh, you can hide a brooch or ring, somethin' like that, and you can spend money without explainin'

where it came from. But if you start rustlin'
stock and *keeping* it, tending the animals
and takin' them to market, then you'd have
to worry every minute about someone rec-
ognizin' this or that one from his neighbor's
place, back when."

"Well, either way, it's bad news if you're
right," the mayor replied. "We've either got
a killer living close enough to tug our
sleeves, or else someone who *deals* with killers, taking blood money. In either case, you
need to root them out."

"I aim to," Eastman promised.

"Would they hang this man you have in
mind?" asked Mathers.

"All depends on what he's done, or what
he's charged with. If he planned or helped
out with the killin', then he'll swing. No
doubt. But if he's only charged with buyin'
stolen property, he could be out of jail in
two, three years."

"And right back here," said Mathers.

"Oh, there's ways to let him know he isn't
welcome," Eastman said.

"And you could handle that? Within the
law, I mean?"

If I'm still sheriff, Eastman thought.

But what he said was, "I don't see why
not."

■ ■ ■ ■

"We have a problem, Clete," Angus McCallister announced.

His foreman frowned and said, "Another one?"

"Part of the same one, if you like. A complication."

"Awright, then."

"I suppose you've heard about this U.S. marshal, in from Enid?"

"Sure have, Boss."

"He's looking more and more to me like one big stumbling block. You follow?"

"Um . . ."

"He's in our way."

"And you want I should move him?"

"It's a thought," McCallister replied.

"If he's there in town, it shouldn't be a problem," Cletus Paxton said. "I'll go in and call him out."

"What, just like that?"

A shrug. "Why not?"

"Well, Clete, for one thing, he's a *lawman.* You can't pick a fight with him for looking at you sideways or insulting you. In fact, I'm pretty sure he's got immunity from calling you a dozen different kinds of sumbitch, if he feels like it."

"I'll think of somethin'," Paxton said. "Lawmen ain't perfect."

"What if you can't take him?"

Paxton smiled at that. "I'll take him, Boss. Don't sweat it."

"Then, we've got another problem, even if you do."

"What's that?"

"You work for *me*," McCallister reminded him. "You kill a U.S. marshal, when they're finished hanging you, they come for me, thinking I put you up to it."

"Well . . ."

"Don't get me wrong, now," said McCallister. "I'm all for getting rid of him. It just requires some thought, and . . . what's the word I'm looking for?"

"Don't know."

"*Finesse.* That's what we need."

"You lost me, there."

"It's French. Means 'smooth,' or some damn thing. Whatever. Clete, I'm saying that we need to think this through before you go to town and make a mess that's bound to cost us everything we've worked for all these years. You understand?"

Paxton nodded. "You want him kilt some way that won't come back on you."

"Exactly!"

"Won't they just send out another one? I

mean, they don't run out of marshals, right? It's not like some hick town where you can shoot the constable and go hog wild."

"That's true. But by the time Judge Dennison finds out his man is dead and sends out reinforcements, we could have a break with Colonel Northcliff and Red Eagle, on the rez. There's nothing like a war to raise some dust and cover tracks."

"I'm thinkin' rifle," Paxton said.

"Say what?"

"Lay back and shoot the marshal from a distance. No one sees who done it, and we're in the clear."

"You're good enough to do that?" asked McCallister. "I mean, of course, with pistols, but —"

"There's nothin' to it," Paxton said, smiling. "He never sees it comin'. You don't even have to draw."

"Where would you do it?"

"Have to be in town," the foreman said. "Too hard to follow him all over God's green acres, waitin' for a shot and never gettin' spotted."

"So, in town, then," said McCallister. "I understand he has a room at the hotel."

"I'll check it out."

"And don't share this with anyone."

"Hey, I ain't stupid!" Paxton said.

"No, no. Far from it! You're the best, Clete. No one finer."

"I won't need no help on this one, anyway."

"I shouldn't think so."

"Either pot him through his window, if I get an angle on it, or else take him when he's goin' in or out of the hotel."

"Sounds like a plan."

"And there's some kinda bonus in it for me?"

"Absolutely. How's a hundred dollars sound?"

"Two hunnerd sounds a whole lot better, now you mention it."

"Then two it is."

Paxton rose from his chair and sauntered to the door, then paused there, fingers wrapped around the knob.

"So who'm I lookin' for, again?"

"The *marshal,* Clete."

The foreman rolled his eyes. "I mean, his *name.*"

"Ah, that. It's Slade. Jack Slade."

"Well, you can scratch him off your list, Boss. It's as good as done."

"I feel better already," said McCallister.

"I aim to please."

Just aim straight, McCallister thought, but

kept his mouth shut as the study's door closed.

Well, it was done now. *Half* done, anyway. He'd passed the order and McCallister saw no reason to think that Paxton would not follow through.

And after that . . .

He didn't know Judge Dennison, except by reputation, but from what he'd heard, McCallister knew that the hanging judge would spare no effort to discover who had killed his deputy, and why. The best thing that McCallister could do, under the circumstances, was to guarantee that Cletus Paxton never had a chance to run his mouth in federal court.

There had to be a way to pull that off, without endangering himself. A shocked discovery of Paxton's crime, perhaps, leading to confrontation . . . and the foreman's death?

Why not?

McCallister's involvement in Slade's death might be suspected, even when he'd dealt with Cletus, but without the foreman's testimony nothing could be proved.

Relaxing, finally, McCallister decided that another shot of whiskey was in order.

It was almost time for him to celebrate.

10

Slade woke before sunrise from dreams that he couldn't recall, but which left him uneasy, feeling as if he'd missed something important that might come back to haunt him.

Shaking off the vague sense of doom, he rose and dressed by lamplight, with the curtains drawn across his window, then sat down to double-check his weapons while he waited for the only restaurant in Paradise to open for its breakfast customers.

Slade found himself hoping that the Mexican chef worked mornings. He felt like huevos rancheros — could almost taste them, in fact, as he finally put on his hat and prepared to step out.

He'd flipped a mental coin, deciding that he'd leave his saddlebags and Winchester in the hotel room while he ate, then make the short detour to retrieve them on his way down to the livery. It wouldn't cost him any time worth mentioning, particularly since the men he hunted — if they slept at all — were likely lighting up a breakfast fire themselves, somewhere off to the west of town.

He had considered riding west, first thing, to cut their trail, instead of repeating his trip to the late Hascomb ranch, but it was too risky. Slade had seen the wagon tracks departing from that slaughter scene in a southwesterly direction, but that didn't mean the killers had continued on in a straight line, indefinitely.

Hell, for all Slade knew they could've gone a couple hundred yards, then changed their minds and struck off in a different direction. Or the tracks he'd seen could be a false lead altogether, laid deliberately to throw man hunters off the scent.

Crossing the hotel lobby, Slade tipped a nod to the desk clerk, then stepped out into dawn's first gray light. The street was nearly empty, just a pair of merchants sweeping off their bits of sidewalk, but he saw lamps burning in the restaurant and took it for a good sign.

Crossing the street, Slade let his mind drift back to the cruel, faceless men he was hunting. More specifically, he went back to the subject of their wagon, and a sore point

— one of many — that was gnawing at his mind.

Slade reckoned that a gang must be responsible for the horrific homestead murders, but the only evidence he'd found of any callers at the Hascomb place were those same horse-and-wagon tracks he planned to chase that day. It seemed a strange way for a gang of deadly raiders to approach their target, one man driving while the others hunched together in the back, waiting to drop and run.

Maybe I've got it wrong, Slade thought, as he entered the restaurant and was surrounded by its welcome cooking smells. *Maybe the wagon was a neighbor's, after all.*

Slade wouldn't know until he found it, though. By which time, he would either have the killers in his sights, or else he'd be lamenting all the time he'd wasted on a wild-goose chase.

There was a different waitress covering the restaurant that morning, older, slow to smile. Slade thought he would be, too, if he was forced to wait on people all day long, carrying food out of the kitchen and retrieving empty plates.

Slade wondered what her story was, for something like a second and a half, then saw huevos rancheros on the menu and chose black coffee to wash them down. The coffee came immediately, and the food about ten minutes later. Slade dug in, found it delicious, and proceeded from the first large bite to clean his plate in something close to record time.

Pale sunlight bathed the street as he began the short walk back to his hotel. It wasn't too hot, yet, but Slade supposed that it would be another scorcher by mid-morning, when he was out in the middle of nowhere.

Chasing ghosts?

He recognized the voice inside his head, and was about to answer silently that someone had to do it, when a bullet sizzled past his face, immediately followed by the loud crack of a rifle shot.

Slade dived and rolled on the wooden sidewalk, coming up with his Colt in hand and cocked. He saw the second shot, a pale puff of smoke from a rooftop three doors north and catercorner from the hotel's entrance. That shot smashed a window, somewhere off to Slade's left, and he heard a woman's scream.

Slade fired once, to keep the shooter's head down, then sprinted off across the street. Most people, in that situation, would've sought someplace to hide, but Slade's instinct took him in a different direction.

First, he was a lawman, and he didn't run from trouble — much less from a sniper bent on killing him.

Second, he guessed the shooting must be linked in some way to the crimes he was investigating, and he hoped the rifleman could shed some light in that direction.

Finally, Slade knew he wouldn't rest until he'd looked into this sneaky bastard's eyes and saw what lay behind them.

No more shots were fired at Slade, crossing the street. He knew damn well he hadn't hit the sniper, shouldn't even have scared him that much, but the would-be assassin had gone off his game.

Slade found a set of stairs that took him to the rooftop sniper's nest, slowing the last few yards before he rushed it, just in case the gunman was there waiting for him. There was nothing on the square, flat roof to hide a cat, much less a man, and Slade soon found the pair of shiny rifle cartridges, abandoned where they'd been ejected from a lever-action rifle.

But where was the shooter?

Slade supposed his quarry might be fleet of foot enough to have escaped using the stairs, before Slade reached the far side of the street. He couldn't get away entirely, but there had been doors along the alley, more around in back, where someone could have ducked inside and hidden for a time. From there, it would be easy slipping out and strolling off, while Slade was busy on the roof.

He also found a ladder on the far side of the building, fastened to the wall and granting access to a narrow alley down below. With *two* escape routes, Slade would have to question everyone on Main Street, to discover if they'd seen a running man after the shots were fired.

And all for . . . what?

Nothing.

The first attempt had missed. Slade owed someone for trying, but he'd have to pay the tab later.

He was already wasting daylight, and the morning wasn't getting any younger.

Cletus Paxton still couldn't believe he'd missed both shots. The second one, okay, when Slade was rolling like some kind of acrobat and grabbing for his six-gun, that was normal for a moving target with a case of nerves thrown in.

But Paxton knew he should have had Slade on the first shot, when the marshal was slow-strolling back toward his hotel.

He'd jerked the trigger that time, when he should've squeezed it nice and easy.

What the hell?

Riding away from Paradise, back toward the spread that he'd called home these past four years, Paxton dissected the events that now threatened his job — perhaps his life.

He'd had a couple of drinks in town last night, first thing, before he went to look for Slade at the hotel. The snotty clerk wouldn't give up Slade's room number, just kept saying he was out with Sheriff Eastman and would be back later. Could the clerk convey a message?

No damn thank you, even if Cletus had known the definition of *convey.*

He'd scouted out the shooting stand, been satisfied with what he saw from the rooftop, then went back for a few more drinks. Just killing time, until the posse or whatever made it back to town. One of the girls at the saloon had sidled up to him, complaining she was mighty thirsty, so he'd helped her out with that.

Being a gentleman.

Long story short, he'd messed around and missed Slade coming back from wherever in hell he'd gone to, and it was full dark by the time that he got back up to his rooftop lookout post.

Four of the hotel's upstairs windows had been showing lights when Paxton settled down to wait; three of them had curtains over them, and number four was occupied by a fat man who *should've* pulled the drapes, considering the way he looked without his clothes. Clete had considered firing through the other windows, randomly, but he had known that was the liquor talking. It would be a waste of lead and energy, blasting a picture off the wall or some damn thing, when he had no idea which room was Slade's.

After an hour or so of waiting, wondering how it could be so chilly, after yet another sunbaked day, Paxton began to wonder if he shouldn't go across the street, orders be damned, and call the marshal out. It was the simple way to handle his assignment — simpler, it seemed, than sitting on his ass and staring at the street — but something kept him from it.

Namely, Paxton's fear of what Angus McCallister might say — or do.

He'd seen the boss horsewhip a thieving ranch hand half to death, one time, then put the bloody mess up on its horse and send it off across the badlands, going nowhere. Sights like that weren't easy to forget.

And still, he fell asleep.

Sometime around midnight, Clete guessed it must have been. He blamed the whiskey for it, and the headache that had roused him finally, as dawn was breaking in the east. He'd jerked upright, forgetting for a second where he was, then swung around in panic toward the street —

And saw his target crossing just below him, walking like a man without a care on Earth.

He'd fumbled with his drooping hat and pushed it back out of his eyes, snatched up his Winchester, but by the time he got the rifle to his shoulder, Slade had cleared the field of fire and disappeared somewhere below him.

Stopping off for breakfast, Clete assumed, since Slade was headed in the wrong direction for the livery and he wouldn't find the sheriff in his office yet. Clete had considered going down to get a bite, himself, thinking he'd eat, watch Slade, then trail the marshal when he left the restaurant and shoot him on the street.

No good. Too many witnesses.

So he had waited, tracking Slade across the street when he had reappeared, thankful to get a second chance. And he had blown it, getting anxious, jerking at the trigger like he'd never bushwhacked anyone before.

Stupid.

After his second miss, when Slade was shooting back, Paxton had known that it was time to go. He'd been afraid to use the stairs but scrambled down the ladder, nearly falling once and getting a hellacious splinter in his goddamn trigger finger, if you could believe it. Slade had failed to spot him, somehow — Paxton's first and only break so far — and now he had to think about what he would tell McCallister.

How he could make it seem that the disaster wasn't all his fault.

"Your courage does you credit, but you are not thinking of your people first," Red Eagle said.

Little Wolf scowled at the aged chief, as he replied, "I think of them. I know the bluecoats blame us for the white men killing one another, and they will not let us rest until they have shed blood for blood."

"They have harmed no one yet," Red Eagle countered.

"Not yet?" Little Wolf challenged. "You mean, not *this time*. When have they ever dealt fairly with any of our people? When have they believed us, when we speak the truth? What do they care about their so-

240

called justice, if a red man can be punished for their crimes?"

Red Eagle understood Little Wolf's abiding rage. What Cherokee — what Indian of any tribe — did not? All had been driven from their homes, had seen their lives uprooted, loved ones shot, starved, raped, or poisoned with the "gifts" that carried smallpox. Who among the proud folk who had once roamed far and wide across the land now called America would *not* have lashed out at the white man, if an opportunity arose?

But there were no more opportunities.

The last battle of the last war had passed them by.

Red Eagle had not been a warrior in his own right, since the Cherokee had been defeated in his father's time, when Red Eagle himself was still an infant. He did not recall much of the brutal trek along the Trail of Tears, had never really known the two siblings who died on the march from Georgia to Oklahoma.

Thus, Red Eagle had become a chief in time, replacing brothers he had lost before their faces were imprinted on his memory. And he had longed to seek revenge — still craved it, sometimes, if the truth be told; achieved it, sometimes, in his dreams — but service to his people meant *preserving* them, not throwing lives away as had been done at Wounded Knee.

"You saw the marshal, Little Wolf. He does not believe we killed these farmers."

"He is one man," Little Wolf answered. "And a *white* man. When he's forced to make a choice, you know what he will do."

"I cannot claim to read his heart," Red Eagle said.

"What does it matter? When he fails to find the killers — or they find him, first — the bluecoats will return and burn our homes."

"And where else would they send us?" asked Red Eagle.

"To our graves," Little Wolf replied. "As at Bear River, and Sand Creek, and Washita, and Wounded Knee. As they have done times without number, and will do again."

Except for Wounded Knee, the massacres that Little Wolf named had all occurred before his birth, and far away, but no red man ever forgot his people's history. No act of vicious treachery was truly swept away by passing time.

Because Red Eagle could not guarantee the safety of his tribe, he changed the subject. "You say that the marshal is one man, and so must fail. *You* are one man.

242

How would you find these killers in the white man's world, where you have never been?"

Little Wolf shrugged off the question. "It is true that I may fail," he said. "But if I never *try,* failure is certain."

"If you leave the reservation," said Red Eagle, "that alone is violation of the white man's law. It may be all they need to fall upon us."

"They won't catch me," Little Wolf answered, with the arrogance of youth.

"They only need to *see* you. On a whim, you would endanger all of us."

"But if I find the killers —"

"I cannot allow it," said Red Eagle. "As your chief, I say you must not go."

Little Wolf seemed on the verge of answering, but held his tongue. He rose and turned away from Red Eagle, swept through the chief's front door, and left it open, spilling bitter sunshine, as he stalked away.

"So you didn't see the man at all?" asked Sheriff Eastman.

"Just the outline of his head and shoulders, as he fired the second time," Slade answered.

They were standing on the square, flat rooftop of the farm-supply shop that had served Slade's would-be killer as a sniper's roost. The line of sight to Slade's hotel was clear. Below them, several residents of Paradise were clustered on the sidewalk opposite, staring and straining in a futile bid to overhear their words.

"Too bad you didn't hit him," Eastman offered, toeing at the rifle cartridges that had been left behind. "There's not much I can do with these."

"You might say I was in a hurry," Slade replied.

"I hear you. Still, too bad. That scream you heard was Emma Gladstone. Bullet missed her, going through the window, but she caught some flying glass. Doc Fisher says a piece of it is in her eye."

"Sorry to hear it." Slade had no idea what else he might've said about a total stranger's wounds.

"Looks like somebody wants you off this case," Eastman surmised. Adding, "Somebody who's got no prize coming for his marksmanship."

"I wondered about that," Slade said. "He had the hotel covered, but he didn't take me on my way across to breakfast."

"What's that tell you?" Eastman asked him,

"Beats me," Slade replied. "Maybe he

wasn't watching when I crossed the first time, or he messed it up somehow and lost the opportunity. Maybe he can't shoot anyone who's facing him."

"He should've had you," Eastman said, stating the obvious. "First shot, with ample time to aim and nothing in his way. You should be dead right now."

Slade thought about that and imagined himself from the killer's perspective. Why *hadn't* the man dropped Slade while he was crossing Main Street toward the restaurant? How had he then missed his next-best shot, if only by a fraction?

"Maybe his heart wasn't in it," said Slade.

"Or his eye, from the bad aim," the sheriff replied. "Why would you say that?"

Slade shrugged. "It's just a thought," he said. "If this was someone with a private grudge, I think he would've taken that first shot. I *don't* believe he would've let it go at two and run away."

"You're thinking someone *hired* the shooter?"

"Maybe *sent* him, anyway," Slade said. "If so, the man behind him's going to be disappointed."

"I'd say. Anyhow" — Eastman turned toward the stairs — "I think I've seen enough."

When they were back at street level, the sheriff asked, "What are your plans today, in case somebody's looking for you?"

"Someone with a rifle?" Slade replied, half smiling.

"Anybody, I suppose."

"I mean to trace those wagon tracks I showed you, leading from the Hascomb place. It may turn out to be a waste of time, but I can't stand to leave a loose end dangling."

"Hell, we've got nothing *but* loose ends on this thing," Eastman replied. "I guess you have to start somewhere."

"And how about yourself?" Slade asked.

The sheriff's eyes skittered away from Slade's, and Eastman scuffed the wooden sidewalk with his boot. "I'm not sure, right offhand."

Slade thought Eastman was lying, but he saw nothing to gain by pressing it.

"Okay, then," he replied. "I'll just be on my way."

"Be careful," warned the sheriff. "They don't call 'em badlands, out this way, for nothing."

"Thanks," Slade said. "I'm catching on to that."

Slade felt the sheriff watching him, as he retreated toward the livery. He couldn't work out what was troubling Eastman, but Slade guessed it went beyond the shots on Main Street.

Did he have a fair idea of who had called those shots? If so, was he planning to visit the person responsible? In short, was Eastman friend or enemy?

With any luck, it wouldn't matter for the next few hours. Anyone who wanted Slade would have to track him down and try their luck out in the open.

Badlands, right.

Slade knew exactly how the territory got that name. He was a part of it, in fact, although a relative latecomer to the game.

But someone had gone overboard, even by Badlands standards, and it was Slade's job to reel them in. Today, if fortune smiled on him, he'd have his chance.

If not . . .

There's always tomorrow, Slade thought, then realized that he was wrong.

There would be no tomorrows for the dead.

"How will you find these white men?" asked Gray Feather.

"The Great Spirit will guide me to them," Little Wolf answered. "I have seen it in my dreams."

"You saw their faces?" Little Owl inquired.

"No, but I recognized them by their bloody hands. When I am close enough, I'll know them by their stink. They smell of death."

Little Owl and Gray Feather nodded solemnly. Stands Watching lived up to his name, studying Little Wolf's face. It moved Little Wolf that his best friends on Earth would come to see him off.

As if reading his thoughts, Gray Feather said, "I will go with you."

"No," said Little Wolf. "It is enough that I be exiled for defying Red Eagle. Our people will have need of you — all of you — when the soldiers come again."

"If you succeed," Gray Feather said, "they have no reason to come back."

"White men *make* reasons," Little Wolf. "Each time they send our people to a reservation, they make promises. 'Take this wasteland and stay forever.' But they always change their minds. It may be gold, the black slime from the soil, or even salt. They *will* return to move our people — or to kill them. When that happens —"

"We will fight!" Gray Feather interrupted him.

"It will be a good day to die," Little Owl declared.

"A better day to *kill*." The utterance from Stands Watching surprised them all.

Changing the subject, Little Owl asked Little Wolf, "When you find the men you seek, what will you do?"

Little Wolf appreciated that his friend had not said *if*. His dreams of tracking down the murderers were incomplete. Their faces had eluded him, and Little Wolf had not seen the end of his adventure, though it felt like death.

Whose death?

"I cannot take them to the white man's law," he said. "No judge or sheriff will accept my word that they are guilty. I will slay them, if the Great Spirit allows it."

"How does that prevent the soldiers from returning?" Little Owl inquired. "They will blame us for yet another massacre of whites. What happens to our people if they catch you?"

"Red Eagle will disavow me. He is skilled at catering to whites," Little Wolf replied.

"Perhaps the marshal . . ." Stands Watching did not complete his thought. He seemed embarrassed by the others staring at him.

"He is only one man," Little Wolf said. "And a white man, at that. You think it means something, because he would not let the soldiers search our homes? How long will he remain? And when he goes, what then?"

Dead silence from the others. Little Wolf stroked his horse's neck and told them, "I must go."

"We watch and wait for your return," Gray Feather said.

"Better that you prepare for war," Little Wolf replied. "Red Eagle cannot see it coming. You must be his eyes, his strong right arm."

Little Wolf clasped hands with each of them in turn. No further words were necessary as he mounted, wheeled his chestnut mare away from them, and rode off toward the rutted track that linked the Saline Reservation with the outside world.

Little Wolf did not look back to see them watching him, because he was afraid his will might falter. That he might abandon his idea, or worse, allow his friends to ride along and die beside him in the white man's world.

It felt like suicide, crossing the reservation's boundary for the first time in his life. He had been born and raised there, like his father and mother before him. Little Wolf had expected to spend all his days within the Saline Reservation's confines. Only the white man's treachery — toward Cherokee and toward his own people — had forced Little Wolf to chart a course that meant exile or death.

Red Eagle would not, *could* not take him back into the fold, once he had crossed that line in full defiance of the chief's command. Little Wolf was now an outcast from his tribe and from his family, who might feel shamed by his actions.

Or, possibly, they would feel proud.

Through him, at least, they might experience what it was like to think, choose, act, without the orders of a chief or "Great White Father." If he found the murderers and punished them, he would find some way to alert his friends and family. Whatever happened, after that, at least the people Little Wolf loved would know he had succeeded in his quest.

For justice?

No.

White slayers of white victims meant no more to him than ants going to war. He acted now, only because their crimes threatened his people with attack and dispossession. If he could postpone their suffering, his life and death would count for something.

And, perhaps, that was a kind of justice, after all.

11

Slade's back itched all the way out to the Hascomb place, a spot between his shoulder blades made nervous by the mental image of a rifle shot from nowhere ripping through him and punching him out of the saddle. He caught himself glancing around frequently, making sure that the country behind him was open and empty, and stopped it after he had ridden out from town a mile or so.

In prior situations, when someone had tried to kill him, Slade had always known who pulled the trigger — or, at least, who gave the order. This time, while he guessed it must be an attempt to get him off the homestead murders case, he didn't know who stood to gain from blowing out his brains.

Had one of the actual murderers come into town for the purpose of killing him? And if so, how did they know who he was, much less that he'd been assigned to the case?

That question troubled Slade the most, due to its implication that the killers either lived in Paradise or had some kind of information pipeline to the town, an ally who was helping them for reasons Slade could not divine.

In his experience, the big conspiracies were always based on greed. A man might plot to kill his lover's husband, or vice versa, but there'd never been an outlaw gang or robber baron that Slade knew of who'd gone out to kill for pleasure. They were always looking for a profit, somewhere down the line.

Now, if the murderers *were* Indians, as Colonel Northcliff thought, the homestead killings made a certain kind of sense. Race hatred was a virulent disease, infecting people of all colors, driving them to do horrendous things. Same thing for the religious bigotry that led some men to rail against a certain church or creed, as if the god they prayed to made a lick of difference on Earth.

But these crimes simply didn't feel like red on white to Slade. He couldn't pin that feeling down, beyond the explanations he'd already given to Northcliff and Sheriff

Eastman, but his mind remained unchanged.

And he was damned sure that the man who'd tried to kill him back in Paradise wasn't a Cherokee.

Which told him . . . nothing much.

Upon arriving at the Hascomb place, Slade let his roan drink from a half-filled water trough and checked his own impulse to make one final walking tour of the murder house. If he'd missed anything the first two times, Slade guessed that he would keep on missing it, and nothing he had seen would help him name the murderers.

The wagon tracks he'd seen before were still intact, and it was plain to him that several horses had been hitched behind the wagon when it left the farm. Beyond that, Slade still couldn't say what any of it meant.

There was an outside possibility that Tom Hascomb had sold his livestock to another rancher, who collected shortly before the family was slaughtered. All by sheer coincidence, of course. Slade didn't buy it, but he'd have to play it cagey if the tracks led him to one of Hascomb's neighbors. Barging in, accusing everyone in sight of murder wouldn't make his case hold up before Judge Dennison.

But at least he would have a suspect —

which was more than he had at the moment.

Slade collected his horse from the trough, mounted up, and followed the wagon southwestward. He wasn't sure what lay in that direction, besides Texas, and he hoped the killers weren't preparing to evacuate the Oklahoma Territory. Legally, his federal badge allowed him to pursue them anywhere in the United States, but Slade wasn't prepared for tracking them through Texas and beyond. If there were borders to be crossed, he'd have to find a town with telegraph connections and alert Judge Dennison, before he traveled any father.

Then again, perhaps the killers had a hideout somewhere close at hand, a place where they stashed rustled livestock prior to selling it, from which they launched their raids.

In which case, he supposed they would be well armed, maybe even have the hideout fortified somehow. If Slade found that he couldn't smoke them out alone, he'd have to break off, ride for reinforcements — and allow them time to slip away.

It was his curse to always probe a situation, pick it all apart, until he isolated the worst-case scenario. That trait made him bad company, sometimes, but it had also saved his life on various occasions. Pessimism's upside was that if you always expected the worst, you were spared certain fatal surprises.

Of course, that didn't mean that someone wouldn't kill you anyway.

Preparedness was only part of tracking killers. Blind luck figured into it, as well, along with speed and skill. And sometimes, Slade felt that the law conspired to tie his hands.

An outlaw could go anywhere, do anything he pleased. The lawman tracking him was bound by rules and regulations, had to stop and ponder every move he made, to see if it was criminal or lawful.

But in man hunting, a split second's delay could get you killed.

Slade rode on, hoping that the killers would stand out like broken dishes on a fancy dining table. Make them hairy, gap-toothed monsters who were slow to think and quick to draw.

Just give me an excuse, he thought.

But something told him that it wouldn't be that easy when the time came.

If it came.

Sheriff Eastman hoped that he was wrong about Heck Riley, but suspicion gnawed around the edges of his mind as he rode out to Riley's spread, nine miles southwest of Paradise. It was a full day's ride for nothing, if his brain was playing tricks on him, but Eastman knew he'd never rest until he had checked it out.

He blamed Jack Slade for pointing out the obvious and blamed himself for having failed to see it earlier. The killers had pulled all their raids so far within a long day's ride of Paradise, and sometimes closer. They were stealing stock each time, and if the animals weren't on the Saline Reservation — where, he reckoned, Colonel Northcliff would have found them with his searching — then they must be somewhere else.

And that was where Heck Riley came to mind.

Heck never used his full name — Hector August Riley — but you'd find it filed away at the territorial prison, in Guthrie. Riley had served two years on a rustling charge, before settling outside of Paradise. One of the warden's circulars had found its way to Eastman's desk, a few months later, and he'd ridden out to have a word with Riley at his modest spread.

Heck Riley wasn't quite a giant, but he cut it close. Eastman supposed he must be six foot seven, anyway, and likely tipped the

257

scales around three hundred pounds. East-man had seen him half a dozen times and noticed that he always seemed about two days beyond the need for shaving. Straight dark hair covered the big man's ears on either side and overlapped his collar in the back. He had small, shifty eyes, but made up for it with a pair of hands the size of skillets.

At their first meeting — and their only conversation — Eastman had explained the facts of life. Told Riley that he didn't judge a man by time he'd served, but recognized that some offenses tended to be habit-forming. Let him know that he'd be under scrutiny if any livestock turned up missing around Paradise.

And yet . . .

The homestead murders hadn't seemed to fit Heck Riley's pattern. He'd been jailed for stealing cattle on the sly, but there was nothing in his prison file to indicate that he was violent, despite his size. It seemed completely out of character for him to slaughter families — as if a pickpocket had started robbing trains.

But there was still his history of trading stolen livestock. If he wasn't in the murder gang, Eastman still felt compelled to have a look around Heck's place and satisfy himself that Riley wasn't buying up the missing animals.

He thought back to his one and only conversation with the big man, nearly three years past. Riley had said, *Don't worry, Sheriff. I'm not going back to jail. Never. No way.*

He'd sounded like a man who meant it, at the time.

But *how* did he mean it?

Eastman cursed Jack Slade again, for stirring up suspicion in his mind and dragging him away from Paradise, when he should be in town, soothing the voters who could take away his tin star come election time.

Assuming that he ran again, that is.

A major part of Eastman's job was keeping up appearances. As long as things ran smoothly on the streets of Paradise, and he offended no one well-to-do or influential, he was likely to be running unopposed. But if he stepped on the wrong toes . . .

In that respect, grilling Heck Riley was a win-win situation. Riley was an ex-convict, and thus a natural suspect for *any* crime, as far as Paradise's leading merchants were concerned. More to the point, he lived well out of town and didn't rank as anybody's steady customer. If it turned out that he was innocent, Eastman and those who paid his salary could go back to ignoring Heck, and no harm done.

But if he *was* connected to the murders somehow, and he named the killers, Eastman could become a hero overnight. He could demand a raise in salary for his next term, or find himself another, better-paying town to safeguard if the mayor and council turned him down.

Win-win.

He topped a rise and saw Heck Riley's place in front of him, a half mile distant. Smallish house, with a ramshackle barn and fairly large corral, a pair of decent shade trees in the yard that might've made Heck choose the spot, to start with.

Here we go, thought Eastman. *Nothing ventured, nothing gained.*

Little Wolf knew that it must be an illusion, but the air seemed cleaner, sweeter, once he'd crossed the line between the Saline Reservation and the free world. He imagined that the sun was warmer, shining on his face, his naked chest and shoulders.

He had strayed across the boundary before, making a game of it as every young man did, but he had never truly *left* the reservation, knowing in his mind and heart that he could not return. A mile across the line, Little Wolf felt truly free for the first time in all his life.

But how long would it last?

He understood the white man's rules, even the ones that were not written down and labeled *laws*. An Indian found off the reservation, anywhere in Oklahoma Territory, was assumed to be a renegade. The rare exceptions covered Native women hired as cooks or housekeepers by whites, or red men supervised as laborers by white foremen.

Little Wolf, riding alone and armed in white man's territory, could be gunned down with impunity by anyone who met him, but that thought was secondary in his mind as he rode out across the gently rolling plains.

First in his thoughts was a question. Where should he begin to seek a gang of murderers?

It seemed to him that he could only start from the last place where they had struck — a risky proposition in itself, since other whites might still be picking through the ashes or considering how to divide the property among themselves. Still, Little Wolf was a hunter, and he reckoned that no white man with a badge could match his skill at tracking prey over the long haul, using sign that would elude most eyes.

He had been present when the chief of bluecoats spoke to Red Eagle, describing where and when the last crime had occurred. The "Hascomb place" meant nothing to him, but he knew the distance and direction he must travel to arrive there. And, once he had seen the place himself, Little Wolf believed he would find something, some clue, that would let him track the killers.

Failing that, he was prepared to haunt the district like the silent predator for whom he had been named, waiting until the raiders struck again, at which time he would find fresh evidence to put him on their trail.

He had already offered prayers to the Great Spirit, asking only for an opportunity to help his people in this matter, even at the cost of his young life.

And if he got to kill some vicious white men in the process, why, so much the better.

Thus engaged in thought, Little Wolf almost missed the riders as they topped a hill off to his left, a half mile distant. There were four of them, outlined in silhouette against the sky. They saw him instantly, exposed upon the plain, and ducked low in their saddles as they spurred their mounts in swift pursuit.

A stranger to this country, Little Wolf had no refuge available. He needed cover he could fight from, or a way to slow the men who hunted him.

Cover might wait for him over the next hill, or the next one after that; he could not tell. As for delaying the pursuit, he only saw one way, under the present circumstances.

Shouldering his Springfield rifle, Little Wolf took aim, willing his horse to stillness as it sat beneath him. He had never killed a human being, but heard the death song in his mind and felt the thrill of battle in his blood. His finger tightened on the Springfield's trigger, slowly taking up the slack.

He longed to kill the men pursuing him, but knew his own abilities, the limitations of his single-shot weapon. The white men had their rifles drawn from saddle leather, probably repeaters, and he had to make each bullet count.

He chose a larger target, therefore, squeezed the trigger, and absorbed the Springfield's kick against his naked shoulder. Still a hundred yards away, one of the charging horses stumbled, pitched its rider forward, then rolled over him.

It was the second from the left in line. Its twisting, rolling fall forced two more animals to veer off course, their riders clinging for dear life. Only the one on Little Wolf's far right held steady, squeezing off a wild shot on the fly.

Little Wolf spun and fled, bent low over his horse's withers, cheek almost against its neck. He kept his eyes forward, sweeping the landscape for a place where he could turn and make his stand against the three remaining white men, seeing nothing yet.

His gun was empty, and he could not reach the pouch of bullets at his waist, just now. He hoped there would be time enough before he died to drop at least one more of the white men.

If not . . .

A sense of bitter disappointment gnawed at Little Wolf's vitals, telling him that he had failed before his task was even well begun. Unless he managed to evade or kill his three pursuers, he would never find the others who had cast a shadow on his people and the Saline Reservation.

He would die a failure, as Red Eagle had predicted.

Stubborn pride made him ride on, cursing the men who followed him and wishing them a thousand ugly deaths.

Monotony was part of every lawman's life.

Slade had suspected it before he ever donned a badge, and it had quickly been confirmed by personal experience.

Dime novels painted a romantic vision of the West as it had never been, with steely-eyed sheriffs of perfect integrity, stalking bad men in black hats across a landscape rife with Indian warriors, cattle stampedes, earthquakes, cyclones, and mighty rivers sweeping men, horses, and wagons over waterfalls. It all led to the high-noon show-down on some dusty street, where Good and Evil met for the last time in a roiling cloud of gunsmoke.

The authors never mentioned time spent filing paperwork with a judge who de-manded letter-perfect reports. They ignored the hours spent in courtrooms, testifying or waiting to testify, and the precious days lost riding trails that led nowhere.

Like now.

Slade didn't need his watch to tell him it was noon and half his day was gone. The sun directly overhead was all the timepiece that he needed, baking his scalp through the crown of his hat. He couldn't push the roan to greater speed, because he needed it alive and there was nothing yet within his field of vision that would justify a gallop.

Stretching out in front of Slade — forever,

as it seemed — the wagon tracks went on and on, drifting a little farther to the southwest, mile by dreary mile. It wouldn't have surprised Slade to glance up and find a pair of vultures wheeling overhead, but he resisted the temptation, knowing that the sun would sear his eyes.

They found a trickling stream, some thirty minutes later, and he happily dismounted and gave the roan a chance to drink and graze a little on a patch of stunted grass. Slade used the time to stretch his legs and work a nagging kink out of his lower back, then scan gently rolling landscape where the wagon tracks vanished from sight.

He'd passed two small homesteads already, wondering what made the raiders choose one farm over another. Did they scout their targets in advance, or take potluck when sundown caught them on the doorstep of some family whose luck was running out?

Try as he might, Slade couldn't put himself inside the minds of men who killed for no apparent reason, other than the lust to rape and slaughter. He'd known others who were similar — had even dropped the hammer on a few, himself — but perfect understanding of their motives still eluded him.

With any luck, it always would.

He thought of Faith, alone on her ranch with a group of male employees that she trusted, both to do their jobs and mind their place. Slade knew a woman's life was difficult on many levels, in the West or anywhere, and sometimes wondered how they bore the curse of being prey to total strangers from the moment they were old enough to walk.

How did they manage to maintain a sweet and loving side, with all the inequalities and hardships they endured? Again, it was beyond him, something he would never truly understand because he wasn't born a woman, couldn't see the world through a woman's eyes.

But Slade had seen enough to know the men he hunted now were no better than rabid animals. No one on Earth would blame him if he shot them dead on sight — assuming that he ever actually *saw* them.

No one but Judge Dennison.

The judge was all for executing them, of course, but there were dots to be connected, rules and regulations to be followed in the law-and-order game. Slade knew the rules and would abide by them as far as possible.

Unless the quarry forced his hand.

Perhaps they'd make it easy for him at the

end, insist on fighting to the death. Slade wouldn't mind, despite the risk and fear of losing any further time with Faith, if he could take such monsters with him into darkness.

But he had to find the bastards, first.

"Come on," he told the roan, hauling himself into the saddle once again. "Let's get it done."

Heck Riley's layout wasn't much to look at, but he seemed to make ends meet. Stock trading, so he claimed, and even with the best intentions, Sheriff Eastman hadn't ridden out to check the jailbird's animals for altered brands and such.

He *would* have made the ride, if there'd been any claims of rustling in the neighborhood, but since there hadn't been — at least, until the homestead murders started — taking off a day to visit Riley's spread had seemed a waste of time and energy.

He'd thought of Riley after the first slaughter, but the mayor and Colonel Northcliff had been set on blaming redskins from the start. Eastman had still considered Riley, for about a second and a half, before remembering that Riley'd never killed another person — that the law knew of, at least — and didn't seem the type to butcher families for half a dozen head of livestock.

Then, there was the sex side of the recent crimes. Women and children both were violated during the attacks, with grim brutality. Eastman had no idea where Riley's interest lay, in that respect, but logic told him that it was unlikely one man's taste ran both to females and young boys.

It *had* to be a group or gang of some sort. Didn't it?

Still, Eastman knew he should have talked to Riley earlier, gone out and had a look around his place to make it known that Riley hadn't been forgotten altogether by the law.

Harassment, some might call it.

Eastman called it an ex-convict paying dues.

When he was fifty yards from Riley's house, Eastman released the hammer thong that held his Smith & Wesson in its holster. He'd need to be careful now, when he dismounted, but it was a compromise in favor of security. He stopped short of unlimbering his Winchester, thinking that might be overplaying it.

Riley came out to meet him on the porch, smiling. "Sheriff Eastwood," he said. "Long time no see."

"East*man*."

"Sorry," the giant said. "It *has* been quite a while."

"I didn't mean to leave you unattended, Heck," Eastman replied. "You may have heard, we've had some trouble lately."

"Terrible," said Riley, wiping off his smile.

"Nobody's come around to bother you, I take it?"

Riley smiled again and answered, "Not until today."

Dismounting, Eastman led his horse to the nearby corral and tied it up beside a water trough. Riley kept pace with him, so Eastman didn't have to watch his back. There were three horses penned in the corral, all staring at him now, and Eastman realized he wouldn't know if they were stolen without brands, since he had no useful descriptions of the Deacon place or Hascomb's.

"I don't guess you see a lot of strangers out this way," he said to Riley.

"Now and then, one passes by. They get a look at me," Heck said, "and don't slow down."

"You're lucky," said the sheriff. "I suppose it must get lonesome, though."

Heck Riley shook his head. "Never been much for company, myself."

"Well, now I see that no one's kilt you in

270

your sleep, there's one more thing I need to do."

"What's that?" asked Riley.

"I suppose you've heard that stock's been missing from the ranches that were hit."

The big man's face went blank. "And you imagine some of them have found their way out here, somehow. Is that it?"

"You've been locked up for rustling," Eastman said. "Doin' my job means checking every*one* and every *place* that might put me in touch with who I'm hunting."

"When the warden sent around his little love notes, did he mention that I never killed nobody?"

"Heck, if I thought you'd been killin' kids and women, I'da shot you on the porch before you said hello."

"That right?"

"Believe it," Eastman said, thankful to hear no tremor in his voice.

Heck Riley had a good ten inches on him, and at least a hundred pounds, but he was empty-handed at the moment. Eastman's heavy Smith & Wesson reassured him, and he kept his hand within an inch of its curved grip.

"I mean to have a look inside that barn," he told Riley.

"You bring a warrant with you?" Riley asked.

"Didn't suppose I'd need one, since you're such a law-abiding man."

"Speakin' of law," Riley replied, "there was a guy locked up at Guthrie, used to be a lawyer. Helped himself to some old lady's bank account, as I recall. He used to get a little jailhouse cider in him and go on about the Constitution, reckoning how it applied to ever'one the same."

"Your friend mention the part about reasonable suspicion? No?" Eastman forced a smile to hide his nerves. "That's when a lawman sees a known offender actin' like he's got some kinda guilty secret. We can stretch the rules a little, and make sure that he don't escape. You follow me?"

"No warrant, then," said Riley.

"That's the ticket. Now, you just walk on ahead of me and open up those big barn doors. We'll have a look inside, and if you got nothin' to hide, I'll leave you with a fancy-ass apology. How's that."

"Don't seem I got much choice," Riley replied.

"You're catchin' on. Let's take a little walk, shall we?"

Heck Riley led him to the barn, with Eastman trailing close behind. The sheriff did not draw his six-gun, but he clutched its grip in readiness. Standing beyond arm's reach, he watched Riley remove the five-foot piece of timber that secured the broad barn doors.

And still, he wasn't ready when the huge ex-convict swung around and slammed the board into his head, dropping the sheriff into darkness like a grave.

12

"Now, weren't that nice?"

The panting animal had rolled away from Jenny Hascomb, leaving her to weep from shame and pain. He drew her knees up nearly to her chest. Too late, now, to protect herself, but the position helped to ease the ache from his incessant thrusting into her.

"I reckoned you weren't broken in," the monster said. "Don't worry none. You'll get the hang of it real soon."

She bit her lip, willing the flow of tears that soaked her blindfold to desist. Crying would only make the bastard feel more powerful. Her best course, she imagined, was to shut down her mind when he touched her, try to go somewhere inside her own head where the beast couldn't reach her. That would cheat him of his prize, if he had any wits at all.

And if he didn't, she might still escape the pain.

A shifting in the wagon told her he was done with her, at least for now. Her feeling of relief was short, however, as a sudden thought produced a wave of nausea.

What if his seed took root inside her, and she had to bear his child?

I'll die first, she decided. *Kill myself before that happens — and his filthy little bastard, too.*

As soon as the thought had formed in her mind, then Jenny realized it likely wouldn't matter. Those who held her captive had already killed her parents and her siblings. They had only spared her life for *this,* the worst torment a girl could suffer, and she guessed that they would soon tire of the sport.

When they grew weary of abusing her, or found themselves another toy, she'd be discarded. They would have to silence her, of course, because she'd glimpsed some of their faces at the ranch, when they attacked the house. That would mean killing her, because no oath she ever swore would stop her telling what they'd done and sending them to hang, if she could manage it.

The certainty of her inevitable death came as a strange kind of relief to Jenny Hascomb. Knowing that she wouldn't have to kill herself was best, since she already doubted her ability to follow through with it.

Self-murder was a sin, her parents always said — or *used to* say — and since you couldn't ask God for a pardon after you were dead, it meant a one-way ticket down to Hell. If you were killed by someone else, though, then the Savior would be merciful, greet you with open arms.

Unless . . .

What they had done — what *he* had done *to her* — was also high up on the list of sins her parents talked about. Without a wedding ceremony, it was an abomination in God's eyes, the very sin that drove the first two people out of Eden.

Did it matter that she hadn't wanted him? That she had struggled, even with her hands tied? She had actually tried to hold her breath and die that way, while it was going on, but self-asphyxiation without rope or something else to choke you was, apparently, impossible.

Her body fought to live, even when Jenny longed for death. Did that mean she had secretly *enjoyed* the torture, somehow, and her mind had kept it from her?

No.

She hated her abuser, everything about him, and the others who were holding her against her will.

Against my will, she thought. That had to count for something, didn't it, when sins were weighed and measured?

For, if not — if she was damned to Hell already — then she ought to do something that warranted eternal punishment. If she could free her hands and find a weapon, she could try to kill her captors. Make them scream as she had heard her mother scream, the night her world came to an end.

Another shifting in the wagon told her someone was approaching. Not her rapist coming back for more; the new arrival didn't weigh as much.

God, not the old ones! Please!

Strong hands hauled her into a seated posture, with her back against some flat, hard surface. New pain flared between her legs, as someone forced her knees down and began to bind her ankles.

"Please . . ."

A fist lashed out, splitting her lips and bouncing Jenny's head off of the hard surface behind her.

"Shut that mouth, you little Jezebel!" the woman whom she feared most among all the others hissed at her.

A second blow landed on Jenny's cheek, an openhanded slap this time, making her left ear ring.

"You come into our family and *tempt* him, like the others," said the woman. "Do you think I'm blind? Did you imagine there would be no punishment? A little whore like you deserves to be —"

"I'm not —"

The clenched fist struck with greater force this time, numbing her jaw after a flare of blinding pain.

"You speak when spoken to! And bear in mind, you won't be with us long. Soon as he tires of you, you're mine. I know a thousand different ways to make you scream."

Little Wolf supposed that the great spirit had forgotten him, or that it had forsaken him because he disobeyed Red Eagle. He would have to help himself, if it was not too late.

A backward glance showed him the three white riders, galloping along his back trail, keeping up as if their horses were invincible. He'd proved that false with their companion, but his lead had narrowed to the point where Little Wolf could not afford another standing shot.

He had no fear of death per se, but dreaded going to his ancestors with no great tales to share. How could he be a hero in the afterlife, if glory had eluded him on Earth?

Above all else, he hoped to avoid the Place of Bad Spirits, reserved for the souls of big sinners who suffered eternal torment. Had he done anything in life that warranted such punishment?

Not yet, decided Little Wolf.

And it had never been regarded as a sin to kill one's enemies.

If only he could find a place to turn and make his stand. Someplace where the three whites could not surround him, pin him in a cross fire with their rifles and six-guns. A little cover, and some time to plot his strategy was all that Little Wolf hoped for.

And so far, he'd found nothing.

Against their guns, he had his single-shot Springfield rifle and forty-nine remaining cartridges. When those were gone, he had his knife, bare hands, and teeth as weapons. If the white men let him close enough to touch them, they were finished.

But they wouldn't.

They would shoot him from a distance, given any chance at all, and only move in closer when they knew that he was dead or dying. Then, they might take time to scalp him, mutilate his body, but they would not deal with him as equals.

As a man.

His horse was tiring now, worn down by galloping over the gently rolling hills. It gained speed on the downslopes, laboring a little more each time it had to climb, while Little Wolf expected each new crest to be his last.

One of the white men would get lucky with a rifle shot, if they kept on this way much longer. If he didn't find someplace to hide and fight.

Another hill, and this time, when he topped it, Little Wolf saw possible salvation on the other side.

Tall trees.

Not just a few of them, but rows and rows, a veritable forest cloaked with shadows.

Feeling sudden exultation, Little Wolf raced toward the tree line, hearing angry warning shouts behind him. Once again, the white men tried to drop him with their rifles, but their aim was not improved by rage or speeding horses.

The trick, thought Little Wolf, was not to *lose* them in the forest, but to stop them getting in at all. He had to reach the tree line, turn, and bring them under fire while they were still exposed. At that point, if he somehow failed to kill them, maybe he could frighten them away — or, at the very least, cause them to seek another angle of attack.

If they tried to encircle him, he knew they would be clumsy in the forest, making noise with every step to give themselves away. A lifelong hunter such as he would have no problem tracking them, ambushing them, taking them down one at a time.

Above all else, he must not let them corner or surround him, where their rapid-firing guns could overwhelm him. He must be one of the forest's shadows, everywhere and nowhere, all at once.

But first, he had to reach the trees alive.

A bullet whispered past his left ear, drawing a curse from Little Wolf as he hunched lower on his horse. He longed to make himself invisible, but could not manage it. If he remained a target long enough, one of the white men *had* to score a lucky hit.

At fifty yards and closing, Little Wolf allowed his hopes to rise and spread their wings.

At twenty-five, those hopes began to soar.

At ten —

Another bullet came so close that Little Wolf could feel its heat upon his cheek. The next one might shatter his skull and send him cartwheeling into oblivion, unless —

He reached the tree line, plunged on through it, hauling on his horse's reins to turn back after they had covered thirty feet or so. Before the animal had time to double back completely, Little Wolf sprang from its back and ran to reach the fallen tree he'd spotted on arrival.

He could fight from there — begin his fight, at least — and if he had to flee again, his feet would carry him. He did not stop to tie his horse, trusting the beast to linger somewhere close at hand until he whistled for it.

Dropping prone behind the log, he palmed a cartridge, reloaded, and peered at his approaching enemies over the Springfield's sights.

Angus McCallister was sipping sweet Kentucky bourbon from a chunky crystal glass when rapid knocking on his study door distracted him.

"Enter!"

Clete Paxton came in as he always did, reminding his employer of a rogue bull in a china shop. He always seemed keyed up, excited about something, but this time his face betrayed a certain nervousness.

"Well, Clete? What happened?"

"Can I get a drink, first?"

"I don't think so," said McCallister. "Talk first, drink afterward."

"Can I at least sit down?"

"Why not."

McCallister circled his desk and lowered himself into his padded chair, while Paxton took the wooden seat directly opposite. It had not been designed for comfort.

"So," McCallister began, "the marshal is . . . ?"

"Out lookin' for whoever kilt those farmers, I suppose," Paxton replied.

"I see."

"It wasn't like you're thinkin', Boss."

"Can you read minds, now? Can you even read a *newspaper?*"

"I had him lined up, Boss, as sweet as anything. Right in my sights, I swear to you."

"If that was true, he wouldn't be out hunting," said McCallister.

"I still don't know what happened," Paxton answered, in a whiny tone that sparked an urge inside McCallister to slap his face and keep on slapping until he was bleeding from the ears.

Icy calm, the rancher said, "Try to explain it, Clete."

"He musta ducked or somethin'."

"So you missed."

"Well, yeah."

"And how'd the marshal take that?" asked McCallister.

"He took a shot at me."

"I guess his aim was no better than yours."

"I was too fast for him," said Paxton, straining for a grin.

"He get a look at you?"

Clete thought about it. Shook his head. "I'll swear he didn't see my face."

"Just like you swore the problem would be taken care of?"

"Listen, Boss —"

"Who saw you leaving town, Clete?"

"Nobody! I swear to God!"

"How would you *know* that, when you're busy running?"

"Well . . . I looked around, and . . . you know . . ."

"Yes, I *do* know."

"It'll be okay, Boss."

"Yes," McCallister said, rising from his chair, "I guess it will."

He circled toward the fireplace, where a half-burned log had shifted, sagging in the grate.

"Take off your hat and stay a while, why don't you," he told Paxton. "Just a second here, and I'll get you that drink."

Paxton removed his Stetson and placed it on the floor beside his chair. The tautness

284

in his shoulders seemed to ease as he relaxed. The odd, obnoxious smile came back.

McCallister picked up a fireplace poker, hefted it, then turned and rushed across the intervening floor toward Paxton. Drew the poker back and whipped it down across his head, sinking the iron barb deep into the useless stew he called a brain.

Paxton bucked once in his chair, then slithered from it to the woven rug below. He twitched and shivered like a victim of Saint Vitus' dance, his right hand slapping at his holster until McCallister moved around and stepped on the wrist.

No point in taking chances, even now.

It took a few more minutes for the last traces of life to wobble out of Paxton. Finally, he lay still on the rug, eyes glazing over as they dried. McAllister retrieved a polished letter opener from his desktop and held it midway between Clete's mouth and nostrils, checking for any signs of respiration.

Nothing.

He was done, and now the grunt work could begin.

The rug was ruined, but it came in handy for wrapping the body. McCallister got down on hands and knees to do the job, wrapping Clete up like one of the pigs in a blanket he favored for breakfast. When he'd finished, he used twine to tie the bundle in four places — at Clete's head, chest, hips, and ankles, sealing him inside.

Surveying what he'd done, McCallister beheld a tube still open on both ends, protruding a good foot or more beyond Paxton's head and feet. He fetched more twine and sweated over it, crimping the ends and tying them off so that no one could peer inside without loosing the knots.

When *that* was done, he had another drink, then went out on the porch and called a couple of his hands away from watching ponies in the main corral. They hurried over to him, anxious as ever to please the boss man.

"I need a wagon brought around," he told them, "and a rug fetched from my office. I'll be taking it to town."

Both of them looked at him like he had lost his mind.

"A *rug*, Boss?" asked the blond one.

"Wagon. Rug. That's what I said."

"*You're* taking it to town?" the balding cowboy echoed.

"If I want to hear a goddamn echo, I'll shout down a rain barrel," McCallister snapped. "Bring the wagon, then fetch the

286

rug out of my office while you've still got jobs."

"Yes, sir!" they both chirped out. The blond ran for the wagon, while the other made his way inside to see the rolled-up rug.

Five minutes later, they were hauling it outside, manhandling it into the wagon bed, with baldy saying, "That's a heavy'un."

"I'll be back when you see me," said Mc-Callister, pulling himself into the driver's seat. "Go find some work to do, and let the ponies be."

McCallister knew he could find a place for Clete to rest and rot away, somewhere between his spread and Paradise. Maybe a nice, deep gully, choked with weeds, where he'd be out of sight but still accessible to ants and buzzards.

After he'd dumped the corpse, McCallister would check the rug again, to see if it was salvageable, or if he should burn it. And once that decision had been made, he would drive on to town.

He had a plan in mind, a way to get things rolling with the Cherokee, and it was time to make his move.

The first shot could have come from anywhere. A rifle's crack, drifting across the plains, was open to interpretation. It could be a hunter bagging dinner, or a deadly ambush claiming human life. A farmer might've been dispensing mercy to a dray horse with a broken leg, or some kid might be getting in a little target practice, dreaming of the day when he'd be old enough to hunt for real.

One shot meant nothing.

But the volley that immediately followed it meant trouble.

Slade turned his roan toward the crackling sound of gunfire, thinking, *What now?* The last thing that he needed was distraction from his search. Not only would it cost him precious daylight, but he'd also have to double back and hope that he could find the wagon's track again, without returning to the Hascomb farm and starting out again, from scratch.

But on the other hand . . .

Slade knew it was too much to hope that the gunfire might mean he'd found the homestead killers. Striking in the middle of the day wasn't their style, and as far as Slade knew, none of their previous victims was shot.

Maybe they've changed their pattern, he thought, hopefully. *Maybe their next intended victim's putting up a fight.*

288

Maybe.

Slade didn't get his hopes up, as he galloped on toward the apparent source of the gunfire. It didn't sound as if the guns were too far off. Maybe across the next hill, or the next one after that.

A lull in firing made Slade wonder if he'd come too late, but then the whiplash of a single shot rang out again, followed by two or three more rifles answering.

He made it one man against several, then — which still told him precisely nothing.

Slade crested the nearest hill and was surprised to see a forest spread before him, with its tree line half a mile away. Off to his right, he spotted puffs of gunsmoke where two tiny figures — no, he saw a third — were firing toward the woods. After they squeezed off half a dozen shots, another rifleman concealed within the trees gave back a single bullet.

Slade had no idea what it was all about, but he knew there were only two lawmen in the vicinity, and he'd be damned surprised to find that any of the shooters down below was Sheriff Eastman. Wearily, sparing a curse for the diversion from his job, he drew his Winchester and started down the long slope toward the gunmen he could see.

Of course, this *was* Slade's job — deterring homicidal violence when and where he found it. If he could prevent a murder here, at least he would have won *something* today, besides chasing a set of day-old wagon tracks across the countryside.

And if it turned out the three riflemen had treed an outlaw, if they could produce some evidence proving a crime had taken place, then Slade would help them try to bag the miscreant and take him back to Paradise.

Alive, if possible.

Above all else, in this kind of uncertain situation, Slade would look out for himself.

He would come in behind the shooters, quiet-like, and try to take them by surprise. That put him in the forest sniper's field of fire, but Slade preferred to take his chances with a lone long-distance gunman when he could, rather than three.

Circling around to find their blind side, he advanced, straining to make out any faces, but the distance was too great, their backs still turned.

Slade hoped it wouldn't come to killing, but he was prepared for anything. If it came down to *them* or *him,* he wouldn't have to think about it twice.

A wave of nausea brought Ardis Eastman retching back to consciousness. He knew, from being knocked out once before, that it was natural and didn't signal any damage to his insides.

On the other hand, his ribs ached, indicating that whoever'd knocked him cold had also put the boot to him while he was down. If he could just remember who the bastard was —

Heck Riley!

Eastman fumbled for his Smith & Wesson, but it wasn't in his holster, where it ought to be.

"Looking for this?" a deep, familiar voice inquired.

The act of sitting up almost made Eastman puke a second time, but he controlled the urge, bracing himself against a bale of moldy-smelling hay. His eyes came into focus, showing him that he was inside Riley's barn, over against the eastern wall. His hat still lay outside, in sunlight, near the threshold of the open doors.

Heck Riley crouched in front of him, fondling the sheriff's pistol with an almost loving, faraway look on his face.

"You shoulda been more careful while you had the chance," said Riley.

"Yeah. I see that."

"Too late now, o'course. But, still."

"Too late for what, Heck?"

291

"You. Me. Ever'thing."

"You punched a lawman, Heck. It could be worse. You catch our justice of the peace in a good mood, you might get off with ten days' easy time."

"It ain't that simple, Sheriff. We both *know* it ain't that simple."

"I'm not sure I follow you," said Eastman.

"Well, you followed *somebody,* to get this far," Riley replied. "You come out lookin' for the stock them nasty killers rustled up. And my, oh, my! What have we here?"

Eastman took time to look around the barn for the first time. He counted eight stalls, six of them with horses standing placidly inside.

"Are these from Hascombs'?" he inquired.

"Two of 'em," Riley said. "The others, I still got left over from the Deacon place."

Eastman made no attempt to hide the loathing in his voice. "Why did you have to kill them, Riley? Women, children. Why'd you have to —"

"Hey, not me!" Riley protested, interrupting. "You had that part right, to start with. I ain't killed nobody — well, nobody you'd know, anyhow. You'll be the first since I got outta prison, Sheriff."

"And you plan on killing me because . . . ?"

"You found me out. Why else? I need some lead time, and I can't afford a posse breathin' down my neck."

"You oughta stop and think about this, Heck."

"I done my thinkin' while you had your little snooze. Once I sell these nags, down in Texas, there'll be nothin' to connect me with the rest of it."

"So when they hang you, it'll only be for killing me," Eastman replied.

"I got it all worked out," Riley replied. "There's gonna be a fire, ya see? We ain't the same size, you and me, but burnin' shrinks a body down some. No one's gonna find your horsc. I'll sell it with the rest and head for Mexico. How's that?"

"Sounds like a plan. There's just one thing, though."

"Yeah? What's that?"

"Well, since you're set on killin' me, no matter what, how 'bout you put my mind at ease first?"

"Meaning?"

Eastman shrugged, a move that amplified the vicious pounding in his skull. "I'd like to know who did the other killings," he replied. "Maybe, one of these days, I'll meet up with 'em down in Hell, and we can settle it."

Riley barked out a laugh at that.

"That's good," he said. "You got a sense a humor. If it wasn't for that badge, we mighta got along okay."

"I guess we'll never know," Eastman replied. "So how about it?"

"Hell, why not. You likely won't believe it, anyway."

"Why's that?" Eastman inquired.

"Because it just don't fit, ya know? That's why you never found 'em. You and ever'body else was lookin' for a bunch of redskins or a gang of border trash. Hell, you weren't even close."

"Who *should* we have been looking for?"

Smiling, Heck Riley told the sheriff what he knew. It wasn't *everything,* of course. The killers hadn't trusted him that far, but it was plenty. Eastman nearly wept, mourning the fact that he would never get to share the information with Jack Slade.

"Ain't that a corker?" Riley said, as he rose from his crouch.

And fired the Smith & Wesson into Ardis Eastman's chest.

13

Slade fired a rifle shot into the air — one of his fifteen rounds wasted — and swiftly pumped the Winchester's lever action to chamber another cartridge. He'd timed his shot as best he could, to fall between rounds fired by the three gunmen up ahead, and thus to capture their attention.

From the way their heads whipped right around to face him, Slade knew it had worked.

This was a risky moment, when the three of them might open fire on him together, but he'd gambled that it might be worse to take them by surprise and make them fire on reflex, fearing they'd been ambushed by a friend of whoever they'd cornered in the trees.

With all three shooters staring at him now, Slade called out to them, "U.S. marshal! Hold your fire! Put down your weapons *now!*"

They thought about it for a minute, while Slade kept advancing, ready with his Winchester in case they tried to go the hard way. Finally, when he was forty yards away and closing, they appeared to reach a mutual consensus. None of them laid down his rifle, but at least they lowered the muzzles.

Slade could only hope the sniper in the woods saw what was happening and understood, that he would hold his fire instead of grasping at the opportunity for one free killing shot.

When Slade was close enough to read their faces, and for them to read his badge, he asked the men, "What's going on here?"

Two held their tongues. The third, and farthest to Slade's left, responded with a question of his own. "What are you doing on the boss's land, lawman?"

"I wouldn't know your boss from Adam in the orchard," Slade replied, "but *lawman* says it all. This badge covers the whole U.S. of A., and your spread's part of it. I heard the shots, and here I am. I'll have your names, and then an answer to my question."

"I'm Zack Lauter," said the first one who had spoken, acting sullen for the benefit of his companions.

"Leland Voss," the middle man replied.

"Will Grayson," said the only shooter left.

"Again, what's going on here?" Slade demanded.

"Got ourselves an Injun, back there in the trees," said Lauter.

"What's he done worth killing for?" asked Slade.

"He left the rez and trespassed on the boss's land, is what," Lauter replied. "Damn near killed Ernie Ford, shootin' his horse from under him."

"Where's Ernie now?" Slade asked.

"Walkin' his gear back to the big house," Grayson said. "We couldn't carry him and catch the Injun, too."

"I'll go out on a limb and guess you fellows fired the first shots in this little party," Slade observed.

"What if we did?" Lauter was getting angry now. "He's off the goddamn reservation, Marshal! He's fair game."

"And where'd you go to law school, Mr. Lauter?"

Lauter blinked at him, confused. "What the hell? Law school? I quit sixth grade."

"You should've stuck around and learned something," Slade told him. "First of all, it may or may not be a criminal offense for Indians to leave the reservation. If it *is,* enforcement of that law falls to the army or a U.S. marshal like myself. It's not your job.

297

You're not entitled."

"But —"

"You'll know it when I'm finished," Slade said, cutting through the cowboy's protest. "*Second,* straying off the reservation doesn't mean you get to kill him, just because you're in the mood. That's murder, same as if you shot a white man on the street, in town. Judge Dennison would hang you for it, and I'm bound to stop you any way I can."

"Christ's sake, Marshal," said Leland Voss. "The redskin's *trespassin'!*"

"And that may get him fined at trial. It's not a hunting license, even if your boss says otherwise. Buying a piece of land and putting cattle on it doesn't make you God, deciding who should live or die for stepping on your grass."

"What kinda lawman are you?" Lauter sneered.

"The kind who's sending you boys home, right now. You want to argue, I can take you back to Paradise and lock you up. Or, if you want to take it further . . ."

As he spoke, Slade let the muzzle of his Winchester swing toward Zack Lauter's chest.

"Hold on, Marshal!" Lauter said. "This whole thing is a big mistake."

"And now's the time to end it," Slade

298

replied. "You hurry, I'll bet you can catch up with your friend."

The three retrieved their horses, mounted up, and rode off to the east. There was a chance they'd try to dry-gulch him, but Slade had a more pressing matter on his mind.

The shooter in the trees.

When Lauter and his men were out of sight, Slade turned toward the tree line and called out, "That's an end to it. Come out and show yourself."

A moment later, he saw Little Wolf, his escort from Slade's first trip to the reservation, moving from the shadows into daylight. He was mounted on a mustang, riding bareback with the reins secured to a hackamore, no bit between the horse's teeth.

"You lost?" he asked the Cherokee.

"I come to help my people," Little Wolf replied.

"By getting shot?"

"I am unharmed."

"So, helping *how?*" Slade asked.

"I seek the men who murder whites and blame it on the Cherokee."

"That's my job," Slade replied.

"And have you found them?"

"I was working on it, when I had to stop and save your skin."

299

"*Red* skin, you mean?"

"I won't pretend I'm color-blind," Slade answered. "But the law's the law, for red or white. You should be heading back, before those yahoos have the army hunting you."

The Cherokee frowned at him, looked surprised.

"You are not taking me to prison?"

"Not today," Slade said, already pulling on his reins to turn the roan around. "You'll have to get there on your own, you want to see the inside of a lockup. I've got wagon tracks to follow and some people with a prior claim on my time."

"Lawman!"

Slade answered without looking back.

"My best advice to you is, go back to the rez. If that's too much to ask, you might want to get off of Mr. Bossman's land, whoever in hell he is."

The wagon felt a good deal lighter without Paxton or the bloodstained rug riding in back. Angus McCallister supposed that was a trick the mind played on itself, a feeling of relief to know he'd gotten clean away with murder, but he didn't care.

Mind trick or not, he still felt good.

And he would feel a damn sight better once he'd put his new plan into play against the Saline Reservation Cherokee.

McCallister was sick and tired of waiting for the army to step in and sweep the red stain from his future property. He'd paid Northcliff enough to do the job, and promised more, but still the colonel blathered on about the law and his *superiors.*

From what McCallister had seen, that group included nearly everyone on Earth.

The problem, as McCallister defined it, was that Northcliff and his soldiers weren't afraid. They had no fear of being hacked up in their sleep like helpless farmers, slaughtered in their homes. Some of the bluecoats might be *angry* at the killers — whoever they were — but they wouldn't move without orders from Northcliff, the sluggard.

Thankfully, that rule didn't apply to the good citizens of Paradise.

McCallister was taking his case to the people. He planned to educate them on the harsh reality of frontier life, where redskins and the army were concerned. Visit the leading merchants who enjoyed his custom and perhaps, if he was in the mood, address whoever happened to be loitering around in the saloon.

Drunks made a nice, responsive audience for killing talk.

The best part, thought McCallister, was

that he wouldn't even have to lie. Just take a moment to remind them of the lives that had been cut short by bloodthirsty savages, with more to come unless some kind of action was initiated to curtail the threat.

What had the army done, so far?

Nothing.

What had their U.S. marshal managed to accomplish?

Diddly-squat.

Who would protect the folk of Paradise, unless they stood up for themselves?

McCallister did not intend to call for any kind of raid against the Cherokee. He wouldn't have to, by the time he finished talking rape, murder, and mutilation to his fine red-blooded friends and neighbors. Men knew what to do about it, when their families and homes were threatened.

They removed the threat. Destroyed it, root and branch.

Of course, it would be foolish to assume that any group of riled-up shopkeepers and laborers could rid the Saline Reservation of its present occupants. That was the army's job, and once townsfolk were bloodied in their first clash with the Cherokee, then Colonel Northcliff would be forced to *do* his job, like it or not.

He'd have to earn the pay he had received

from Washington *and* from Angus McCallister.

Belatedly, McCallister thought that he should've saved Clete Paxton's body, hauled it into town, and blamed the unknown slayers for his foreman's cruel demise. It was too late, though, and a part of his mind knew it wouldn't have worked.

He would've had to butcher Paxton like a hog at slaughter time, for one thing. For another, no one would believe the murderers had risked their lives against his ranch hands, just to kill one cowboy.

Let it go, he thought. And just like that, the thought was gone. Paxton could rest in peace — at least, until the buzzards and coyotes found him.

McCallister was smiling when the town came into view. He started whistling, working up and down the scale with "Dixie," and rehearsed what he would tell the sheep in Paradise.

An hour after leaving Little Wolf, Slade finally decided that the wagon tracks were leading him somewhere, instead of simply rolling out across the hills and plains forever, going nowhere.

They were headed for a farm.

And he could see it, up ahead.

303

It wasn't much to look at, but most homesteaders began with modest homes and barns, adding corrals and suchlike as they went along. Great spreads were not discovered; they were built from the ground up, with muscle, sweat, and tears.

Sometimes, with blood.

It wasn't that the place laid out in front of him was small, but rather that there seemed to be a general untidiness about it that bespoke a certain laziness. That didn't fit the homestead lifestyle, as he'd seen it practiced, and it put Slade on his guard.

Even before he saw the big man drag a body from the barn.

Slade put the roan into a gallop, down a long slope toward the farmhouse and its outbuildings. The breeze was in his face and blew away the sound of hoofbeats for a moment, but when he was still a hundred yards or so out from the house, the man dragging the body heard him coming, raised his head, released his flaccid load, and drew a pistol from his belt.

Slade drew his own and fired a shot before the stranger could aim. It missed, as he'd expected, but it made the big man duck and run, spoiling his shot at Slade.

So far.

Slade dismounted on the fly, stumbling

for cover on one side of the corral as his
roan kept running, seeking safety for itself
behind the farmhouse. He knew it wouldn't
go far, and Slade focused his thoughts on
the gunman before him.

Where was he?

A shadow ducked into the barn, leaving
Slade in the yard with a body stretched out
on its back. A closer look revealed the face
of Ardis Eastman, half turned toward Slade
with eyes open, mouth slack.

Was he dead?

The blood staining his shirt showed where
Eastman was wounded, but Slade couldn't
tell if the sheriff was breathing or not. Moving forward to check for a pulse would
expose him to fire from the barn's open
door.

First things, first.

Slade reversed direction, jogging in a
crouch around the corral until he reached
its farthest point from the open barn doors.
Risking a look in that direction, he calculated that his hidden enemy would have two
seconds, give or take, to hit him on the run
while firing from an awkward angle.

Good enough.

Slade broke from cover, running flat out
over open ground, braced for the bullet that
could drop him, but it never came. He slid

into the barn's north wall, flattened against the earth, and *then* the shooter fired, punching two bullets through the wall a yard above Slade's head.

Two out of six shots gone, and Slade remembered that the gunman had drawn from his waistband, not from a holster. Slade had seen no cartridge belt, which meant that even if the shooter had spare ammunition in his trouser pockets, it would be a slow and fumbling process to reload.

Test it.

Slade reached above his head, straining his shoulder for a solid, openhanded slap against the wall. Dust rained down on his hat brim from the blow, and from a third shot that immediately followed.

Then the shooter called out to him, "If you're feelin' lucky, come and get me! 'Cuz I sure as hell ain't comin' out to you!"

Slade took a chance and answered him. "You really want to shoot a U.S. marshal, after what you've done already?"

"Might as well," the disembodied voice came back. "Bastards can only hang me once."

"There's still a chance you might not hang," Slade lied, "if you explain yourself."

"Your friend already marked me for a rope," the shooter said. "He knew I'd helped 'em."

Shifting closer to the barn's broad entry-way, Slade felt a chill run down his spine.

"Helped *who?*" he queried. "I don't follow you."

"Bullshit! You're out here for the same thing he was. I go in with you, I'm dead meat."

"You could make a deal," Slade answered. "Testify against the others when they come to trial, and maybe get away with life."

The shooter laughed at that. "You think you're gonna bring 'em in?" he asked, his tone mocking. "That bunch? The bitch alone would skin you like a rabbit. She might even make you *like* it."

What the hell . . . ?

"I'll take my chances," Slade replied.

Two more shots drilled the dusty wall above him, putting Slade in motion. Three long running strides, and he was through the barn's door, down again and rolling, watching for a movement or a muzzle flash to mark his target.

When the last shot came, death's whisper at his shoulder, Slade was ready. He fired twice and heard both bullets strike the shadow figure that was lurching toward him. When it fell, he vaulted up and rushed forward to kick away the wounded shooter's gun.

It was as bad as it could be, both lungs shot through, and bloody froth already forming at the gunman's lips and nostrils. Slade shook the dying man back to the edge of consciousness.

"Where can I find them?" Slade demanded.

"Where you . . . least . . . expect . . ."

"Who *are* they, dammit!"

"Fambly . . . it's your . . . funeral."

The shooter died wearing a crimson smile.

Fambly? Now, what the hell . . .

It hit Slade, then, and nearly sent him reeling from the barn back into daylight, where he found the air still smelled of death.

Little Wolf had never known a white man he could trust. Pale hands extended in the guise of friendship meant that other hands held guns and knives and lying treaties clutched behind their backs. In Little Wolf's experience, no white man ever kept his word, unless that word was threatening.

But now, he was alive because one white man had prevented others of his kind from killing Little Wolf. Beyond that, even though the white man wore a badge, he had ignored the fact that Little Wolf was off the reservation.

How were such things possible?

What did it mean?

After reflecting for a moment, while the lawman rode away and passed from sight, it came to Little Wolf that he had met a very strange white man indeed. Perhaps there were no others like him in the world.

This man, Jack Slade, was searching for the very men whom Little Wolf himself pursued. He wanted to arrest or kill them — that part was unclear — for slaying other whites. And Little Wolf, though he cared less than nothing for the farmers who were murdered, yearned to stop the unknown men before their crimes led to destruction of his tribe.

So far, his search had been all aimless wandering, and it had nearly cost his life. But if Jack Slade knew where to find them, why should Little Wolf not follow him — discreetly, at a distance — and discover where they were?

And so it was that he'd begun to trail Slade, staying far enough behind the lawman that his own sharp eyes could barely recognize the tiny mounted figure, constantly alert for the return of those who'd tried to kill him once before, or the appearance of more whites along the way.

It pained him, understanding that the world now opening before him would forever be denied to those he'd left behind, trapped on the Saline Reservation. Little Wolf wished he could call or beam his thoughts to them from where he sat, astride his pony, and encourage all of them to scatter, find their own place in this world they often spoke of but which most of them had never seen.

Perhaps he should forget the white-man killers and ride on alone until he found a place where men ignored the color of one another's skins and always spoke the truth.

Did such a place even exist?

But duty kept him on the lawman's trail, mile after weary mile. He knew that they were coming to a farm, perhaps before Slade did, because his nostrils plucked the scent of gathered horses from the air. His keen ears might have heard a distant shot, but if they did, it came from too far off to trouble him.

Little Wolf knew that he must not approach the farm. He let Slade crest a hill that overlooked the spread, then trotted forward for his own look, once the lawman had descended, passing out of sight.

The next gunshots were close enough to

make his pony shy, before Little Wolf jerked the reins to assert his authority. Edging toward the crest, he saw Slade dismount and run for cover, while a larger man retreated to the barn.

During the fight that followed, Little Wolf considered going down to help, but then dismissed the thought. Slade only faced one enemy, and he had shown that he was brave enough to handle three. If anything went wrong, and Slade was killed, then Little Wolf would seize the winner and determine whether he was one of those who'd killed the farmers.

If the white man didn't want to talk . . . well, there were ways to *make* him share whatever knowledge he possessed.

But in the end, Slade killed his enemy inside the barn, then came back out to kneel beside another dead man lying in the sunshine. Little Wolf observed as Slade dragged that body inside the barn, came out again, and closed the doors behind him.

The lawman whistled loudly, and his horse came trotting toward him, from behind the farmhouse. Little Wolf felt disappointment, knowing that Slade must now ride to find the nearest town and have white shamans come to tend the dead.

But Slade was looking down at something

on the ground, which Little Wolf could not make out. He mounted, and instead of turning toward the town white fools called Paradise, the lawman kept on in the same direction he'd been following before he stopped to shoot the farmer.

Traveling southwestward.

Little Wolf rode down into the silent farmyard, seeking whatever it was that fascinated Slade and made him leave the corpses unattended. When he found it, Little Wolf could only wonder.

Wagon tracks.

Fambly.

Or, if your ruptured lungs were quitting on you, leaving you to mutter with your dying breath, it could be *family.*

What else?

The bitch alone would skin you like a rabbit. She might even make you like *it.*

It was very nearly too much to accept, laid out in front of Slade that way. There were families all over Oklahoma Territory, all over the U.S. of A., and some of them bred criminals. The James and Younger boys were all related, and they had been cousins of the Daltons, too. For some clans, it appeared that crime was in their blood.

As far as *bitches* went, Slade reckoned any

312

family that robbed and killed to get along must have its share. Hard women paired with vicious men, bearing their children, maybe sharing in their butchery.

Slade thought of Belle Starr, born Myra Shirley, who'd been one of Cole Younger's lovers, then tried her luck with badman Jim Reed, and finally married a Cherokee outlaw — Sam Starr — in Oklahoma Territory. Sam had died matching guns with a lawman, and Belle had served six months for helping him steal horses. She was best known for her own unsolved ambush murder, at Eufaula, in 1889.

But Belle had never killed a man, as far as Slade could tell — much less women or children. The James boys, Youngers, Daltons, all had killed when it seemed necessary, during robberies and feuds.

But not for sport.

Slade's quarry was a family that killed for pleasure, and one member of it was, apparently, a "bitch" who thrived on bloodshed.

Then again . . .

He only had the dying word of a man he'd shot, a man who'd tried to kill him. And, for that matter, a man whose name Slade didn't even know.

Could it have been a lie? Some kind of parting shot to throw him off the trail of those he hunted?

Slade considered it, but didn't buy it.

No. The lung-shot gunman had been *taunting* him, predicting Slade's grisly demise if he rode on and found the killers. What would be the point of that, when laying a false trail?

Slade imagined Ardis Eastman and his killer lying in the barn together, going ripe while horses whickered in the nearby stalls. He justified his snap decision based on urgency, a feeling that he had a chance to overtake the killers if he just pressed on a little longer, but Slade knew he couldn't just abandon Eastman and the unknown gunman.

It he hadn't found the wagon he was following by sundown, he'd turn back toward Paradise — ride through the night, if need be — and send Hezekiah Grimm to fetch the bodies. Someone else would also have to see about the gunman's horses, if they *were* his, feed and water them, determine what to do with them.

Somebody else, Slade thought. *Not me.*

Eastman had a deputy in town, though Slade had yet to meet him. Presumably, he'd be in charge of local law enforcement until the mayor or someone else chose a replacement for the murdered sheriff. In the meantime, Slade was not prepared to guard the shopkeepers, while there were killers still at large for him to catch.

The bitch alone would skin you like a rabbit.

Slade had never arrested a woman, but there could always be a first time. And if that woman was a vicious killer, he would treat her just the same as he would any man who threatened Slade's life or the lives of anybody else.

The thought repulsed him, but he didn't plan to die for chivalry.

Before he started dealing with the killers, though, Slade had to *find* them. Maybe at the end of these damned wagon tracks.

How long until he lost the sunlight?

It was past noon, now. The sun was creeping westward, but he still had hours left before night fell.

With any kind of luck, it would be time enough.

And if he had to start from scratch, tomorrow, then so be it. One day or another, it was all the same to Slade.

Unless the killers chose new targets in the meantime, claimed more lives while he was dawdling along behind them on the trail.

Go faster, then, he thought, but didn't want to kill his roan when there was no end to the trek in sight.

Slade felt a sense of being watched, but shrugged it off. At this point, his imagination could turn out to be his own worst enemy.

He rode on, following the trail wherever it might lead.

14

Angus McCallister was on a roll. Since hitting town, he'd made four stops — first at the barber's shop, where gossip was a given, then at three stores where his generous expenditures ensured receptive ears.

At each, his message was the same: the good people of Paradise and its surrounding farms had suffered long enough under a reign of terror that should've been nipped in the bud, after the first family fell to prowling monsters.

If the local sheriff couldn't handle it — which, plainly, he *could not* — he should've asked for help. And not a solitary U.S. marshal, either, but the trained and ready troops from Fort Supply.

Of course, the soldiers only dealt with Indians, but who were the most likely suspects in this string of grisly mutilation murders, after all? Would any *white* man do such things, unless his mind was totally unhinged? And where would anybody find a *gang* of raving-crazy white men, in this day and age?

The answer was painfully obvious. Redskins were responsible for the attacks, and if the army unit under Colonel Northcliff was restrained from taking action by some stupid rules laid down in Washington, some thirteen hundred miles away, who *would* respond?

Who else, besides the brave, red-blooded citizens of Paradise?

McCallister stopped short of calling for a mob to organize. In fact, he didn't even *recommend* a course of action to his listeners. Instead, he simply questioned how their fathers and grandfathers would've dealt with such a situation in the good old days, when men were still entitled to defend their homes and families.

The message got across.

Handing his money to the dry-goods dealer, Chester Simms, McCallister remarked, "Of course, I don't have much to fret about, at my place, with the hands and all their guns around. It must be troubling, though, for someone like yourself, what with a wife and — is it three girls, now?"

"We've got a fourth child on the way," said Chester Simms. After a guilty glance around the store, he almost whispered, "I've been hoping for a boy, this time."

"Well, sir," McCallister replied, "let's hope that he grows up without a cloud of danger hanging over him. Let's hope that he *grows up!*"

"Amen to that!"

"If you'll just put the beans and flour in my wagon, there, I think I'll step across to the saloon and have one for the road. Here's something extra for your trouble, Chet."

"Thank *you*, Mr. McCallister!"

"Please, make it Angus. We're all neighbors here. We're all in the same leaky boat together, after all."

Smiling, he walked across Main Street to the saloon and pushed his way through batwing doors into a murky atmosphere that smelled of alcohol, tobacco smoke, and cheap perfume.

The place was doing decent business for an early weeknight, half a dozen earnest drinkers standing at the bar, while two round poker tables boasted four men each. Two painted floozies tried to keep the fellows drinking at the bar, or tempt them for a hike upstairs.

Angus McCallister was known in Paradise, as rich men always manage to be known around small towns. He didn't own the place, by any means, but there was no doubt that his money had a solid impact on the town's economy, both through his own direct expenditures and through the salaries he paid to his ranch hands — which most of them immediately spent in town. He knew Rance Mathers well and had donated cash to the political campaigns that put Rance in the mayor's office and then kept him there.

There was a reason why McCallister was stopping last at the saloon. Liquor, anger, and fear were volatile components. Mix them in the right proportions, and an agitator could produce a powerful explosion. It required a master, though, to channel that destructive force toward a specific target and make sure that it didn't run out of steam before a satisfactory result had been achieved.

McCallister moved toward the bar, acknowledged the bartender's friendly greeting, and ordered a beer. When it arrived, he raised his voice to ask, "What news about the killings?"

It was plain that little else had been discussed in the saloon that day. The hush that fell, in answer to his question, lasted for the better part of half a minute, then a drinker to his left replied, "No goddamn word at all."

"That's right," another said. "Getting straight answers around here's like panning for gold in my barn. All you get are horse turds."

McCallister sipped his cold beer, raised an eyebrow, and asked, "So you think something's been covered up?"

"Who knows?" a third patron asked. "The mayor and sheriff keep on sayin' they don't know who's doin' it. The soldiers from the fort don't know, and —"

"*I* know," said a fourth voice, from the far end of the bar. "It's redskins, sure as hell. Just think about it, what was done to all them kids and women. Redskins. Had to be."

"I don't know," said the bartender. "Seems like the army would've done something by now, if it was Injuns, plain and simple."

"Now you mention it," McCallister chimed in, "I've had some thoughts on that, myself. Barkeep, a round for the house, please . . . on me."

Slade was about to lose the daylight, and he knew he couldn't chase the wagon tracks once night descended on the plains. His choice, then, was to either double back to Paradise as planned and send the undertaker out for Sheriff Eastman and his killer, or to let the bodies wait and camp right where he was, to start his trek fresh at sunrise.

It wouldn't rain that night. A clear sky promised Slade the tracks would still be visible tomorrow, but he wasn't sure that he could find this spot from town, without retracing his whole journey to that point and winding up exactly where he was at dusk, trapped in a waking nightmare where he was condemned to repeat the same movements over and over, making no progress.

A sickly feeling of uneasiness had built inside him since he'd heard the dying gunman's words back at the ranch, now miles behind him. He was trying to imagine what kind of demented family would live by theft and murder, entertain itself with torture, sexual assault, and mutilation of the dead.

Not Cherokee, he knew for certain, now. Not any kind of Indians.

When he was little, Slade had read a story set in Scotland, said to be a true report. It told about a man named Sawney Beane, who took a whore to wife and raised a pack of feral children, then went on through incest to produce grandchildren and great-grandchildren. Living in a cavern by the sea, the Beanes slipped "back to nature," if a sane person could call it that, killing and *eating* hapless travelers until one of their would-be victims got away and brought back soldiers to annihilate the tribe of cannibals.

Of course, all that had happened — if it ever did at all — back in medieval times. Was such a thing conceivable, in the final years of the modern nineteenth century?

At least, he thought, *they haven't started eating people yet.*

As far as he could tell.

Slade was about to flip a coin, let dumb luck choose if he rode back to town or camped beside the wagon's track to wait for morning, when he saw a flare of light ahead, perhaps a mile distant.

That would be a campfire, he supposed. Somebody else deciding they should ride no farther into dusk and darkness. Slade knew that it could be anyone. He couldn't even guess the odds against finding the killers, just like that.

But if he didn't even check, when twenty minutes at a steady pace would put him there, how would he face himself tomorrow and forever after, as the massacres went on?

Slade cursed and slipped the Liberty

Head fifty-cent piece back into his pocket. He urged the roan forward at a walk, taking no chances as shadows stole over the landscape, concealing stones and prairie dog burrows, gullies and rattlers that came out to hunt at sundown. Slade took his time, half certain that he'd find a solitary drifter or a clutch of cowboys slouched around the fire, trying to figure how he'd handle it if he was wrong.

If it was something else.

Slade had his badge and its authority. He had his Winchester and Colt, both fully loaded. And he had a spyglass in his saddlebag, through which he could eyeball the campers from a quarter mile, if there was light enough and nothing in his way.

If he saw them from a distance and it *was* them, whoever *they* were — if it looked and felt like he'd found the right people — Slade supposed he'd have to leave his horse and do the final stretch on foot, preserving the advantage of surprise. Depending on how many people were in camp, he'd do his best to get the drop on them, and . . . what?

How many wild-eyed killers could he actually control, through fear alone? Wouldn't it just be easier to lie back in the dark and use his rifle, pot them from a distance, and concoct some story afterward, to justify it?

No.

Slade wouldn't trust himself to judge a person's long-range guilt or innocence through rifle sights. How could he, if he didn't catch them trying on their latest victim's scalp or some such lunacy?

He might peer through the glass and see a group of rough trail hands who *might be* killers, or a normal-looking family that *could* have bloody secrets, but he'd have no proof of guilt until he faced them, spoke to them.

Slade might wind up a murderer, himself, unless he played it straight.

Look first.

Dismounting in near darkness, Slade removed the spyglass from his saddlebag, extended it, and raised it to his eye. He found the campfire in the lens and brought it into focus.

"Damn!" he muttered to the night and felt his stomach turn.

"Here's your supper. Make the most of it."

It was the hated woman's voice again. Jenny had missed her cloying scent, distracted by the rich aroma from the stewpot. Cautiously, she raised her hands — still bound together at the wrists, but now in front of her, so she could eat — and felt a tin plate settle on her upturned palms.

"You need to keep your strength up for tonight, at least." The woman's voice turned sly and mocking, then, adding, "Don't count on making it to breakfast."

Jenny considered letting fly, flinging the plate of food into the woman's face, maybe scalding her eyes, but with her own eyes covered by the blindfold she'd be guessing on the distance and direction to her target. It would mean another beating, at the very least — and, anyway, the stew would be her first meal since she had been kidnapped. She was hungry now, in spite of everything.

She felt around the edges of her plate, found no utensils, and began to feed herself by hand. The stew was hot enough to make her wince at first, but Jenny knew that wouldn't last, sitting out in the open air, with nightfall coming on.

Darkness was relative, but she could tell where there was daylight on the world beyond her blindfold. And tonight, if they forgot to tie her hands behind her back, she'd have a chance to reach up, push the cloth aside, and glimpse her kidnappers.

If they were *really* careless, she might even have some small chance to defend herself, next time one of the men —

"That stew not good enough to suit you,

princess?" asked the woman, taunting her again.

"It's fine," Jenny replied, and pushed a bite of stringy meat into her mouth, hoping that it was beef. Who really knew, with animals like this? It could be horse or dog . . . or something else.

"*Fine,* is it? Good enough for a last meal?" the woman asked.

Jenny kept quiet, thinking of her parents and her siblings. All dead, now, and what would happen to her if she *did* escape somehow, from her kidnappers? She had an uncle Joseph, on her mother's side, but he was somewhere up in Kansas or Nebraska, and she couldn't even think of his last name.

She willed her thoughts to slow down and untangle while she ate the stew, one gristly morsel at a time. She needed time to think, but how much time was left before they tired of her and left her for the buzzards?

She focused, finally, upon the idea of a weapon. Something, anything, that she could use in self-defense — or even self-destruction, if it came to that, a quick escape from pawing hands and worse. Jenny had killed her share of chickens at the farm, had watched her father butcher hogs. If she could find a knife . . .

Then, what?

Cut through the bonds around her ankles, while they slept, for one thing. Slip her blindfold off and grip the knife between her feet or knees, to free her wrists.

And then?

She didn't know if her abductors took turns standing watch, throughout the night, or if they felt secure enough to sleep straight through. If she was armed, untied, she'd have a choice of tackling them alone or slipping out of camp and running for it, praying that they wouldn't wake and follow her.

Better to kill them first, she thought. *It's what they all deserve.*

It would require more speed and will than strength, she realized. Even a child could stick a knife in someone's throat while they were sleeping. But to kill four in a row, before one of them woke and reached a weapon of his own — *her* own — would take both speed and nerves of steel.

She caught herself imagining the spray of blood, half smiling at the mental image, then remembered that she didn't have a weapon, couldn't cut or club them with her two bare hands.

Change the priority. Try easing up the blindfold, just enough to peek around the camp without alerting any of her tormentors. Check out their stock of guns, knives, whatever they had, and see where they were kept at night. If she could just —

"All done with din-din?" asked the male voice she had quickly learned to hate. "Ready for beddy-bye?"

She shook her head, afraid to trust her voice.

"Aw, sure you are. C'mon, darlin'. I'll tuck you in."

She tried to spin away from him, but he was quick and strong. A heartbeat later, Jenny found herself thrown easily across his shoulder, sobbing, as he bore her toward the wagon.

"If it was me," Angus McCallister proclaimed, "I don't believe I'd wait around until the army got its marching orders. Hell, we all know how things work in Washington. The Capitol needs painting, Congress sets up five committees to discuss it, and it takes a year to choose the color."

Murmurs of assent ran up and down the bar. McCallister winked at the barkeep to dispense another round.

"*Mean*while," he said, turning to let the poker players hear him, "we could all dry up and blow away before they notice it, back East. Can't blame 'em, really. They're all busy wondering what they should do with

Cuba and the Philippines. Who's got the time to think about some farmers getting killed in Oklahoma Territory, anyhow?"

"Bastards!" one of the drinkers at the bar spat out. "And we can't even vote 'em down, without statehood."

"That could take years, *decades*," McCallister pressed on. "And while you're waiting for it, how many more men, women, and children will be lost?"

"So, what?" one of the cardplayers inquired, folding his hand. "You think we oughta ride out to the rez or somethin'? Fight the cav'ry *and* the Cherokee?"

Before McCallister could answer that, a slim, familiar figure entered the saloon. Rance Mathers spotted him and made his way across the sawdust-littered floor, circling around the poker tables. His dark eyes locked on McCallister's and held them fast.

"What's this about?" the mayor asked, when he'd closed the gap enough to speak without raising his voice.

"A friendly chat," McCallister replied. "We're discussing events of the day."

"Something special?" asked Mathers.

"We're talkin' 'bout the killin's, *Mayor*," one of the bar-side drinkers said.

Mathers ignored him and focused squarely on McCallister.

"What are you hoping to accomplish, Angus?" he inquired.

"Accomplish, Rance? Why, nothing whatsoever. Have we reached the point where talking is illegal, now?"

"I don't see anyone arresting you," Mathers replied. "But since you raise the subject, there's a statute on the books against inciting riots."

"We could ask the sheriff, or the U.S. marshal," said McCallister. "Any idea where they've run off to, by the way?"

"Tending to business, I expect," said Mathers. "Just as you should be."

McCallister felt angry color rising in his cheeks.

"Meaning, I take it, that *my* business has nothing to do with Paradise, or families getting slaughtered everywhere you look, around the countryside."

"Meaning that we have Sheriff Eastman, Marshal Slade, *and* Colonel Northcliff's soldiers working on this problem. And the last thing anybody needs is half-baked vigilantes with a snoot full, getting in the middle of it, making matters worse."

"Mayor, I beg to differ with you," said McCallister. "First up, as far as I can see, the folks you named aren't *doing* anything to help this town. And second, I don't see how things can get much worse. How many dead folk is it now? Twenty? Thirty?"

"Too damn many!" said a voice from somewhere down the bar.

"And you can multiply that by a hundred," Mathers answered, "if a bunch of yahoos on the prod stir up a war against the Cherokee."

"*Yahoos,* he says." McCallister played to his audience. "The men who vote you into office and can vote you *out.* Let's ask the slaughtered homesteaders about your war, Mayor. If they could talk, I'll bet they'd say it's already started."

Most of the cardplayers were on their feet now, joining their friends at the bar, but McCallister saw one making tracks for the exit. The look on his face told McCallister that he was off to spread the news — or gather reinforcements.

"I'm warning you, Angus."

"*You're* warning *me?* You should've warned your people there were killers in the neighborhood and that there's nothing you can do about it. Maybe they'd feel better with their fate in someone else's hands — that is, the ones who're still alive."

"Angus," the red-faced mayor replied, "don't make me arrest you for breaching the peace."

332

"Arrest me?" McCallister joined in the general laughter. "You and whose —"

The first swing caught McCallister in the solar plexus, driving the air from his lungs and doubling him over, fighting for breath. A rising knee collided with his forehead, and the barroom tilted, reeling.

McCallister hit the floor on his left side, felt sawdust on his cheek, and heard a pistol cocking somewhere, miles above his head.

"The rest of you stand back!" he heard Rance Mathers saying, then a strong hand clutched his collar and began to drag him like a sack of laundry, toward the door.

Slade recognized the wagon first, and then the faces ranged around the campfire. All but one, that is. The stranger was a girl with long dark hair, a blindfold covering the top half of her face, feeding herself from a tin plate and struggling with it, since her wrists were bound.

The Bowdens.

Slade felt sick, knowing he'd shared a meal and night with them, then let them go along their merry way to kill again. There must be, he supposed, some way to live with that.

But now he had them. More or less.

Slade folded his spyglass. He tethered his

roan to a low mesquite bush with a slipknot that wouldn't hold long, if he didn't come back. Pulling his rifle from its saddle boot, he marked a course across the open ground and started moving toward the Bowdens' camp.

The darkness covered Slade's advance. He took his time, watching his step, both to avoid unnecessary noise and keep from stepping in a hole or rut where he might snap an ankle. Jenny Hascomb needed him in fighting form, right now, not sprawled out at the mercy of her kidnappers.

Slade's momentary thrill at finding her alive had quickly faded, when he thought about what she had likely suffered in the hours since she'd been abducted. He recalled John Junior's brutish, leering face and didn't want to think about him touching Jenny Hascomb, or . . .

And what about John *Senior?* He was older, granted, and he had his silent wife, Helen, but would she intervene if the old man got randy? Would she even care?

A family that slaughtered strangers by the wagonload was clearly operating on a different set of rules from normal folk, whatever *normal* meant these days.

The Bowdens had no extra horses with them, just the wagon team, which they'd unhitched and tethered off to one side of the camp. Slade guessed there would be grass there, and perhaps a spring to quench their thirst.

The path he'd chosen led him toward the far side of the camp, directly opposite the horses, minimizing any risk that they'd give him away. He stayed well out from the ring of firelight, sheltered by the night. They could glance up and never see him, with the firelight in their eyes.

So far, so good.

At thirty yards, Slade took his pace down to a crawl, testing each step before committing to it, painfully aware of gritty sand and pebbles underfoot. If he could reach the wagon, he'd have cover and could get the drop on them, no problem. Nothing they could do about it, then, but raise their hands or die.

When he was twenty yards away, Slade saw John Junior lift the Hascomb girl and carry her around behind the wagon. Moments later, he could hear and see the wagon groan beneath the added weight.

Slade had no difficulty picturing what Bowden had in mind for Jenny Hascomb, but a clumsy rush to save her from it might produce the opposite effect, might even get her killed. Slade bit his tongue to keep from

335

cursing and edged forward.

Slow and steady as it goes.

Two more minutes, and he crouched beside the wagon's falling tongue, the main bulk of the wagon shielding him from view of those who still remained around the campfire. Moving closer with exaggerated steps, to rule out any scuffling sounds, Slade heard a kind of sobbing whimper from the wagon, overridden by a deep voice muttering.

Suppose he stepped up on the wagon's doubletree and shot John Junior, *then* threw down on the remaining Bowdens. Could he justify it to Judge Dennison. Would anybody even question why he'd dropped a rapist in the act?

Temptation nearly overcame him, but Slade reckoned it would have the same effect when he called on the others to sit still and raise their hands. Junior might have a weapon with him — likely did, in fact — but if he tried to use it, either on the girl or Slade himself, there would be time enough to kill him.

Wouldn't there?

But if he struck the girl without a warning, *then* came after Slade, the nod toward rules and regulations would've cost her life. Slade took a beat to think about it, had decided it was best to take no chances, when he heard the whisper of a scraping sound behind him and began to turn.

"That's far enough, Jack."

As she spoke, he heard Kate cock the pistol she was carrying.

"I see you couldn't stay away," she said.

"Miz Bowden," he replied, coldly.

"Oh, Jack, don't be so formal. Anyway," she said, "the name's Bender."

15

"I assume you've heard our story," said Kate Bender.

"You mean Cherryvale?" asked Slade.

"Just kill him, will you?" said Kate's brother.

"Shut up, Junior!" Kate snapped at him. "Or get back up in the wagon with your little whore. I guarantee you, it's your last night with her."

Slade, disarmed, was seated with his back against one of the wagon's wheels. Kate stood before him with a pistol in each hand, one of them his. The others — John, Helen, and Junior — sat around the stoked-up campfire, watching him with eyes as cold and dead as chips of flint.

"And yes, Jack," Kate resumed, "the story you're familiar with *did* happen up in Cherryvale."

Kansas, that was, a hundred and fifty miles north as the crow flies. Or the vulture.

Take your pick.

Slade had been a child, then, in 1873, fresh out on the road and running from home. He recalled how the Benders had captured headlines — and then dropped from the news when the posse that pursued them came back empty-handed.

Stalling for time, he said, "The way I heard it, you set up some kind of inn or way station, a few miles out of town. Somebody stopped by on his own, you'd offer him a meal, then John or Junior there would sneak up on their blind side with a mallet."

"Always liked the ax better, myself," said Junior, grinning.

"Kill them, rob them, plant them. Sit back waiting for the next one," Slade observed. "Kind of like trapdoor spiders."

"It was sweet, all right," Kate said. "But all good things come to an end."

Slade knew that part of it, as well. One of their victims — a doctor, if Slade had it right — had a wealthy brother who'd come looking for him, traced him as far as the Benders' inn, and wasn't satisfied with the answers they gave him. When the brother came back with Cherryvale's sheriff, the inn was abandoned. And out back, they'd un-earthed . . .

"Eleven bodies, was it, that they dug up?"

Slade inquired.

"They found eleven, then quit looking," Kate amended. "Once, I almost wrote the mayor a letter, telling him where he could find the rest, but I decided it would be a bad idea."

"You've held up pretty well," Slade said, "all things considered."

"Meaning what, exactly?" she demanded.

"Well, the time that's passed, for one thing," he replied. "And, then, the talk that went around, about that posse."

"Oh? What talk is that, Jack?"

"Some folks say they caught you on the prairie and decided not to bring you back for trial. Shot mom and dad and Junior, there."

"What about me?"

"The story I heard claims they took turns with you, then burned you alive."

Kate laughed at that, standing before him with the pistols at her sides. Behind her, there were smiles around the campfire.

"That's what I call wishful thinking," she told Slade. "The truth is, they were never even close, despite Governor Osborn's two-thousand-dollar reward. Poor bastards had to tell the people something, I suppose, to let them sleep at night."

"You all were pretty slick, I guess," Slade said.

"The one that made me laugh the hardest," Kate replied, "was when they brought that woman and her daughter from Detroit, thinking that it was me and Ma. Talk about stupid, eh? That takes the cake."

"I'm guessing Kansas soured you on innkeeping," Slade said.

"You're guessing right. I had to quit the fortune-telling, too, once I got famous for it on the circulars. Too bad. I used to like the settled life."

"So you've been traveling for sixteen years?"

"What's with the questions?" Junior interrupted. "Are we killing him, or not?"

Kate spun to face her brother, raising Slade's Colt with furious speed and making John Junior flinch backward, scuffling away from the fire.

"He dies when *I* say so, goddamn it! Now, shut your piehole!"

Her tired face wore a smile as she turned back toward Slade. "I grant you, all this wandering can wear a body down," Kate said. "But mine's held up all right, don't you agree?"

"You've just been traveling around the country, killing people," Slade replied. He was surprised that he'd heard nothing of it previously, through Judge Dennison.

Kate waved the other gun dismissively, saying, "Oh, we were down in Mexico awhile. We had a little inn down there. But here's a secret for you, Jack. Most beaners don't have two pesos to rub together. I was getting run-down, living off of rice and beans. A girl needs prime meat every now and then, you know?"

"So how long have you all been doing . . . this?"

"The farm thing? Off and on since '77 or so. We work a territory, make some money to relax on, then sit out a year or so. Montana, Colorado, California, Arizona, Texas. Time flies, when you're doing work that you enjoy."

"You don't have any trouble finding someone who will take the livestock off your hands?"

"Why would we, Jack? People are rotten, everywhere you go. They sing their hymns on Sunday, after getting drunk on Saturday, and spend the other five days cheating friends and neighbors any way they can."

"You'll need another buyer," Slade informed her. "Yours went out of business permanently, earlier today."

"Your doing?" Kate inquired, one eyebrow

raised. "Well, never mind. We've done this territory, anyway. The money we've got squirreled away, I'm thinking we won't have to work again before 1901."

"It's nice to plan ahead," Slade said.

"And I've got plans for you, Jack. On your feet! Now turn around and put your hands behind your back."

"You've made a huge mistake, Rance. You must see that, now. But there's still time to put it right."

"Shut up, McCallister!"

The mayor was pacing back and forth across the sheriff's office, with a sawed-off scattergun tucked underneath one arm. Angus McCallister could see him from the cell he occupied, when Mathers passed the open door connecting Ardis Eastman's office proper to the jail in back.

McCallister was seated on the cell's hard cot, hunched forward, favoring his gut, where Mathers had punched him. McCallister's nose and lips were swollen, too, but they hurt too much to probe them with his fingers.

"You can still come through this in one piece," McCallister told Mathers. "I can let it go, you sucker punching me. The folks outside just want me free again, so we can finish off our little talk."

Mathers swung into the connecting doorway, glaring at McCallister. "You've talked too much already," he replied. "I won't let you use *my* town for your dirty work. You want to raise hell on the reservation, use the men you pay to do your bidding."

"That's too obvious."

"The soldiers, then."

"They've let me down. Look, Rance, I thought we understood each other on this thing."

"Moving the Cherokee for public safety," Mathers said. "That's what *I* understood. Now Ardis has gone off, saying he isn't sure the tribe had anything to do with all these killings."

"Where *is* Ardis, by the way?"

"He's gone to see about the missing livestock," Mathers answered. "Wouldn't tell me where, until he'd checked it for himself."

"He's got no jurisdiction on the rez," McCallister replied.

"He wasn't going to the reservation, damn it! Don't you listen? If that stock was on the reservation, Northcliff and his soldiers would've found the animals by now."

"If they were still alive, maybe. You don't think redskins will eat horse meat, quick as beef?"

"I think you need to shut your mouth, Angus."

"I'm sitting in a jail cell," said McCallister. "I've got a right to hear the charges."

"So far, it's disturbing the peace. If things get any worse, outside, we'll call it inciting a riot."

"Riot, my ass!"

Just then, a knocking on the door distracted Mathers. He moved cautiously to check the door's peephole, then hastily unbolted it, admitting Deputy Buck Coleridge. As the door opened and closed again, the angry murmuring outside turned into shouts.

"They're getting antsy," Coleridge said.

"They'll weary of it," Mathers told him. "Wait till it starts getting cold, around eleven, twelve o'clock."

"The way they're drinking," Coleridge answered, "most of 'em won't feel it."

"Grab a rifle, then. Be ready if they rush the door."

"Rance, this is just plain foolish," said McCallister. "You have to realize that *someone* out there must be riding to my place, by now. They'll bring my men back, and you know damn well *they* aren't afraid of you. They take orders from me, and no one else."

"Then you can order them to turn around

and go back home," said Mathers.

"Oh? Like hell, I will!"

The mayor stepped closer to the wall of bars that separated them. He held his shotgun leveled from the waist, its twin muzzles a perfect fit between two of the upright bars.

"That's your call, Angus. But I promise you one thing, right now. Whoever breaks in here to spring you, they'd be wise to bring a mop and bucket. They'll be swabbing up your guts from now till Sunday week."

"I don't believe you'll do it," said McCallister. The tremor in his voice belied his words.

"You'd best believe it," Mathers said. "Whatever else happens tonight, if anybody storms this office, you *will* be the first to die."

"This is better," Kate remarked, when they were twenty yards or so out from the wagon, well beyond the fire's light. "Now we have some privacy."

"For what?" asked Slade. "Something you couldn't tell me with the family listening?"

She laughed at that and said, "Something we couldn't *do,* with all of them *watching.*"

"I guess it's a problem, meeting men, when you're so quick to kill them."

"I'm still looking for the man who can keep up with me," Kate said.

"I heard they had one, back in England. The newspapers called him Jack the Ripper."

Kate jammed one of the pistols underneath his chin and said, "That's not what I call courting talk."

"The only courting talk you'll hear from me is when I hand you over to Judge Dennison, in Enid."

"Jack, we both know that won't happen. Even if you had the drop on me — on us — we'd never let you take us in alive."

"That's good to know."

"Pa did some time, when he was younger, and he's told us all about it. Living in a cage . . . well, that's not really *living,* is it, Jack?"

"For all you've done, I don't think you'd be caged too long," Slade said. "Judge Dennison won't keep you waiting for the necktie party."

"So you want to see me dead?"

"I don't want to see *anybody* dead," he told her. "But if someone has to make the choice, I'd rather save the innocents you've slaughtered and the ones you're planning to."

"You sound just like a lawman, Jack."

"Comes with the badge, I guess."

"All holy and self-righteous. Well, I guess you can afford to be, drawing your paycheck from the government."

"I've had this job a year," Slade said. "Before that, I was on my own and never saw the need to rob or murder anyone."

"Well, aren't you special!"

" 'Normal' is the way I'd phrase it."

"Who's to judge?" Kate asked. "Your church folk? Have you ever read the Bible, Jack?"

"I tried it once. Got lost in the begats," he said.

"You should've stuck it out a little longer," Kate replied. "Get into Deuteronomy and go from there. God's chosen people killing others by the tens of thousands, just for standing in their way. Women and children, young and old. You think we're bad? I reckon we're just being godly, Jack."

"I don't know if the Bible's true or not," Slade said. "But I don't worship anyone who kills just for the hell of it."

"I don't want you to worship me," she said. "Just give me a few minutes of the time you still have left."

"Not if I had a hundred years."

"Being self-righteous doesn't suit you.

You've killed people, Jack. I see it in your eyes."

He almost told her all of them deserved it, but Slade guessed that wouldn't send the proper message.

Instead, he told her, "I enforce the law. Someone resists arrest, I use the force required to bring them in, one way or another."

"Dead or alive."

"It comes to that, sometimes."

"I think you killed *before* you had that badge. Tell me I'm wrong."

"Only in self-defense," Slade said.

"And who defines it, Jack? You've never been a woman in the West. You've never been a girl who couldn't say 'no' to a pig and make it stick. I'll bet you've never had some filthy bastard hold a razor to your throat, while he —"

She stopped abruptly, blinked at Slade, then smiled. "Oh, what the hell. We may as well drop it."

"Kate, listen —"

"And speaking of dropping things, it's time you dropped those trousers."

"Talk about your wishful thinking," Slade replied.

"Oh, I forgot. You're indisposed," Kate said. "Here, let me help you."

Tucking Slade's Colt underneath her right arm, while she held the other pistol pressed against his ribs, Kate used her left hand to attack Slade's belt. The trouser buttons were more difficult, making her fumble at his groin.

"One-handed's never easy," she said, smiling, knuckles rubbing him, "but I guess you won't mind."

Another moment and she had it, yanking Slade's pants down around his ankles. Any chance he'd had of kicking out at her was lost.

"Well, now. It seems you're glad to see me, after all."

Slade wished for better self-control, but the insistence of her stroking fingers overcame embarrassment, his sense of violation. When he tried to back away, she clutched him and her pistol jabbed against his ribs.

"Play nice," she said, "and maybe this won't have to be the last time."

This time, when he tried to pull away, Kate let him go and swept a foot around behind him, tripping Slade. He toppled over backward, landing painfully upon his hands and elbows.

"See?" she grinned. "I knew you'd fall for me."

Straddling his lower body with a six-gun

in each hand, Kate Bender settled down on top of him.

Patience was not a young man's virtue. When he'd left the reservation, Little Wolf had hoped to quickly solve the mystery that had ensnared his people in a web of lies that might yet lead to their destruction. The attack by white men had delayed him, and he'd chafed at trailing the lawman who had saved his life — or theirs — but he had seen no better option.

Now, after hours of following old wagon tracks, Jack Slade had found a group of travelers who held his interest. Little Wolf sat back and watched Slade use the spyglass as night fell, watching the tiny figures hunched around a campfire, near a wagon.

Could it truly be the wagon they'd been following?

What did it mean?

Did Slade believe these people were the killers?

Little Wolf waited. He was watching when Slade left his horse and went forward on foot, drawing inexorably closer to the fire. The young brave used that opportunity to walk his own horse closer to the camp, where his sharp eyes could watch events unfold without need of a telescope.

There were five people around the fire, at first. Three women and two men. One of the women — younger than the rest by many years — was blindfolded and ate her food without utensils, fumbling with the plate because her wrists were tied.

Aside from that, the campers looked like any normal family that Little Wolf could imagine. What did he know of parenting among white people? Did they bind and blindfold children who had misbehaved?

Based on the way they treated Cherokee, it seemed to Little Wolf that anything was possible.

When Slade was halfway to the camp, still well off to the left and not exactly watching, Little Wolf saw one of the women without a blindfold leave the others. She rose and left her plate, then walked around behind the wagon, out of sight. Presumably, a call of nature had distracted her.

Soon afterward, the younger of the two men took the girl with the blindfold into the wagon. Little Wolf, at that point, guessed that either they were not related, or that whites were even more perverted than he'd thought.

Moments later, Slade approached the wagon. He was careful not to let the campers see him, but from Little Wolf's perspective it was plain the lawman had not seen the woman leave.

Where was she? What would happen if she saw or heard Slade first and raised a general alarm?

But it was worse than that, and Little Wolf was watching when the woman suddenly emerged from darkness behind Slade and aimed a pistol at his back.

Little Wolf had aimed his Springfield rifle, ready to kill her without compunction and settle his debt to Jack Slade, but the woman spoke instead of firing. She disarmed Slade, took him prisoner, and marched him out to meet the others. Soon, the younger man returned to join the circle, but he left the girl inside the wagon as he moved to bind Slade's hands.

It was a bit confusing, watching these white people without hearing anything they said. Little Wolf followed Slade's example, trusting his horse to stand alone while he crept closer to the fire.

He heard them now, the younger woman questioning Jack Slade, but much of what they said still made no sense to Little Wolf. He gathered that these people *were* the killers whom he sought, but otherwise . . .

They spoke of murders and a place called Cherryvale, which meant nothing to Little

Wolf. The younger of the men was anxious to dispose of Slade, but he did not control the woman with the pistols. Nothing passed between Slade and the older couple, who observed the scene without displaying any visible emotion.

Finally, the standing woman ordered Slade to rise and follow her. Slade did as he was told. They walked some distance from the fire, with Little Wolf their shadow, then they stopped and spoke again.

The woman wanted Slade, that much was obvious even to Little Wolf, who had not yet been with a woman in the carnal way. Slade argued with his mouth, but when the woman took his trousers down, it seemed to Little Wolf that she must win.

And then what?

Would she kill the lawman?

Could he let her do it?

Little Wolf had come to find these people and destroy them, as a way to save his tribe. The woman had confessed their crimes to Slade, but if she killed him, Little Wolf would have no witness to that fact. Even if he went on to kill them *and* to free the girl held captive in the wagon, who was there to differentiate between those killings and the rest?

He might be blamed for all of them, the

wrongful judgment of his people thus sub-stantiated.

No. He needed Slade alive, and there was still the matter of his blood debt to the law-man, unresolved.

He saw the woman trip Jack Slade, then pounce upon him, settling on his lap. She laid one gun aside and reached beneath her skirt to find him, make him fit, as Little Wolf moved forward through the darkness.

"There, now." Kate sighed, as they fit together. "That's just right."

She squirmed a little, then was rising on him when a shadow loomed out of the night behind her. Slade was startled by the sud-den blur of movement and the solid clunk as something heavy struck Kate's skull and spilled her sideways, sprawling on the grass.

Slade half expected Junior, felt himself indecently exposed and vulnerable to at-tack, but it was Little Wolf who bent and grasped one of Slade's arms, lifting him to his feet. The Cherokee was grim-faced as he stepped around behind Slade, drew a knife, and freed Slade's hands.

"Dress now," he told Slade, being wise enough to whisper. "Then we kill the oth-ers."

Slade hurried with his trousers, cinched

his belt, and didn't bother with the buttons, as he answered Little Wolf.

"I have to try and take them in alive."

"You *did* try," Little Wolf reminded him.

"I'm not done trying."

Slade retrieved both pistols from the ground, tucked Kate's under his belt, and pressed the fingers of his free hand to her throat, seeking a pulse. He found it, strong and steady, but she didn't stir.

"Sorry you don't have time to finish," Little Wolf remarked. Was that a smile making his lips twitch?

"Never mind that," Slade replied, surprised to feel a surge of guilt as he imagined telling Faith about tonight. "If they start shooting, there's a hostage in the wagon."

"Girl with blindfold," Little Wolf replied. "Is she not one of them?"

"Not even close."

Slade couldn't see the other Benders from where he and Little Wolf stood over Kate, but he devised a hasty plan.

"One of us needs to go around behind the wagon, so we have them in a cross fire. Just in case."

Little Wolf nodded and was gone, without another word. Slade didn't have a chance to caution him, or order him to hold his fire unless the Benders reached for guns.

Uneasy about leaving Kate, he had no choice. He couldn't tie her with the rope that Little Wolf had slashed to free him, and he couldn't wait around to think of something else, leaving the Cherokee to face the other members of the family alone.

Cursing, Slade jogged back toward the wagon, found the place where Kate had caught him unaware the first time, and eased back the hammer on his Colt.

He heard Junior complaining, "Damn it, Pa! She's takin' chances with that bastard!"

"Watch your mouth, boy," growled the Bender patriarch. "Your mother's sittin' here, if you're too dumb to know it."

"Sorry, Ma. But we should —"

"Freeze right there," Slade ordered, stepping out to show himself.

John Senior sized him up and said, "Your fly's undone, lawman. What you been doin' with my little girl?"

"I'm giving you a chance to raise your hands," Slade said.

"That's mighty generous of you," said Junior, smiling like a man who thinks he has the upper hand.

"Under the circumstances, I believe it is," Slade told him.

" 'Spose we don't feel like surrendering," the old man said. "You reckon you can take all four of us?"

"One's down already," Slade replied. "That just leaves three."

And then, it went to hell.

Kate's mother shrieked like a demented banshee, leaping to her feet with an agility Slade found amazing. She dove toward the big Sharps rifle propped against the wagon, while her menfolk went for weapons of their own.

Junior drew a pistol that he'd hidden underneath his shirttail, at the back, while the old man whipped a knife from his right boot. As Junior fanned a shot at Slade, his father hurled the pigsticker and Helen Bender snatched the rifle, letting out another high-pitched squeal.

Slade ducked beneath the tumbling knife, as Junior's bullet plucked at his left shirtsleeve. He fired first at Kate's brother, saw a spout of crimson burst from Junior's shoulder as the big man toppled over backward, cursing a blue streak.

A rifle shot rang out, and Slade saw Helen Bender standing with the big Sharps at her shoulder, looking down the barrel at him, but her face was slack, her eyes unfocused. Crimson blossomed on the bodice of her dress, just as her knees folded and she collapsed into an awkward pirouette.

She got the shot off, even so, the bellow of her Sharps a hammer stroke on Slade's eardrums. He ducked instinctively, but it was angling back across the campfire as her lifeless finger jerked the trigger, and the heavy bullet struck her husband as he rose, punching a half-inch keyhole through his forehead.

Slade saw the old man's skull burst like a ripe melon, emptied in a heartbeat. Dead before he realized it, Papa Bender lurched forward and landed facedown in the campfire, where his beard and bloody hair caught quickly, giving off a cloud of smoke.

John Junior struggled to his feet, his left arm hanging useless at his side, but he still clutched the six-gun in his right hand, triggering another shot at Slade. It struck the wagon, sparked a scream from Jenny Hascomb, and sprayed Slade with wooden slivers as he dropped into a prone position.

Slade fired from the ground and saw his bullet punch through Junior's chest. The big man staggered, was about to fall, when Little Wolf fired from behind him, making sure. The rifle shot put Junior on his face, arms splayed as if he had been crucified.

Slade rose, surveyed the scene — and wondered why in hell the Cherokee was leveling his Springfield at Slade's face. The wildcat scream behind him froze Slade for a second, long enough for Kate to stab him in the back.

Her knife's blade wasn't long, but it was double-edged and razor sharp. It cut Slade's denim shirt and scored his flesh like they were nothing, scraped across his shoulder blade, and angled toward his spine. He bellowed from the pain, twisted away from her, and then the blade was slicing toward his throat.

The Springfield spoke again, and Kate leaped backward, as if yanked by ropes, tumbling across the sod and coming to a stop ten feet away from Slade, her skirt and petticoats rucked up around her hips.

Slade felt himself begin to fall, but Little Wolf was there beside him, gripping his left arm, helping Slade sit, instead of sprawling on his face.

"You should have killed her sooner," said the Cherokee.

16

Colonel Hollis Northcliff was finishing his second whiskey of the night, considering a third, when someone rapped sharply on the door to his private quarters. Although half out of uniform, wearing a simple shirt instead of his blue tunic with the polished eagles on its collar, Northcliff opened his door to the night.

A weathered-looking sergeant stood before him, flanked by a civilian on his left.

"Beggin' your pardon, sir," the sergeant said, after a quick salute. "We got a rider here from Paradise who claims they got a situation you should know about."

Slade didn't feel like asking either one of them inside. He eyeballed the civilian, saying, "And you are . . . ?"

"Deke Walker, Colonel."

"Mr. Walker, what exactly is this 'situation'?"

"Well, sir, it appears the mayor's done lost

his mind and dragged Mr. McCallister — my boss, sir — off to jail for no good reason I can think of. Now, a bunch of people from the town and all are workin' theirselves up to storm the jail and turn him loose. Fact is, it may be done by now, since I've been ridin' for a while."

"This is a matter for your sheriff, Mr. . . . Mr. —"

"Walker, sir. And Sheriff Eastman ain't been seen since he rode out this morning, goin' who knows where. His deputy was with the mayor inside the jailhouse when I left."

Northcliff wished that he'd skipped the whiskey, which was slowing down his thought process. Officially, he had no jurisdiction in civilian matters unless local law enforcement officers requested help with something like a riot or a natural disaster. On the other hand, if lawmen were unable to communicate for any reason — whether they were missing, dead, or under siege — Northcliff supposed that he could offer minimal assistance without jeopardizing his career or pension.

Then again, Angus McCallister's involvement was a complication fraught with danger. If Northcliff's superiors decided he had intervened without authority of reason, they might take a closer look at Angus and his history with Northcliff. There was nothing down on paper to prove anything against them, but . . .

Northcliff addressed Deke Walker once again. "You say the mayor arrested your employer for no reason. What exactly was the charge?"

"I ain't *exactly* sure," Walker replied. "Somethin' about sighting a riot, disturbin' the peace. I forget."

"And at the time he was arrested, what was Mr. McCallister doing?"

"I wasn't there, but someone told me he was talkin' to some folks in the saloon, about the redskins and these killin's."

Bloody idiot!

Northcliff could see it in his mind's eye. Angus, tired of waiting for him to remove the Cherokee, buying the house a round or ten and telling the assembled drunks they should do something for themselves. Ride out and teach the damned redskins a lesson, maybe run them clear out of the territory.

It could be tough to prove incitement, with a hometown jury fond of McCallister's money, but the trial would be held in Enid, before Judge Dennison. McCallister might lose, and if he drew a prison term . . .

What would he do? Sit back and take it like a man, or try to bargain with the law? Serve up a colonel, maybe, on a silver platter, if it shaved his time or got him off the hook completely.

And if Northcliff had to face a court-martial, it meant his whole life had been wasted. The conviction rate in military trials was overwhelming, since the army rarely went to trial without an airtight case. Upon conviction of accepting bribes, Northcliff would first be stripped of rank in a humiliating public ceremony, then dishonorably discharged from the service. He'd be lucky not to spend the next five years in Leavenworth.

"Sergeant," he said at last, "call out a dozen men. We leave for Paradise at once, and pray it's not too late."

"Yes, sir!"

The sergeant left their visitor standing alone on Northcliff's doorstep.

"Colonel, sir," Deke Walker said, "you want me to, I'll ride on back to town and let 'em know you're comin'."

"No!" The last thing Northcliff wanted was to telegraph his move. "I would prefer that you ride back with us . . . for safety's sake."

"Okay, sir."

"Just wait there," said Northcliff, as he

closed and latched the door.

McCallister could pose a problem, North-cliff realized. And it was one that he would have to solve this very night, before the rancher dragged him down.

Perhaps, if Northcliff took McCallister into protective custody, but then, McCallister tried to escape . . .

Who could predict what happened next?

"I don't know whether I can do it," Deputy Buck Coleridge said.

"Do what?" Rance Mathers asked.

"Gun down those people in the street. I know 'em all. Some of 'em were my friends, before tonight."

Scowling, the mayor replied, "You hit it on the head. They were your friends *before,* not now. They'd rather free McCallister and go off killing Cherokee than stay at home and mind the law."

"Speaking of law," Coleridge pressed on, "I'm still not clear on why we've got Mr. McCallister locked up."

"I *told* you, Buck. I made a citizen's arrest for disturbing the peace and inciting a riot. Hell, call it inciting a *war* and you'd be closer to the truth."

"Mayor, everybody and his dog in town has spent the past two weeks talkin' about these murders. Most of 'em believe the red-skins are responsible. You can't arrest them all."

"Most of them weren't recruiting for a private vigilante army to go out and raid the rez tonight. I hope you recognize the difference, Buck, since you're wearing a badge."

"That's something else," said Coleridge. "Shouldn't Sheriff Eastman be the one arrestin' folks, if it's required? Or me, for that matter?"

"Buck, we still don't know where Ardis went this morning, and you weren't at the saloon. A citizen's arrest is perfectly legitimate, as you should know by now."

"I understand it," Coleridge answered, "but I don't feel much like dyin' for it."

"Most of those are good people, out there," Mathers reminded him. "They're scared and angry, some of them are liquored up, but all they really care about — most of them, anyway — is living peacefully and sleeping through the night without somebody coming in to cut their throats. They think McCallister can help them, but they'll cool off pretty soon."

"I hope you're right, Mayor," Coleridge said, "because I'm not sure I can shoot 'em."

They were back to that.

Mathers explained, "You've got two basic kinds of jailhouse mobs. One, the most common kind, wants justice in a hurry. What they *claim* is justice, anyway. They storm a jail to lynch your prisoner, and never mind the little details, like a trial."

Coleridge was nodding, fiddling with his scattergun.

"The other kind," Mathers went on, "I call the mercy mob. They want to break somebody out of jail to set him free, either because they think he's innocent, or else his crime should be excused. We've got the second kind, out there, but one thing both mobs have in common is their total disrespect for law and order. Understand?"

"I guess so," Coleridge said.

"Don't *guess,* damn it! "You swore an oath in front of me and Sheriff Eastman when you got that badge. You promised, with your right hand raised to God, that you'd uphold the law without fear or favor. There was nothing said about ignoring crimes committed by your friends, was there?"

"No, sir."

"You're damned right, no! You have a duty to perform, by God! If you can't do it, leave your badge and weapons on that desk, and

367

take your ass outside to join the mob."

Buck Coleridge blinked at him, surprised, as color blossomed on his cheeks.

"I'll do my duty, Mayor," he answered stiffly. "But that doesn't mean I have to like it."

Mathers allowed his voice to soften. "That's why it's called duty," he observed. "If it was fun, they'd call it 'play.'"

The moment stretched between them, silent but for the insistent mumbling of the crowd outside. Then, Coleridge asked him, "Do you really think they'll rush the jail?"

"I hope not, but you have your orders, if they do."

"And you meant what you told Mr. Mc-Callister? I mean, the part about him bein' first to go?"

"I mean it," Mathers said. "You'd best believe I do."

Slade's shoulder was on fire, aching and burning all at once. There'd been no way to stitch the gash Kate Bender had inflicted with her knife, but Little Wolf had bound it tightly with strips of cloth cut from clothing they found in the wagon.

That came *after* they had untied Jenny Hascomb and removed her blindfold, Slade assuring her that she was safe and that she had nothing to fear from him, or from the young bare-chested Cherokee. She had relaxed a little when she saw the bodies strewn around the campfire, but Slade guessed that she would be a long time overcoming what she had experienced.

Assuming that she ever did.

The girl sat off to one side, with her back turned, while Slade and Little Wolf summoned their horses, then cleaned up the camp. Slade had to take the bodies with him, back to Paradise, and that meant loading them inside the wagon. He would drive it, Jenny helping if she could, and he would tie his roan to the tailgate. The Cherokee who'd saved his life could then decide if he was going with them, back to town, or if he'd choose some other course.

Whatever Little Wolf decided, Slade wasn't about to interfere. He owed the younger man too much and wasn't going to make any trouble for him, come what may.

Loading the corpses was a struggle, since Slade had to work one-handed, but Little Wolf was strong and far from squeamish. They packed away the two men, first, after a pause to douse John Senior's smoking head with water from the wagon's barrel. It would take a miracle for anybody to identify him, by his face, but Slade's would be the only testimony on that score, and Bender was in no shape to deny his name.

They loaded up the women next, Kate going last into the wagon. Even through his pain and weariness, Slade still experienced a pang of guilt at handling her, recalling those last moments when she'd tried to force herself upon him.

Tried?

He thought of Faith again, but couldn't deal with that just now. Fresh blood was leaking through his shirt before he finished tying his horse to the back of the wagon, bracing himself for the climb to the tall driver's seat.

If they held a steady pace, Slade guessed they should be back in Paradise within three or four hours, say ten or eleven o'clock. With any luck, most of the townspeople would be asleep. Slade could reserve his answers for the mayor and Ardis Eastman's deputy, while someone fetched the town's doctor to stitch him up.

At least he knew there would be no more homestead murders in the interim. That reign of terror was ended . . . or was it?

Jenny Hascomb sat beside him on the driver's seat, wrapped in a blanket, shivering and weeping softly to herself. Slade could imagine what she'd been through

370

since her kidnapping, but could he ever really *understand?* Despite what Kate had done — or tried to do — with him, he knew that it was different for a woman, young or old.

Could such things be forgotten? Would the ordeal color the rest of her life and twist it somehow? Turn her into a spinster, perhaps, or spin her off the other way entirely?

Speculation served no purpose, so Slade concentrated on his driving, glancing over now and then to find Little Wolf still keeping pace with the wagon. Slade hadn't asked the Cherokee what he was planning to do next, now that the mystery was solved and there was no reason for any further finger-pointing toward his people.

It would take time for the word to get around, of course. And what would happen then? Would the momentary resurrection of the Bloody Benders bring reporters flocking into Paradise, or would it pass unnoticed? Had the homestead murders even rated coverage outside of western Oklahoma Territory?

Slade had no idea, and if the truth be told, he didn't care. He didn't plan on granting any interviews, in the event that someone asked. He'd let town spokesmen do the talking, or perhaps Judge Dennison.

Raising a weary hand, he beckoned to Little Wolf, bringing him closer. There was still one question that required an answer.

"Are you coming into town with us?" he asked the Cherokee.

Smiling without much humor, Little Wolf responded with a question of his own. "Will I be shot on sight?"

"I'll do my best to see that doesn't happen," Slade assured him.

There was no sign of the smile when Little Wolf replied, "White men may not be happy that I shot the woman, even if she was loco."

"You want me to," Slade said, "I'll take that on myself."

He couldn't tell what thoughts were churning in the space behind those dark brown eyes, but Little Wolf *was* thinking, there could be no doubt of that.

"Ask me again," the warrior said at last, "when we can see the lights."

"I thought you said they'd break it up when they got cold," Buck Coleridge said.

"Guess I was wrong," Rance Mathers glowered. "Whiskey keeps them warm."

"They've had enough, some of 'em, that they should be falling down by now."

"Something to wish for, anyway," the

372

mayor replied.

The mob outside the jail had grown, which he supposed was no surprise. Before the murders, nothing much out of the ordinary had occurred in Paradise, and since the killing started, a majority of townspeople stayed off the streets at night. The mob scene at the jail gave them a reason to come out, a feeling of safety in numbers, and — for some, at least — a sense that they were *doing something,* even if they couldn't explain what *it* was.

"We want McCallister!" one of the men in the mixed crowed called out, and it became a chant in nothing flat.

"We want McCallister!"

"We want McCallister!"

"You hear that, Rance?" Angus McCallister called out, from his jail cell. "You can't hold me forever."

"One thing you should bear in mind, Angus," Mathers replied. "Forever's just a finger twitch away for you, first time your friends out there try coming through this door."

A stirring in the crowd distracted Mathers from his prisoner. Heads turned out there, facing northward along Main Street, but Mathers couldn't see what had distracted them. Two or three members of the mob tried cheering, but the noise fell flat into an unexpected silence broken by . . . hoofbeats?

Pressing his cheek against the office door to get the most out of its narrow peeping slit, Mathers saw mounted soldiers trotting into view, with Colonel Northcliff leading them. Beside him rode a cowboy Mathers didn't recognize.

"What's going on?" McCallister inquired.

"Shut up," Mathers suggested.

The double line of army horses stopped outside, squeezing the mob between their dark flanks and the sidewalk fronting on the jail. If trouble started now, the crowd — with most constituents unarmed, as far as he could see — would be caught in a cross fire.

Mathers saw Northcliff dismount and make his way toward the sidewalk. The crowd parted to let him pass, no questions asked. A moment later, he was at the door and knocking.

"You come in, and no one else," said Mathers through the door.

"Agreed."

Buck Coleridge raised the bar that double locked the door, while Mathers turned the latch and eased it open. Northcliff slipped inside, and Mathers slammed the door again, waiting for Buck to put the crossbar

374

back in place. Outside, the muttering re-sumed.

Northcliff glanced at the shotgun Mathers held and said, "It seems I got here just in time."

"For what?" the mayor inquired.

Northcliff nodded toward Angus in his cell. "To take him off your hands and place him in protective custody."

"He's safe, right where he is, Colonel."

"That mob out there —"

"Wants to release him, so that he can lead them on a raid against the Saline Reserva-tion. Or, more likely, tell them what to do while he stays nice and comfy at his ranch."

Northcliff looked troubled now. "A raid, you say?"

"I guess he's tired of waiting for your men to make the redskins disappear. Decided he should take a hand in it, himself."

McCallister piped up, "I never said —"

"Shut up!" Mathers ordered, punctuating his command with a jerk of the shotgun in McCallister's direction.

"If this is true —"

"It's true, Colonel," Mathers replied. "I'm charging him with incitement to riot and sending the case in to Judge Dennison, soon as that marshal has time to report it."

Why was the colonel looking nervous now?

"Ah, Marshal Slade," he said. "And where *is* he, just now?"

Before Mathers could voice his ignorance, a shout went up outside the jail. He shoved past Northcliff, pressed his face against the peeping slit once more, and saw approximately half the crowd moving together, south along Main Street.

"Stay here!" he snapped at Buck Coleridge. "And bar this door behind us!"

On the sidewalk, Colonel Northcliff at his elbow, Mathers stopped and stared at the tall wagon rumbling down Main Street. He recognized Jack Slade, slumped in the driver's seat, but who was that beside him, blanket-swaddled?

Jesus! Could it be the Hascomb girl?

And why, in God's name, was an Indian riding beside the wagon, with a rifle in his hand?

The mob was surging into Main Street now, blocking the wagon. Mathers snapped out of his momentary trance and left Northcliff behind him, on the sidewalk. Bulling in among them, jabbing with the shotgun's butt and shoving bodies off to either side, he jostled toward the wagon.

"Get the hell out of my way!" he snapped, forgetting for a moment that the men, at least, were voters. "Move it! I'm the god-

376

damned mayor!"

Slade told his story once, briefly, before the bluecoats went to work and cleared the street, ordering people back into their shops and homes, or into the saloon, whichever suited them. He had a mounted escort to the doctor's office, after telling Northcliff's men that Little Wolf had saved his life, along with Jenny Hascomb's. Then, the mayor took over, stalking up and down the street beside them with a shotgun, barking at the mounted troops to *give the boy some breathing room.*

Slade started on his tale a second time, including Ardis Eastman's death and where the body could be found, while Dr. Enoch Stone examined Jenny Hascomb. When the doctor had her doped and resting for a bit, he came back with a grim expression on his face and started talking while he cleaned Slade's wound.

"I'd normally speak only to the girl's parents," Stone said, "but since her family's all gone, she'll need an adult's care. Rance, possibly your wife —"

Colleen Mathers chimed in, "I'm standing right here, Enoch. And of course, I'll help in any way I can."

Blushing, the doctor said, "She's been . . .

assaulted. If she's lucky — and I'd say she is, to be alive — then time won't find her in a family way. Aside from that, she's young. She'll heal, at least in body. Mind and spirit may require more time and tender care."

"She'll have it," Colleen Mathers said, without consulting husband Rance.

"Now, Marshal, it may smart a bit when I start stitching."

Smart, hell.

Once again, Slade felt as if his back and shoulder were on fire, but he sat through it, knowing that each suture put him that much closer to the long ride home from Paradise.

"You don't know who it was that killed the sheriff?" Mathers asked him.

"We weren't exactly introduced," Slade answered, through clenched teeth. "But you should find them both together, at his spread southwest of town. I'll draw a map, if it'll help."

"Sounds like Heck Riley," said the doctor, between stitches. "It's been nine or ten months since he came to see me, with a broken arm, but the description fits, and that's about where you should find his spread."

"Riley?" Mathers echoed. "Ardis talked to me about him when he settled here, must be two years ago. The man's a jailbird."

"Was," Slade said, correcting him. "He won't be going back."

Behind him, Colonel Northcliff cleared his throat. "About this Little Wolf . . ."

"I've told you twice," Slade said. "The girl and I would both be dead, if not for him, and you'd have murders going on for God knows how long, while you kept searching the reservation. If you're smart, you'll thank him. Maybe give him whatever reward's still current on the Benders, if there is one."

"And on that subject," Mathers said, "I think we're all agreed that nothing good can come of having Paradise made famous as the town where the Bloody Benders met their well-deserved comeuppance. I, for one, don't want to read about our town in dime novels that can't tell truth from . . . from . . . a load of horse manure. We don't need crazy strangers traipsing in and out, asking directions to the spot where Kate Bender was killed, for God's sake. We'd become notorious!"

"That isn't up to me," Slade told him, as the doctor finished stitching. "I report directly to Judge Dennison, not to the newspapers. I don't know what they've published on the crimes, so far, or if they'll carry any follow-ups."

"But if somebody *asks* you . . . ?"

"I'll refer them to the judge and leave it up to him," Slade said.

"That's fair enough. I'll write Judge Dennison myself, and make our feelings on the matter known."

"What about McCallister?" asked Slade.

Mathers was clearly having second thoughts about jailing the richest man for miles around. His face was close to beet red as he said, "As long as there was no harm done, perhaps I should dismiss the charge."

"Since it was never filed, officially, that shouldn't be a problem," Slade replied.

He thought about the sniper who had tried to kill him, but he knew the triggerman would likely never be identified. He had likely been one of McCallister's men, perhaps one of those who'd gone down in the past few days. If not, Slade took it as a given that the man would be in flight for parts unknown. Tracking a nameless, faceless fugitive would be a waste of everybody's time, and he was anxious to get out of Paradise as soon as possible.

"When can I get out of here?" Slade asked.

"Another day or two, at least," said Dr. Stone, in answer to his question. "And you'll have to take it easy, even then."

"Easy's the way I like it," Slade replied.

His shirt was ruined, but he slipped his jacket on over his bare skin and the bandage on his shoulder, wincing at the pain it cost him.

One more day in Paradise, or maybe two.

Slade would be glad to see the last of it, see Faith again, even to see Judge Dennison.

"Is something wrong, Marshal?" asked Colleen Mathers.

She had caught him frowning, but Slade wiped it off his face.

"No, ma'am," he lied. "I can't think of a thing."

The employees of Thorndike Press hope you have enjoyed this Large Print book. All our Thorndike, Wheeler, and Kennebec Large Print titles are designed for easy reading, and all our books are made to last. Other Thorndike Press Large Print books are available at your library, through selected bookstores, or directly from us.

For information about titles, please call:
  (800) 223-1244

or visit our Web site at:
  http://galc.ccngagc.com/thorndike

To share your comments, please write:
  Publisher
  Thorndike Press
  295 Kennedy Memorial Drive
  Waterville, ME 04901